Stories of Hope

Helen McAlley

First published by Busybird Publishing 2023

ISBN: 978-1-922954-19-0

Cover design: Busybird Publishing

Layout and typesetting: Busybird Publishing

Busybird Publishing
2/118 Para Road
Montmorency, Victoria
Australia 3094
www.busybird.com.au

CONTENTS

THE GIFT

I cuddle my daughter close to me. How very precious she is. Just six weeks old, and yesterday I had the joy of seeing her first smile. She is not smiling now, just sleepily snuggling up to me after her feed. Looking warm and snug in my arms, she looks totally at peace as if she knows already how much I love her and want to protect her from all harm. A strong feeling of tenderness fills my heart. How beautiful she is. What soft cheeks! As I gently touch one of them, a thought comes to me so strong that it makes me give an involuntary gasp. Then I feel relieved as though rescued from some great danger like being drowned. Everything is all right. She is here and safe with me. I do not need to worry. My thoughts, like stragglers on a bushwalk following their whims rather than the map, wander back over the past year, pondering all that has happened.

Twelve months ago, I was just starting to feel settled again. My two sons John and Michael also seemed happier and more settled after the trauma of the divorce. Only that week, I recalled, John's teacher had said how at last, John's schoolwork was beginning to improve again. And I could see that Michael was happier. The nightmares were becoming less frequent. His appetite was better and he seemed less withdrawn. Of course, the boys still missed their father's presence in the home. There was a gap in their hearts that would never be totally filled. But at least they were coming to terms with what had happened.

My mind went back a further ten months to that day when James had made the unexpected announcement that he was leaving us. He was sorry he said, but he had met a girl at work and gradually they had come to realise that they were deeply in love. He knew it was hard on us, but, as far as he could see, there was no alternative for him but to leave me and marry her. He did not love me anymore, so what was the point of us remaining married? Yes, he knew the children would suffer, but children are resilient. They would get over it eventually and maybe even come to see what a sensible thing he had done. He hoped all arrangements would be amicable. He wanted the boys and me to remain in the family home and for us all to be as little disturbed as possible. He wanted the boys to spend every second weekend with him and his new wife.

How can you remain undisturbed when a huge rock is rolling over you crushing the life out of you? How had I been so blind as not to realise what was going on? Yes, James had been working back a lot lately. And he had seemed a little distant at times when we were talking together. I had thought he was preoccupied with his work situation which was indeed demanding. I felt grateful that he earned a good salary and we were comfortable as far as money was concerned. My first thought was that it was my fault that he wanted to leave us. Maybe I hadn't been working hard enough on our marriage. Was that it? Had I only been half listening when he wanted to speak to me, perhaps too concerned with my own responsibilities to give him my full attention? Maybe it was my housekeeping that was at fault. I have never been a tidy person and I find cooking a bit of a struggle.

I never did work out what it was. A week later, James moved out. The boys and I were left feeling lonely and betrayed. They did spend every second weekend with their father, but nevertheless, they missed him so much at other times, as he had played such an important part in their lives. After all, we all still loved him. We couldn't turn off love like someone would turn off a tap that had has been mistakenly left running. It doesn't happen that way. Our mealtimes were lonely; our weekends were lonely; bedtimes were lonely. At any moment, grief could be triggered, like the times when I remembered the happy early days of our marriage when we knew we were invincible. The boys too were vulnerable. Even seeing a couple playing with their children in the park could trigger strong feelings of sadness. The boys so wanted James and me to be back together again and continued to hope that it would happen.

But I did not have a lot of time to indulge my grief. James had always been a good provider, and even now wanted to support the boys as much as possible. But this would not be enough for us to live on. My part-time job was not a well-paying one, although that had not mattered so much when James was with us. I was indeed fortunate that, just at the time of our separation, the company I was working for was going through a time of expansion and was able to offer me full-time work.

How hard were those days just after our separation! How tired I felt all the time, not only with the extra work but with the grief I was feeling. Coming home at night, I just wanted to put my feet up and relax for a while, but was aware that the boys needed me more than ever before. I needed to spend time with them, sometimes just listening as they shared their grief or anger at what their father had done.

It was as if we were going through a long, dark tunnel which would never end. I wondered if we would ever feel normal again, able to join in life's ordinary activities without that ache that we all felt in our hearts. When I met a friend in the street, would I ever again be able to have a quiet enjoyable chat, catching up with the news without fearing that I would burst into tears? Would I ever again find enjoyment in my reading and the tapestry I had loved to do so much? Somehow, I didn't think so. It felt as if my life were over. The work I had to do I did mechanically, seeing each day as futile and life itself as pointless. I had always had a strong faith in God, but now it was as if He had deserted me too. I felt lonely like an abandoned child, rejected and left in the cruel weather to die.

Only gradually did things improve. The day came when I woke up without that feeling of extreme dread at having to face yet another day. My friends Phyllis and Ron had asked us to go to their home for Sunday lunch and, in spite of myself, I found myself looking forward to it. I was also sleeping better at night and was less likely to be tearful when meeting old friends. Like a butterfly crawling out of its cocoon, I was tentatively looking forward to beginning life afresh. The beautiful natural things around me, the sky with soft, white, fluffy clouds, the flowers in our picturesque old garden, the restful green of the grass to which I had been temporarily blinded, now seemed to come to my senses afresh, soothing me and acting as a balm for my wounded spirit.

I was also getting used to working full-time. My boss was appreciative of my efforts and I was developing more confidence in my abilities. Then, the unthinkable happened.

One night, I was asked to work late to complete some urgent reports. It was after eight-thirty when I finally packed up and made my way to the deserted car park relieved that my work was finally done for the day and looking forward to getting home to have something to eat before putting my feet up. A neighbour had promised to check on the boys. I had left a meal for them and hoped they would have done their homework and be preparing for bed by the time I arrived home.

In a flash, my thoughts were interrupted as a dark figure with a knife in his hand suddenly materialised before me. Was I going to be murdered? I thought of my beloved boys. How would they cope with losing a mother as well as a father? But I was not given much time to reflect. I quickly learned that I was not to be murdered but raped. I still find it extremely difficult to speak of that humiliating experience. In fear of my life, I went along with what was required, relieved at last when it was over and I was left bound in the carpark while my attacker fled.

As I waited for help, I felt numbed by my experience, unable as yet to comprehend the full enormity of it. I wondered vaguely if the boys would be anxious. Would they call the police perhaps? They were not used to being on their own and I hoped they would call our neighbour for help.

I finally managed to attract the attention of a passer-by who took me to the police station. They took down the details and arranged for me to have DNA testing. Later, I was driven back to the car park, the officer waiting until I had driven away. I was given the address of a counselling centre which gave special care to the victims of rape.

In the weeks that followed, it seemed that my old wounds had been opened afresh. I felt terrified to be on my own and had a deep sense of grief that something very precious had been taken away from me. I felt very angry with my attacker. Why would anyone do this to me? Dreary day followed dreary day. All around me, the world seemed grey and lifeless. How hard it was to get up each morning. Only my boys were a comfort to me. They seemed to understand how I was feeling and their little acts of kindness, like preparing coffee for me when I came in from work, were like a soothing ointment to me.

The counselling was also a blessing as I worked through the intense feelings I was experiencing. It was good to have someone who cared about me and who would listen warmly and uncritically as I poured out my thoughts and feelings.

My lowest point came a few weeks after the assault. With a sudden realisation, the thought came to me. What if I were pregnant? I had not until then allowed myself to even consider such a thought. It was too horrifying to contemplate. But the symptoms were all there. Maybe I was just imagining it. I would have to take hold of myself and wait another couple of weeks.

Two weeks later, I knew for sure. My first thought was to get rid of this little creature which so reminded me of my humiliating experience – to crush it out as one would stamp on an insect likely to bite and cause inconvenience. But I had always been taught that abortion was wrong. Something seemed to stop me from taking that desperate action. Although I told myself I would take that step, I kept postponing the appointment which would terminate the little life forever.

One evening, my friend Phyllis called to see me. As I saw the deep compassion in her eyes and knew that she cared for me so much, I sobbed out the whole story. For a long time, Phyllis did not say anything. She just sat there holding me and listening. Finally, she said, 'Mary, I'm going to pray for you. We've always believed God is good and He hasn't changed even if your circumstances have changed so much. I'm going to pray that He will heal the terrible hurt you've suffered and give you the grace to forgive that man. And I'm also going to pray that God will give you direction for the days ahead.'

Although I was feeling angry with God, I did allow Phyllis to pray for me. And the next day, the first little miracle occurred. I knew for certain I could not have an abortion. I still felt very angry and grieved and certainly did not want to have the baby but I knew I could not make the decision to terminate its life. Well, perhaps it could be adopted. There were hundreds of couples out there who would be only too glad to adopt it. Surely no-one in their right mind would expect me to keep it after all I had been through.

Weeks passed. I had to explain to the boys what was happening. They were distressed at what I had been through but also very interested in the thought of a new baby. I explained firmly that we would not be keeping it.

The first time I felt the baby move, I felt shocked as if I were becoming aware of the reality of it for the first time. How was I to go through with it? A feeling of revulsion quivered through me. The whole thing seemed like a bad dream. Could this be really happening to me?

Week followed week. I found it embarrassing to explain to people how I, as a single parent, had become pregnant. I avoided people if I could. With my other babies, I had enjoyed buying the little clothes and other items they needed, but, as this one was to be adopted, no such preparations were made. I tried to go on with my life as if I were not pregnant, telling myself that, when it was all over, I would look back on the situation as one looks back on a severe dose of the flu – unpleasant but finished with.

Finally, I went into labour, with my kind next-door neighbour taking me to the hospital and my friend Phyllis looking after the boys. Throughout the labour, there was only pain with no sense of joyful anticipation. I felt angry that I had to go through this difficult experience – for what?

Eventually, she was born. The nurse on duty did not realise she was to be adopted and placed her in my arms. As I held her, I had, for the first time, a feeling of wonder. What a perfect little creature she was. What perfect little feet with those tiny toes. How trustingly she lay in my arms. Now she was beginning to cry a little. I drew her to my breast and she sucked confidently. I sat for a long time holding her and pondering. Tomorrow she would be gone, but today it would not hurt to hold her for a while....

The next day, I woke up with the feeling that something good had happened to me. What was it? Then I remembered that tiny little life and my arms ached to hold her again. It was then that I realised that, however inconvenient, I could not give her up. Holding her and feeding her again, it was as if I had been reborn. My fears and anger were gone. A miracle had occurred within me.

Later that day, Phyllis brought the boys in to visit me. When I told them of my decision, I expected they would be puzzled. Instead, they were overjoyed. They so much wanted me to keep this new little sister. They also noticed the change within me and I could see the relief in their eyes. My heart went out to them. What a difficult few months they had been through. I wanted to hold them in my arms and reassure them that things would be different from now on.

I continue to hold my peacefully sleeping baby and ponder how Phyllis's prayers were answered. I know now that God is good. This new little one, whatever the circumstances of her conception, is still a precious gift from a loving Father. And, to my surprise, I do not hate my baby's father anymore, feeling instead a deep sense of concern and compassion. I remember with a smile my baby's first smile yesterday. Maybe, when she wakes up, she will give me another treasure like that.

I place baby Grace gently in her bassinette, cover her and tiptoe quietly from the room.

UNFINISHED BUSINESS

When the telephone call came, Ruth was sitting quietly in her lounge-room sipping a cup of tea while she read a magazine which she had bought while shopping that morning. She felt relaxed and comfortable like a cat who has just drunk a large saucer of milk and is now lying in the warm sunshine.

Ruth's husband Ed had died twelve months previously and, while she still missed him terribly after a marriage of forty-five years, she had to admit there were times when she found she was enjoying life on her own. For example, she could have meals exactly when she liked and she could cook what she wanted rather than what Ed liked. Her tastes were simple – a chop and vegies or homemade soup with beef casserole. Ed had liked more exotic dishes like Beef Wellington. Well, she had to admit, it did taste rather good, but it was definitely no better than a simple beef stew, and what a hassle it was to prepare it just as Ed had liked it! It had seemed to have a mind of its own.

And then there had been Ed's love for lawn bowls. Ruth had played too to keep him company, but sometimes she smiled fondly as she thought how much the game meant to him. Wet Saturdays had been a real problem to him and nothing else would do as a substitute. He would wander around the house with that look of not knowing what to do, that people sometimes have when they are embarking on a major project like establishing a garden. Ruth would feel distracted and unable to concentrate on anything else herself on those days. It was good now to be able to make her own decisions about how the weekend should be spent.

Nevertheless, they had been a devoted couple and had shared much together. Ruth often felt lonely as she remembered Ed's genuine love and affection for her. She even missed his faults sometimes, like his unpunctuality.

Now she went unwillingly to answer the persistent ringing of the phone. It was her sister Margery.

'Hello Ruth. I've got some bad news. The doctor says my angina has got worse.' There was a quiver in Margery's voice. 'In fact, he says I shouldn't be living on my own anymore. He wants me to go into a nursing home, but I couldn't. I just couldn't! Not after what happened to Mum. I don't really need a lot of nursing care, but just someone to be around in case I have an attack. Wouldn't it be more sensible if I came and lived with you? There's more room in your house now that Ed's gone. I wouldn't be any trouble and we could be company for each other. And we could share the work. We could have it on a trial basis at first and then reassess the situation after a few months. Please think about it seriously.'

'Just give me a while to think about it, Margery,' said Ruth. 'I'll ring you back tomorrow afternoon'.

She hung up with a hundred thoughts vying for her attention. It was true that Margery had had an irrational dread of nursing homes since their mother's unfortunate experience nearly thirty years earlier. It had been a difficult decision for their mother to make to go into a home but she knew she was getting frailer and was almost totally incapacitated with arthritis. She did not want to be a burden on either of her daughters, then in their forties. At any rate, Margery and her husband Geoff were overseas. 'I couldn't expect Margery to do anything for me,' their mother had said at the time. 'I just hope they're having a wonderful holiday.' Margery and her husband were enjoying long service leave.

Ruth had offered half-heartedly to have her mother while wondering at the same time how she would manage it. Her two teenage daughters Jennifer and Beverley were in a private school and Ruth helped to earn the money to pay the school fees by doing some dressmaking. She was an excellent dressmaker and had the reputation for making top quality bridal clothes. Her life was very full and busy and she knew her mother would need a lot of help, time and patience. It seemed her mother knew that her offer was half-hearted and was hurt by it. Ruth had thought at the time sadly that more was always expected of her than of Margery. Her mother had decided quite quickly then to go into a nursing home and the matter had been settled.

When she visited her mother each week, Ruth was aware of a new coldness in her mother's attitude to her. Nothing much was actually said, but her mother's tone of voice said much. She took even less interest in Ruth's activities than she had done previously. Ruth felt really hurt by this, knowing the interest her mother always took in Margery and Geoff's activities. Ruth's husband Ed had been a source of much comfort to her during those times. It had been a relief to share how she was feeling and to know, as she felt his arm around her, that nothing would alter his love for her.

Then six months after her mother had gone to the home had come the terrible news of the accident. A carer had been helping her mother to get out of the shower. There had been some water on the floor and her mother had slipped and been hurt badly, breaking her hip. She had never fully recovered from this accident. Ruth had visited her more often, taking small gifts and trying to get her out of the depression that had enveloped her. But it seemed that her mother had lost the will to live. Two months later, she had slipped quietly away.

To make matters worse, one of the other residents believed that the carer on duty that day had been slightly drunk. It was difficult to prove anything, but it added a drop of bitterness to an already full cup of sorrow.

And then, when Margery and Geoff had returned from their extended time overseas, Margery had bitterly blamed Ruth for allowing their mother to go into a nursing home at all. As far as Margery was concerned, Ruth was responsible for their mother's death. The matter had been a source of conflict between them for some years, but, with the passing of time, Margery's attitude of hostility and Ruth's resentment had softened somewhat.

Ruth thought even further back to when she and Margery had been children together. Somehow, she could not remember a time when there had not been rivalry between them. In particular, they always seemed to be competing for their mother's attention, and, Ruth thought bitterly, Margery usually won. She remembered a time when they were playing a game together, and she was winning. Margery had been so angry that she had, on impulse, messed up all the pieces.

'Look what she's done, Mum,' had cried an anguished Ruth.

'Oh, Ruth! You take things far too seriously,' her mother had replied impatiently. 'It's only a game after all.' But Ruth had known that it was not fair and had nursed the hurt for years.

Then there was the time that Margery had won a prize in the local show for a painting she had done. How their mother had fussed over her that time – telling all the neighbours about it and, so it seemed, endlessly praising Margery's effort. Ruth knew that she would not have got that sort of attention if she had won a prize. In fact, when she had won first prize for running on the school sports day, her mother had hardly seemed to listen when Ruth had told her. She had seemed preoccupied and Ruth had felt like saying, 'Did you hear me Mum?' But she knew her mother would have considered that to be rude.

Then, when Aunt Elizabeth had asked if just one of the girls could go on a special holiday with her, of course it had to be Margery. 'Her health is more delicate and she will benefit from the time away,' their mother had said, and that settled it.

It was true that Margery's health as a child had seemed rather delicate. She had never seemed to be as strong as Ruth. In retrospect, Ruth wondered rather grimly if it were partly a ploy to get out of the jobs the girls were expected to do. But then, at ten years of age, Margery had become really ill with polio which was sweeping through the area at the time. In the early fifties, a vaccination against polio had not yet been discovered. Even now, as an older woman, Ruth could remember that terrible time very clearly. How well she remembered the anxiety and fear on her parents' faces, and how quickly and angrily they told her to be quiet if she unwittingly raised her voice. At that time especially, she believed that she was not at all important to her parents, whereas Margery was of paramount importance. In later years, after she had become a parent herself, she was able to see this time more clearly from her parents' perspective, but that realisation only partially deadened the pain which occasionally stabbed at her heart.

During the worst times of Margery's illness, Ruth would slip away to her room, quietly close the door and read for a while. She was an avid reader and always tried to have library books available. After a while, her tears would stop flowing and she would feel calmer. Besides her feelings of sadness at her parents' preoccupation, there was also the genuine feeling of concern that Margery might die. Nobody had actually mentioned this as a possibility, but Ruth knew that some children in the district had died. And if it happened to Margery, maybe she would be partly to blame for having those mean feelings towards her sister when Margery was such a delicate child.

Gradually, Margery grew better, but their mother, because of Margery's illness, became increasingly solicitous. For a while, she was afraid to let her older daughter out of her sight. This developed into a general concern that Margery should have the best of everything, or so it seemed to Ruth who felt increasingly neglected. At times, their father noticed their mother's overconcern for Margery and sometimes he even ventured a comment, 'It would be good Jane if you remembered to praise Ruth for her schoolwork as you do Margery,' This comment was made when her parents did not know that Ruth was within earshot. She felt angry yet resigned by her mother's reply, 'Oh George, anyone can do well at school if they are not kept away by illness as Margery has been. Yes, Ruth has done well, but she's had none of the terrible setbacks that Margery has had.'

Ruth also noticed that her mother referred to Margery as 'Sweetheart' whereas she was just plain Ruth. Then there were all those special foods their mother would cook to tempt Margery's appetite. Ruth knew it would be useless to ask for *her* favourite dishes as they would never be cooked.

And if Ruth ever mentioned, ever so respectfully, to their mother that Margery was favoured, how indignant she would be. She was completely unaware of it. Their father, on the whole, went along with their mother, only occasionally making a comment to correct an obviously wrong statement.

Most of the time, he was passive, involved with his own affairs and his work.

Ruth pulled herself up with a jerk as she realised it was now 2pm and she had been so wrapped up in her thoughts that she had neglected to have any lunch. She slowly got up and began to prepare herself a sandwich still deep in thought as she went to the kitchen: It just wouldn't work and that's that! I wouldn't have the patience to have her here. It's a time in life when I have to think of my own needs. It wouldn't even be good for Margery herself to be here. She probably needs expert care that I wouldn't be able to give her.

Although she had made this decision, Ruth still had the uneasy feeling that something was wrong — not sorted out or dealt with — and she couldn't work out what it was. I'm probably worried about explaining this to Margery, she thought. I'll feel better after I've spoken to her tomorrow.

But the niggling feeling remained with her although she busied herself with her sewing that afternoon. The feeling was still there when her daughter Beverley and family visited her that evening. Ruth went to bed that night perplexed and did not sleep well. But, when she woke up in the morning, she knew what the problem was. I haven't forgiven her, she thought. That's what it is. But that's impossible. How can I forgive her after all she's done? It's impossible.

As she thought about the situation a bit more, Ruth realised that she had not forgiven her parents either — her mother for taking her for granted while favouring Margery and her father for being passive and failing to challenge his wife more about her attitudes and behaviour. Forgiving them seemed impossible too.

Still a small voice within seemed to be saying that forgiveness was what was needed. Ruth knew she could not change her feelings, but she remembered a sermon at her church recently when her minister had said that forgiveness, like love, was a decision. We can choose to forgive. Was it really that easy? wondered Ruth.

Then she remembered the example her minister had given recently in one of his sermons at church. One of his male friends, who was often in their home, had initiated an affair with his wife. The two had gone off together and his marriage of twenty-five years had been broken up. His three children had been broken-hearted and he himself had felt utterly devastated to the point that he felt he could never be happy again and could never be able to live a normal life and continue with his ministry.

He continued like this for some time, but one day he came to the realisation that unforgiveness was like a poison in his soul and even in his body. He knew that he could not forgive the terrible wrong he had suffered on his own so he prayed for God's help in achieving forgiveness. He made the decision to forgive in spite of his feelings and found himself declaring aloud that he forgave his wife and her new partner. He remembered also the words of Jesus to pray for our enemies and those who treat us wrongly and he prayed for the couple to be blessed, affirming that he refused to judge them anymore for their actions. His feelings were not much different from before, but he knew that eventually they would soften if he continued to affirm forgiveness.

Then he believed God showed him to go on with the routine of his day and not to worry about his feelings. When the thought of his wife and partner came back into his mind, he would again affirm forgiveness and pray for them to be blessed and once again he would continue with the tasks of the day, trusting that eventually his feelings would catch up with his decision.

It took a few months but eventually he realised that the feelings of resentment were coming less often and were less intense. If those feelings did come back, he would simply affirm forgiveness and blessing. Having practised forgiveness, he felt much better within himself, as if he had been released from carrying a heavy burden.

By lunchtime, Ruth knew that she too needed to forgive her parents and Margery. If her minister could forgive his wife and her new partner with God's help, then surely she would be able to forgive those who had wronged her. It was not that she was saying that no wrong had been done, but it was a decision to begin what might be a long process of forgiveness. She prayed as her minister had prayed, forgiving and blessing her parents and Margery. She knew she would have to repeat those prayers again, but she also knew she had made a start in the process.

Suddenly, she felt peaceful as she had not felt in years. What an unnecessary burden she had been carrying all that time. And really the only person she had been hurting was herself. On impulse, she picked up her telephone and dialled Margery's number.

'Is that you Margery? It's Ruth here. Can you come over for dinner tonight? We must talk this over and work out what would be best for both of us'.

A FRESH BEGINNING

'Robert!' exclaimed Faye. 'How dare you speak to me like that!'

Faye was Robert's maths teacher. Robert had become annoyed when she pointed out a mistake he had made and had attacked her in a verbally abusive manner.

Later in the staffroom, Faye sat quietly pondering on the outburst. She felt very shocked and very fragile, like a fine china teacup that has had a battering and is in danger of shattering.

'What's the matter Faye?' asked her friend and colleague Roger. 'You look as if a tornado had struck you.'

Faye told him her story. She had begun teaching at the Christian school that year determined to do her very best for her students, but Robert had not responded to her attempts to take a caring interest in him. Instead he had been defiant and angry whenever she spoke to him. And worse still, some of the other students were taking the cue from Robert and becoming very difficult to handle. Faye was beginning to dread having to teach Robert's class. She would have a feeling in the pit of her stomach when she anticipated each lesson. She was not a very experienced teacher and knew she had much to learn about disciplining her classes. It seemed Robert would take advantage of her inexperience and would attack her like a cat attacking a wounded bird. As Faye thought about it a bit more, she reflected that Robert needed a strong, caring person in his life who could give guidance and direction but who would not be intimidated by his rude manner.

One day, after another difficult time with Robert's class, Faye expressed this thought to Roger.

'Faye, that sounds just what Robert needs and I'm thinking there might be some way to get someone like that in Robert's life. Have you heard about the mentoring system?' Faye had not heard about this scheme. Roger continued, 'I heard about it at my church the other week. Mentors receive training and then they come into the school system to befriend a student who is vulnerable and needs some support and friendship. They spend an hour a week with their mentee, maybe doing an activity together or even going to a local café.'

'Well, Robert certainly needs something to help him. That sounds like a great idea. I'll mention it to Renata and see if she knows about the program.' Renata was the school principal.

As it turned out, Renata had heard about the mentoring scheme the previous week. She explained to Faye how the Inter-Church Council had contacted her and spoken with her about the scheme and offered mentors if she thought anyone in the school would benefit from them. 'I think that would be an excellent idea for Robert,' she said. 'I've been so concerned about him and he's making life difficult for a number of his other teachers too. I've seen him in my office too many times this term. He's a very angry young man!'

In due time, Robert was assigned a mentor whose name was Allan. Allan was thirty years old and had been a rebel when he was younger himself. He had been angry about the breakup of his parents' marriage and had expressed this anger at school towards his teachers. His life had been veering out of control when an uncle took him under his wings and asked him if he would like to be his apprentice at his car repair business. Allan had always had practical skills and he had been only too glad to leave school and become his uncle's apprentice. Uncle George was a man of few words, but Allan respected his ability and his kindness. And somehow working with the cars helped Allan to feel better about himself. He felt proud of his growing skills and his self-esteem increased as he realised that his uncle really believed in him and was proud of his achievements.

When Uncle George had eventually decided to retire, he had offered to sell the business to Allan and Allan had jumped at the chance. He was then in his late twenties and had saved enough money to pay a good deposit on the business.

By this time Allan had become a Christian and was praying that God would use him to bless someone else. He knew that his life could have been very different if Uncle George had not taken him in hand. He thought he would like to help another young person, just as he had been helped by his uncle. When he heard about the mentoring scheme through the local church that he had attended with his uncle, he knew that this was just the right thing for him to do. He applied and completed his training and then was asked if he could mentor Robert.

It was arranged that Allan would have his first meeting with Robert on Wednesday at lunchtime. As Allen owned his own business he could be flexible with his time.

However, when Allan first met Robert, he was taken aback. Robert had agreed reluctantly to see him but, when they met, the teenager was very rude and surly. Allan asked what he would like to do suggesting they could go to a local café, kick a football or sit somewhere quiet at school and have a talk together. Robert's response was, 'I don't care.' He also accused Allan of being a 'do-gooder.'

Allan felt rather baffled but suggested they go to the café where Allan bought some lunch for them both. It was very difficult conversing with Robert who answered most of Robert's questions with, 'I don't know' or 'I don't care' or even 'That's a stupid question.'

Allen went back to work feeling heavy like the time when he had been carrying a large backpack on a hiking trip. Was it worth persisting in this relationship which seemed doomed from the start? He was deep in thought as he worked on the cars in his workshop that afternoon.

That evening he decided to ring his friend Jeremy. Jeremy had done the mentoring course with him and they discussed how things had gone in their first session with their mentees. Jeremy was enthusiastic. His mentee was a nine-year old boy who had been thrilled to have one-on-one time with him. They had played a board game together at the school, but had still had many opportunities to talk and the young boy had shared how his younger brother had been diagnosed with a serious illness and how he had felt left out when his parents were so busy and preoccupied. At the end of the conversation, Jeremy said to Allan, 'Why don't you give it at least one more try? Maybe it was too confronting for Robert to have to make conversation for the hour. Could you try a board game or a computer game with him? If he's concentrating on something like that, it might be less intense for him.'

So, the following week, Allan met Robert again, and this time he asked him if he would like to play some games on the computer. He had found out that Robert was interested in cars and Robert agreed to play a game which involved car racing. There was an activities room at the school where the students were welcome to go at lunchtime, and they made their way there.

Robert was still not very forthcoming as far as talking was concerned, but he seemed to enjoy the games and Allan went away feeling pleased that this was a more satisfactory session and he would definitely return the following week.

The following two weeks went by in a similar fashion. Allan was wondering if this would be all that would ever happen but resolved he would keep going anyway. He did not want to abandon Robert and hoped Robert would understand that he genuinely cared for him. He remembered too how, as a teenager, his uncle had persisted in taking an interest in him.

The next Wednesday, Allen and Robert were walking towards the activities room when they heard shouts and scuffling in the schoolground. Looking across the quadrangle, they saw a younger boy being menaced by an older boy with several other students calling out and egging on the older boy. Allan immediately ran over to them and pulled the younger boy towards him. 'Don't you dare touch him,' he called, 'and don't think I won't be able to stop you if you try anything stupid.'

The group of boys dispersed and Allan made sure that the younger boy was all right before they continued walking to the activities room. As he glanced at Robert, Allan could see that the teenager was distressed. 'Are you all right, Robert?' he asked. 'You look upset. Do you want to talk about it?'

It was the first time that Allan had seen Robert with his guard down. It was as if he had been wearing a mask of hardness and surliness. Now his true self was apparent in his face. He explained to Allan how his parents had been fighting a lot lately and his father could become violent and attack both him and his mother. The threat to the young boy in the school yard had brought his feelings to the surface. And seeing Allan so protective of the other boy helped him to see that his mentor was someone he could trust – someone who was safe to talk to, who would not hurt him or take advantage of him. Tears came to his eyes as they talked quietly together in a secluded corner of the activities room.

For Robert, it was a relief to be able to share the strong feelings that had burdened him for so long. He spoke of the helplessness he had felt as he would watch his mother being beaten, how at times they would go to a neighbour's house for shelter when his father came home drunk and abusive. He described how his mother was too much in fear of his father to leave him even though *her* mother had often urged her to do so. Robert had felt so angry with his father but knew that confronting him would only provoke further violence. That anger had been bottled up inside him and would sometimes reveal itself in an action out of all proportion to the event that triggered it. If a teacher corrected a mistake or asked for his attention, Robert could pour forth a stream of abuse that was very obviously inappropriate.

For so long, Robert had not had anyone to talk to about his home situation but now he knew that Allan really did care for him. Allan listened carefully showing deep concern in his eyes. Robert had never felt anyone cared for him like this and in fact had believed that he could never trust anyone.

After the session finished and Robert had gone to his next class, Allan thought carefully about what had been disclosed. He felt prompted to see if the school principal Renata was free to talk about what had happened. As it turned out she was free. She had been very interested in how the mentoring scheme was progressing and had got to know each of the mentors.

'Hi Allan,' she said. 'I've been meaning to contact you to find out how you are going with Robert. What's happening?'

Allan told the story of what had happened. Renata was thoughtful before saying, 'I think we need to report this to the child protection authorities. In fact, it is part of my job to report the abuse of children to them. I will call them today and explain what is happening. They will not tell Robert's family who has rung, but they will investigate in a confidential and thorough manner.'

Allan felt relieved. He had not been sure what to do in this difficult situation. He hoped that Robert would be helped to escape from the abusive situation.

The weeks went by. Each Wednesday, Allan and Robert continued to see each other and Robert was now a changed person. He knew he could confide in his mentor and they began going to the café to buy some lunch and talk together. Nothing had changed in Robert's home situation but he began to open up and share some of his hopes and dreams for the future. He had always been a practical person and he hoped to go into a trade where he could use his skills.

Then one day, Robert came with a different story. The child protection authorities had gone to his home and his mother, Janine had admitted her concerns about the way her husband was being violent as well as verbally abusive to both herself and Robert. With the support of the authorities, they had moved to a women's shelter. One of Janine's concerns was how she would manage financially if she were to leave her husband. He had forbidden her to work as he had an irrational fear that she might meet someone in the workplace and have an affair. His solution had been to keep her at home as much as possible. He even timed her shopping trips and if he thought she was taking too long, he would ring her and order her to come home straight away, assuming she was meeting with another man.

The authorities had arranged for Janine to go to a class which would give her confidence in returning to work or study. She had worked as a secretary before her marriage and she was also to be given help in getting her secretarial skills up-to-date. This would include computer training. Then, when she was ready to look for work, she would be helped with writing her CV and to prepare for job interviews. Once she could get a job, Janine could look for suitable accommodation for herself and Robert.

It was also arranged that Robert and Janine would have some counselling as they had been through some very difficult times and needed some help in working through these experiences and making a fresh start. At first, Janine was very fearful that her husband would try to find them, but as time went by, she became more confident within herself and these fears receded.

As Allan continued to see Robert each week, he marvelled at the changes he was seeing. It was like seeing a butterfly emerge from a chrysalis. He knew the process of healing might take a while, but it was encouraging to see that so much progress had been made in such a short time. Robert had also begun to go to church with him and also to attend the youth group. The youth group leader had taken a particular interest in making sure that Robert felt at home in the group and that the other young people included him in their activities.

Some months later, Allan's apprentice finished his apprenticeship and decided he wanted to move on to another capital city. Allan wondered about offering Robert the opportunity to become his apprentice. He knew that Robert would be reliable and he knew their continuing friendship would be beneficial to Robert, especially as he did not have a father who would be able to guide him through to manhood. One Wednesday, he suggested that, after Robert had finished his school year, he could begin his apprenticeship. Robert jumped at the chance.

One Wednesday at the end of the school year, Robert and Allan were having lunch at the café discussing how the year had gone and the changes that would happen in the following year. Allan could not help noticing how very different Robert was from the angry teenager he had met months earlier. Robert's face was glowing as he described how happy and settled his mother was and how he was looking forward very much to his apprenticeship beginning only weeks away now.

'There's one more thing I need to do before I leave school,' he said.

'What's that?' asked Allan.

'I want to apologise to the teachers I gave such a lot of trouble to. It won't be easy, but I really think I need to do it. They were just doing their job, after all, and I treated some of them terribly. If I apologise, I'll feel more ready to move on from school to my apprenticeship. It will help me to make a fresh start.'

Looking at Robert's earnest face, Allan knew that his friend had come a long way and was grateful for the part he had been able to play in helping Robert to get to the place where he was now.

THE DECISION

'Dad, I'm so happy,' said Angela. 'I don't know that I've ever been happier in my whole life.'

Terry looked lovingly at his daughter. Her happiness was one of the things he had wished for the most. He knew that Angela had a new boyfriend, Kevin, whom she had met at the legal firm where they both worked. Life had not always been easy for Terry as a single father. His beloved wife Sharon had died of cancer ten years previously, leaving him with two children to raise on his own. Angela had been just ten years old and was really missing her mother. Michael had only been eight and Terry still remembered the nightmares his son had experienced in those early days after Sharon had passed away.

Although he did not feel confident to act as both mother and father to his children, Terry had resolved that with God's help he would do the very best that he could. During Sharon's illness, he had changed jobs. His previous employment had meant a lot of travelling. Now, he managed to secure a job as a manager of a department in a local store. This meant he was able to care for Sharon in her illness until she became too ill to stay at home and he had moved her to a local hospice for palliative care. Sharon's mother Elizabeth, who lived nearby had been a tower of strength to Terry and the children in Sharon's last days. Her own grief had naturally been very strong, but she had done her best not to let it overwhelm her because she knew how much her family needed her at that time. She had looked after the children after school and helped them with their homework. She had tried to make life as normal as possible for them, sharing her Christian faith, that God is faithful and that, although we have troubles in this life, God always cares for us. She explained how Jesus, through His death and resurrection, had conquered death and has a home prepared in heaven for those who love him.

Elizabeth also knew that it was important to listen to the children's feelings at that time. They had all shared together how sad they were feeling to see Sharon so ill. Terry was grateful that his employer had allowed him to have more and more time off work as Sharon's illness progressed.

On the day that Sharon had died, all the family had been able to be with her. The children had been taken out of school and Terry and Elizabeth were also by her bedside. Sharon had looked very tired. She knew that her time was short. She told them all how much she loved them and said she was looking forward to being out of pain and going to be with the Lord. Then she had turned to Terry and said, 'I know it will be hard for you on your own my darling, but I want you always to look after the children,' Terry, with tears in his eyes, had promised that he would always do his best and Elizabeth had also promised that she too would do the best she could to help Terry. Then Terry had suggested that they pray the Lord's Prayer together, and, during that time, Sharon had quietly slipped away.

The weeks following Sharon's death had been a blur. Terry had taken a fortnight off work and during that time they had been busy arranging the funeral which had been a lovely tribute to Sharon's life. The children had been home from school during that time, but eventually, the time came for them to return. The teachers were aware of their situation and tried to give special care to them during their time of grief. They also had some counselling as a family and this helped them to understand the stages of grief they were experiencing, especially to be aware of their feelings, to give themselves permission to feel them, and not to suppress them. Elizabeth would pick up the children from school each afternoon and stay with them until their father came home. She would cook the evening meal which they would share together before she returned to her own home.

Terry also had a time each week with each of his children. They would go out for dinner at a family restaurant and share one-to-one about how they were going as they mourned for their mother. In time, the children developed a very loving bond with their father. They learned to talk with him about their problems and this helped them as they went through the turbulent adolescent years.

Now Angela, at twenty, was sharing about her new boyfriend, Kevin. She and her father were having a meal together in a restaurant as had been their habit over all the years since Sharon had passed away.

'Tell me a bit more about him, Angela,' said Terry.

'He's so kind, Dad,' replied his daughter. 'Do you know what he did yesterday? It was a month since the first time we went out together. He invited me to go with him after work to that little café in the next street and, for afternoon tea, we had delicious chocolate cake. He knows it is my favourite. Then he gave me a beautiful present.' She showed her father the lovely bracelet that Kevin had given her. 'I want us to spend the rest of our lives together. Do you know what, Dad, sometimes Kevin reminds me of you? You're always so kind to me and listen to me when I have something on my mind. That has helped me such a lot – especially when we were all going through that sad time after we lost Mum.'

Terry felt his eyes moistening. It had not always been easy at times to set aside his own needs to care for his children, but now he could see that any small sacrifice he had made was now bearing fruit.

The months went by and Angela continued to be in a world of her own as the romance with Kevin continued. Terry did not think he had ever seen her so happy. At their weekly visits to the café, he would hear more and more stories of Kevin's love and kindness.

'Do you know what he did this week, Dad? He bought me chocolates and flowers and left them on my desk with a little note that he wants us to be together forever.' Terry looked at Angela's starry eyes and felt grateful to Kevin for being so kind and thoughtful to his daughter.

More time went by, a year, eighteen months, two years, three years and by this time Terry began to sense a look of concern in Angela's eyes, like a storm cloud appearing on the horizon after a beautiful clear summer day. 'Is everything all right with you and Kevin?' he asked one day. He knew there was something not quite right, but had wanted Angela to tell him in her own time.

Angela was looking forward to attending her cousin Joy's wedding. Joy and Eric had been planning it for ages and all the family were looking forward to attending this special occasion. Angela saw it as an opportunity to introduce Kevin to the extended family. She was looking forward to them being at the wedding together like a child looking forward to Christmas. She also thought it might prompt Kevin to start thinking about when *their* wedding might be.

It was the night before the wedding. Angela was sharing with her brother Michael how she could not wait until the next day, when her phone rang. Michael heard her say, 'Oh, really. That's so disappointing. Couldn't you change your mind? They will be expecting you. What about the catering?'

Angela got off the phone and burst into a flood of tears. 'He's not coming, is he?' said Michael. 'What happened?'

Between sobs, Angela explained that Kevin was not coming but he did not really seem to have a good reason for his absence. Michael felt angry at the way his sister was being treated. He knew how much she had been looking forward to attending the wedding with Kevin.

Angela had to ring Joy at the last minute and explain that Kevin was not coming. She felt embarrassed that she did not even have a good reason to give for his non-attendance.

At the wedding the following day, Angela tried to look happy and normal for the sake of the happy couple. But her father and Michael were not deceived. As the day wore on, Angela determined that she would have to talk through the problem with Kevin and work out what was going on.

The following Monday, when they were both at work, she asked Kevin if they could have dinner together that night and he agreed to do so. He seemed just as loving as ever towards her which was puzzling. She decided that she would make the effort to listen to what he had to say before launching into any accusations.

Immediately after work, they went together to their favourite restaurant. Kevin began by reassuring her that he loved her. Then he explained why he had not attended the wedding.

'Mum needed me to do some urgent work in the garden. She had a load of soil coming and needed me to spread it out for her.'

'But couldn't it have waited until later?'

'Well I'm at work all week and she wanted it done for next weekend when her sister is arriving from England to stay for the next month.'

Angela thought it was a poor excuse. 'You knew how much I was looking forward to us being together at the wedding,' she exclaimed.

'I know and I'm really sorry Angela. You know I really love you but I didn't want to let Mum down.'

As they continued speaking, Angela knew something was not right but felt confused. After all, Kevin was assuring her of his love. Was it unreasonable of her to expect him not to help his mother? Could the situation be described as an emergency – that need to get the garden right? Or was Kevin being unreliable? Shouldn't an event like a wedding have priority? She knew she needed time to think about it.

Angela found it difficult to sleep that night. She thought about what had happened and tried to find answers, like a scientist grappling with a challenging hypothesis. Yes, Kevin had always been very loving towards her. The only times he had cancelled events were when his mother needed him. Surely, his mother had a right to his time sometimes.

Kevin lived with his mother. Angela was fond of his mother Janet, yet there were times when she thought Janet meant more to Kevin than she did. Kevin would often speak of Janet and Angela had valued his care for her. After all, didn't she value her relationship with her father? They had always been so close but especially since her mother had died. Was there a difference?

Suddenly, Angela sat up in bed as she realised that, yes, there was a difference. Her father loved her very much, but she knew he would never make unreasonable demands of her. He would not expect her to cancel going to an event with Kevin because he wanted her to do something at home, however important.

Small incidents began coming into Angela's mind helping her to see the matter more clearly, just as a jig-saw puzzle becomes clearer as each piece is put in. Kevin lived at home and she knew he paid his mother a generous amount for his board. Janet had sometimes said that she could not live without it. It had been a struggle for her financially when Kevin's father had left her a few years previously. After this event she had become quite possessive of Kevin. In her desire for financial security, could it be that she might be manipulating Kevin into staying with her rather than leaving to get married?

Angela remembered that there were other times when Kevin had cancelled an outing he was due to have with her because his mother had suddenly been coping with an 'emergency'. Were they really emergencies? How serious were the sicknesses that Janet often had just when Angela and Kevin were planning something special?

Was she reading too much into it? Angela decided she needed to have her father's opinion and the next morning asked if they could have some time together after the evening meal that day.

As she poured out her fears to her father and he listened sympathetically, Angela felt more and more convinced that her suspicions were correct. How had she not been able to see what was going on before this? Terry too confessed that he had wondered about some of the incidents that had taken place. He could see, along with Angela, that Kevin was very loving and caring. And his caring nature actually made it easier for his mother to manipulate him. He loved her too, and had believed he needed to step into his father's shoes when his father had left the home.

'I don't want to lose him, Dad,' said Angela. 'I do love him. But this is a problem. What do you think I ought to do?'

'Angela, I think the only thing you can do is to talk with him about it. He may not even realise that Janet is manipulating him. Ask him if he would be willing to put you first. It doesn't mean that he would stop caring for his mother, but caring sometimes means being tough and not giving in to manipulation. Think what it would be like for you in five years time, if you were married and had a child or children, if he were to put his mother first all the time? Remember how the Bible says that a man must leave his mother and father and be joined to his wife? Would Kevin be willing to do that?'

Angela agreed that she needed to talk to Kevin. She thanked her father for his wisdom and immediately phoned Kevin. They agreed to meet after work the next day. She wondered how Kevin would react. Would he be dismissive of her suspicions? Would he perhaps be blind to the truth? Would he acknowledge that she was right and decide to stand up to his mother? Whatever the outcome might be, she was determined to confront him with what she honestly believed to be the truth.

As she explained her point of view to Kevin, she could see some defensiveness in his expression and realised that he did not think there was a problem.

'Of course, I've got to care for Mum, Angela,' he said. 'I love you both but I have been the man of the house since Dad left.' As tactfully as she could, Angela tried to explain how she believed that Janet could manipulate him by magnifying sicknesses and by being 'too sick to manage' on many occasions when Angela and Kevin had planned a special event together. 'It's happened so often, it can't just be coincidence,' she explained. Kevin seemed doubtful and unwilling to believe that his mother would ever act like that.

Angela tried another strategy. 'Kevin, you always say that you want us to spend our life together,' she said. 'When do you think we could get engaged?' It was not a very romantic thing to say but she needed to know. Kevin looked uncomfortable. 'Well, er…' he stammered.

'Would it be next year, or the year after? And what about marriage? We've been so much in love. Surely engagement and marriage would be the next reasonable step.'

Kevin could not give her an answer. 'I'm really not sure when,' he said.

'What about if we have a week to think about it and then discuss it again?' suggested Angela. Kevin reluctantly agreed.

Things were a little strained between them during that week. The days seemed slow, but eventually they met up again to discuss the issue.

Kevin said, 'I've thought about it a lot Angela. And I really don't think I can suggest a date for our engagement or wedding. I know Mum still needs me to live with her and that has to be my priority.'

So that was that. Angela knew that he would not change. She had loved Kevin dearly but knew she had wasted over three years of her life on a man who might never be prepared to marry her. He would always put his mother first and he genuinely believed it was the right thing to do. Kevin reluctantly agreed to a parting of the ways. He was finding it difficult to see what all the fuss was about. They parted amicably but sadly.

Later that night, Angela told Terry what had happened. 'I am so sad for you Angela,' he said, 'But I believe you have made the right decision. And it is a courageous decision too. I know you were so much in love with Kevin. It must really hurt the way it has happened. It is important that you allow yourself to grieve. Allow yourself to feel those strong feelings of grief because that is the way you will eventually get through this difficult time. And who knows? Later on, someone else might come into your life and you will be so glad that you made this decision. And remember not every man is going to be like Kevin.'

Angela sadly agreed with him. She felt sadder and wiser. She found it difficult to imagine falling in love again but who could tell what the future would bring? In the meantime, deep down in her heart, she knew she had made the right decision.

SOMETHING PRECIOUS

'Mummy, you've just *got* to buy us a DVD player. Everyone else in my class has got one. How can I ask my friends to come to a sleepover without being able to show them a DVD?'

Emma sighed as Kylie, her eight-year-old daughter, stamped her foot and went off to her bedroom slamming her door on the way. She had explained to Kylie many times that she simply could not afford to buy a DVD player, but Kylie could not seem to understand. If the other children in her class had one, why couldn't she? If Emma had enough money each week for basics like food and clothing as well as paying the rent, she had to be satisfied. Buying new car tyres after a puncture would stretch her income seriously. Luxuries like a recorder were out of the question. They would all have to be content with what was available free to air on the television.

As she continued to prepare the evening meal, Emma felt a pang of desperation, like a knife suddenly piercing her heart. Was she being a bad mother after all not giving her child what everyone else had? She thought of Kylie's friend Susie. Susie always had the best brands of clothing and, every day, would come to school with money to buy a special treat at the school tuckshop. Emma's children had a lunch order only once a fortnight as a special treat. Many of their clothes were second-hand and Emma dreaded the days when extra money would be required for the children to go on an excursion.

Fortunately, her other children, Leanne aged 12 and David 10, seemed to understand their situation better than Kylie. Although they sometimes grumbled about not having enough money, on the whole, they seemed to understand and accept that most of the other children at school had more than they had.

Emma resolutely put the matter out of her mind and concentrated instead on the meal and supervising the children as they did their homework and got ready for bed.

But the topic would not go away altogether. The following day, as Emma was working at her cleaning job, she found herself thinking again about Kylie's request. Were her children being deprived after all? Would they be happier with a DVD player? She remembered Kylie's friend Veronica whose family would enjoy watching a DVD together. Everyone in the family would take turns to choose one. Sometimes, when Emma and the children would visit them, the children would all sit and watch a movie while the adults talked, and then they would all have supper together. Now she felt sad as if she had lost something precious. It wasn't the actual machine that was so important but the happy family times it would generate.

Emma sighed as she thought of John, her husband who had left her three years before. He had never been very good at coping with the responsibilities of raising a family. How wonderful he had seemed when he was courting her – so attentive. It seemed he couldn't do too much for her – concerned if she were hot or cold, so often taking her out for a meal or maybe for coffee. He frequently remembered to send her flowers too. She smiled sadly to herself at the memory. After their wedding, he had undergone, or so it seemed, a personality change. Was he insecure and afraid that he would lose her? Emma did not know. He didn't even like her going out with her girlfriends anymore and got into bad moods so easily. It was hard for Emma to believe that this was the same charming man that she had married. And then, when Leanne was born, it had been so difficult. John had seemed jealous of Leanne and unable to cope at all with being a father.

How desperately had Emma tried to have everything in order in the house so that John would not be disturbed too much by the baby. She did her best to have meals at regular hours and to have time to talk with her husband as well as having the house as clean and tidy as possible. But nothing ever seemed good enough for John. He would criticise if the meal were late or overcooked, or if the house were untidy, or if Leanne cried, until Emma felt trapped like a moth in a box – eager to get out but thinking that there was no way to manage it. She was a good-natured person, but with all the verbal abuse, she had started to lose confidence in herself and think that there was something wrong with her after all.

As she dusted, Emma thought back to her own childhood. They had lived comfortably then, she, her brother Ken and her parents. Her father had had a well-paying job and her mother had worked part-time as a nurse. The house and furniture had been of good quality and she and Ken had gone to private schools. The family was able to afford money for enjoyable holidays and they were always well dressed.

What a shock it had been for the rest of the family when Emma had announced, with a starry look in her eyes, that she was going to marry John. She was just 18 years old. She explained that she was not interested in a career, only in getting married. Her parents had pleaded and argued with her, but Emma was adamant.

Somehow, her parents, not blinded by infatuation like Emma, had seen through John's veneer to the selfishness carefully hidden beneath the surface. In the end, her father had been so angry and frustrated that he had shouted that if Emma were to marry John, they would have no more to do with her.

Emma and John had married quietly at a registry office, and soon afterwards, John had been sent interstate with his work. Emma had been too proud to contact her parents, fearing a rebuff, and they did not even know her present address, or that John had left her. Nor did they even know about the children. The ties with her parents had been completely cut.

Emma felt very much alone as she finished her work and went home. She made herself a cup of tea and sat down to drink it before the children came in from school.

Soon she heard them at the door, full of energy as usual. Kylie ran into the lounge-room first. 'Mummy,' she said excitedly. 'We're thinking about families at school and it's such fun. Do you know what we're having next Friday? A grandparents' day. But Mummy,' she added quietly, 'We don't have any grandparents. I wish we did. Susie's got two grandmas and two grandpas and they're all able to come to school next Friday. We're going to make tea and scones for afternoon tea and then give them a concert. But it won't be much fun if I don't have a grandma or grandpa to be there for me.'

When the children had gone to bed that night, Emma sat alone with her thoughts. In fact, John did have a mother, but she was interstate like Emma's own parents and somehow she had never liked Emma whom she saw as taking John away from her. Emma had told the children that they didn't have any grandparents and the children had assumed they were dead.

Now, like a tender new shoot growing and developing in rich soil, an idea began to grow in Emma's mind. What if she contacted her parents and tried to be reconciled to them, even if it did mean admitting that she had made a mistake? She dismissed this thought instantly. Of course she couldn't. Hadn't she had enough rejection already without asking for more? How ridiculous!

Emma did not sleep well that night and when she awoke the next morning, she felt exhausted as if a battle were being waged within her. And indeed, there was a battle going on. Couldn't she humble herself and ring her parents? After all, it was only one phone call. She had usually got on well with her parents after all, except over the matter of her marriage to John.

Eventually she came to a decision. She would ring her parents that evening when the children were in bed.

As she keyed in the numbers, she had a sinking feeling. I'm mad. What will I say to them? I won't be able to think of anything.

She heard the phone ringing at the other end and then her father's voice, 'Hello.'

'Dad, it's me, Emma, your daughter.' Silence. What angry words was he going to come out with?

'Oh, Emma!' Her father's voice broke as if he were about to cry. 'We'd given up hope of ever hearing from you again. It's been so long. I'm so sorry we got so angry with you. We should have just accepted your choice of a husband. We've missed you so much. Oh, Emma, where are you?'

Now Emma herself was in tears as she explained to her father what had happened – finishing with how lonely she was and how she had been prompted to call because of the grandparents' day at school. She heard her father talking to her mother in the background explaining what was happening and then she heard his voice saying firmly, 'We are coming to that grandparents' day. Nothing will stop us. We'll ring you as soon as we know about the final arrangements.'

Emma found it hard to sleep again that night, but this time it was because of excitement. The following morning, she broke the news to her children, explaining about the quarrel with her parents and how she had been too proud and also nervous to contact them. 'So you see, you do have grandparents after all,' she said. 'And they are even coming to Kylie's grandparents' day at school.'

How Kylie's eyes danced at that news and she couldn't wait to tell her friends what was happening.

Emma's parents arrived at the airport late on Thursday afternoon. There were many hugs, kisses and tears and Emma felt enveloped in love – like being in a warm bed with a cosy electric blanket on a very cold night. As she watched her mother smiling and chatting with Leanne, while David listened avidly, and her father walked with his arm around Kylie, Emma felt ready to burst with happiness.

Suddenly, Kylie danced over to Emma. 'Mummy, this is the best day of our lives. I can't wait until tomorrow to introduce Grandma and Grandpa to all my friends. And I'm going to make them the best afternoon tea they've ever had.'

Emma ruffled her impulsive little daughter's hair and smiled at her. This was the girl who had thought that the height of happiness would be to have a DVD player. She knew she was still unable to afford this machine, but, as she looked at her parents and children together, she knew that they had all gained something of inestimable value – something much more precious than a DVD player.

Years later, Emma would look back on that day as the best day of her life – the day that brought her parents back into her life and into the lives of her children.

FRIENDSHIP

'I don't like the colour of that blouse Hazel. It doesn't suit your complexion at all.'

Hazel felt confused. He friend Jacinta was always making remarks like this nowadays. If it wasn't Hazel's clothes, it might be her hair, or maybe the way she had approached a problem. The two of them worked together as teachers in a primary school. If Hazel suggested a different approach to teaching maths, it seemed that Jacinta was always the first person to criticise until Hazel was becoming almost afraid to have a conversation with her friend.

When Jacinta came to Hazel's place for a meal, she would criticise Hazel's housekeeping, or the meal itself. She might say, 'This dish is far too salty, Hazel' or 'When are you going to tidy up that mess in the corner?'

Hazel could feel really hurt by Jacinta's comments, like a small animal wanting to bury itself in the ground to avoid a dangerous situation.

One evening, as she sat alone in her recliner, after Jacinta had left and not before criticising Hazel's choice of crockery as being over colourful, 'People are choosing plain white sets these days, not floral designs,' Hazel pondered what was happening. Yes, Jacinta was being critical, even more critical than usual. What could Hazel do about it?

The two women had met when they were training to be teachers. They had spent a lot of time together during their course and had often discussed assignments together as well as sharing reference books. Jacinta had always been rather forthright but Hazel could not remember her being so critical of her in those days. After they had finished their courses, they had been sent to different schools, but had kept in touch with each other. And eventually they had both applied for positions in the same primary school and both had been given a job.

Now they were both in their late twenties, and both single, but Hazel had a steady boyfriend called Phillip and they were thinking of announcing their engagement soon. Jacinta had had various relationships but was currently single. Hazel loved teaching and not long beforehand had received a promotion and a rise in salary, but Jacinta had not received the promotion she had wanted so much. She was disappointed not least because she believed she needed the money. She loved going out for expensive meals and holidays and was not very good at saving money. On the other hand, Hazel was careful with her money. She had been raised in a large family of six children. He father had only had a modest salary as a bank teller and her mother had mostly stayed home to look after all the children, although she did do some casual work from time to time when it became available.

Money had been in short supply, but the family had been happy. They had enjoyed inexpensive camping holidays and the children had taken it in turns to have a meal out at a family restaurant with one of their parents. It gave them good one-on-one time together. Their parents were caring and her father Nathan in particular had a really good sense of humour, so they often had a good laugh together. Hazel had been the oldest in the family and had loved helping to look after her younger brothers and sisters. Looking back, she thought that her family situation was definitely a factor in her becoming a primary school teacher.

Now Hazel was saving her money so that she and Phillip could put a deposit on a house and be able to move into it when they got married. In the meantime, she was living in a small flat not far from her parents' home. Phillip was a physical education teacher and they had met at their local church where they were both teaching Sunday school.

Hazel and Phillip were very much in love and had shared many hopes and dreams together. They were looking forward to having a large family, although that dream was not so fashionable nowadays. They discussed many times the kind of wedding they would have and what their lives would be like once they were married. Hazel did not believe anyone could be as happy as she was with Phillip. Sometimes it seemed as if they were floating on a cloud together, above all the cares and worries of the world.

But then there were the problems she was having with Jacinta. Even thinking about it, Hazel could feel anxious and overwhelmed as if she had been tipped off that cloud and was landing back on the earth with a painful bump.

Of course, she had discussed the situation many times with Phillip. He was not sure how to respond, but suggested Hazel could ignore Jacinta's comments and act in her usual kind and friendly way with her friend. Maybe then the problem would go away.

But the problem would not go away. One day, Jacinta noticed that Hazel had a new pair of shoes and made an unkind remark about them. 'I wouldn't wear those shoes if I were you Hazel. They make your legs look so fat.' Hazel had always been rather self-conscious about her legs which were somewhat large in proportion to the rest of her body.

She often wore slacks to hide her legs, but on this occasion had worn a dress to school. Tears came to Hazel's eyes at this unkind remark, although she hid them from Jacinta. For the rest of the day, she was imagining that all the other teachers, and the children too, were thinking how ugly she was.

Hazel went home that night still feeling tearful. When Phillip rang after dinner, he could tell she was worried about something. He was concerned. 'Tell me what's bothering you Hazel,' he said. And the story had all come out with a flood of tears.

'I'm coming straight over,' he said. He had been planning to use the evening in preparation for his classes that week, but that would have to be done later. 'Put the kettle on and I'll be there in a few minutes.'

As they sat together on the sofa, Phillip gently ruffled Hazel's hair as she continued to talk about the problem. 'You know Phillip, I've always been taught to be kind to people, but it seems the kinder I am, the more unkind Jacinta becomes. I really don't know what to do. I can hardly avoid her. Our desks are close together in the staffroom. I don't know what's got into Jacinta. She's always been good at giving an opinion about things, but I can't remember her being so unkind like she is now.'

They sat drinking their tea and eating their biscuits. Phillip looked thoughtful. 'I'm not sure how to advise you,' he said, 'but I wonder if it would be a good idea for you to have a session or two with James. Do you remember how they announced at church on Sunday that there is a new counselling service at church and the counsellor is James?'

'Do you really think I need that?' asked Hazel. 'It's not *that* big of a problem. I thought people went to counsellors with bigger problems than that.'

'It's becoming a bigger problem than I'd like,' commented Phillip. 'I hate to see you so unhappy. Just give it a try my darling. And, by the way, your legs are beautiful.'

The next day, Hazel decided to ring to make an appointment with the counsellor. She felt a bit nervous and hoped the counsellor would be understanding. It was arranged that she would go after school on the following Wednesday. During the intervening days, Hazel found herself pondering her problem and wondering what James the counsellor would suggest. She hoped he would be accepting of her and not think that she was wasting his time.

When she went in for her session, she knew from James's smile and the look of acceptance in his eyes that her fears had been groundless. He invited her to share the issue that had prompted her to arrange counselling and listened patiently as she shared her story. She could see that he understood her situation by his body language. He was giving her his full attention. Occasionally he would ask her to elaborate on something she had said or would give a small summary of her story.

Finally, she said, 'I know that Christians have to be loving and accepting of people, but I just don't know what to do when Jacinta makes those unkind comments.'

As they continued talking together, James said that Hazel could choose her behaviour. She could let things go on as they were, but the downside to that could be that she might feel resentful, and that would certainly not be good for the friendship, as Hazel had already seen. There was a danger that resentment could build up to such an extent that Hazel might lose control and explode with anger. Hazel remembered that there were occasional times when she had lost control and reacted in an angry way that the particular occasion did not always justify.

James went on to explain further how some people did not know what to do with their anger, so they would bottle it up inside them until a trivial event might cause an explosive outburst.

James suggested to Hazel that an alternative way to respond might be to share her feelings politely with Jacinta. He explained that this course of action is usually the best as we can deal with anger as soon as we become aware of it. That might mean explaining to the person who has offended us how we are feeling, but this needs to be done with 'I' language rather than 'you' language. You might say, 'When you left all those dirty dishes around, I felt frustrated and angry' rather than 'You never clean up your dishes'. 'When you share how you feel like that,' James explained, 'You are taking responsibility for your own feelings. You might feel frustrated and angry because of those dirty dishes, but it is possible that another person might not be bothered by them. People are not mind readers so it important for us to let them know how we are feeling, otherwise they may not realise that they are offending us.'

Hazel thought about what James was saying. She realised she had never been good at responding in a positive way like this when someone had hurt her. She had tended to retreat into her shell not knowing what to do with the hurt and consequently saying nothing.

She thought about her parents. How had they responded when someone had said something hurtful to them? She realised that had tended to dismiss it as trivial and not say any more about it. But there were some people whose behaviour they resented and maybe this would not have been the case if they had felt free to share their feelings in the way that James had described. And occasionally her parents could become angry and aggressive about something trivial, as if they were releasing something that had been building up inside of them.

When she told James about the way they had reacted to hurts, he explained that our parents are our main role models, especially the parent of the same sex and Hazel could see how her mother could sometimes hold on to hurts and this was the example she had passed on to her daughter.

'But isn't it wrong to be angry?' asked Hazel. James explained that anger, like all other feelings, is neither right nor wrong. Morality comes into the situation in the way that we react or respond to what has happened. A simple 'I' statement or a polite request that something be changed was quite different from abusive or violent behaviour.

Hazel thought about her friend Hilda whose husband was violent at times as well as being verbally abusive. 'But he is so sorry when he gets over it,' she explained to James. 'He's always bringing her flowers and chocolates. It's very confusing for her.'

'He's probably got a backlog of anger,' said James. 'Maybe he's had an unhappy childhood and had a parent who was abusive. Children in that situation are not allowed to express anger. They have to bottle it up.'

'How can someone like that be helped?' asked Hazel.

'It's not always easy,' explained James. 'If they are willing to come for counselling that can be helpful, but many are not, maybe because they don't perceive themselves as having a problem. They tend to blame their partner's behaviour rather than their own over-reaction. Deep down, they also might have a sense of shame and try to keep their behaviour secret. You know the old saying "street angel – home devil?"'

'If they came to me, I would try to get them to talk about any situations that caused anger in the past, which they were unable to respond to appropriately. Sometimes people can spend many sessions going over all the hurts they suffered in their childhood. Expressing them like that gets those hurts out of themselves. If the hurts remain bottled up, they can cause problems as we said. Many people have thought the emotion of anger itself was wrong. They need to see that anger is an appropriate response when we have been violated in some way. In fact, it is a God-given gift. Jesus was angry at times, for example, at injustice. You might remember how he overturned the tables of the money changers in the temple. That area was the only place where the Gentiles could worship, and it had been changed into a place where people were being taken advantage of.

'I would suggest that my client share with me the whole story of what has made them angry. That might take quite a while, but it is really good to pour it all out sometimes. They need to feel heard and to know that their anger is valid.

'For the Christian client, I would suggest asking God's forgiveness for any wrong reactions and suggest that they eventually consider deciding to forgive those who have hurt them. That is tricky. I have to be careful not to jump in too quickly with that one, but forgiveness is so important in our own healing. We do it as much for ourselves as for the one we forgive. I always say it is a decision not a feeling, and we do it with God's grace. It's also important to ask God for healing too and also people need to forgive themselves. It's a process.

'Then people need to learn how to share how they are feeling with others, as I suggested before. This can be difficult. If we were in a situation where we were not allowed to share our feelings, we might think it is wrong to do so. We might confuse being assertive with being aggressive. Remember though that Jesus said that if we have something against someone, we should talk to them about it. Then we have the opportunity to have the problem solved.

'For people like Hilda's husband, there are also men's groups available and that is often very helpful to feel the acceptance of their peers, and to be able to be honest. But if he continues to be abusive and refuses to get help, I am seriously worried about Hilda's safety. She may need to leave him for her own protection. No one should stay in a situation where they are not safe. She may need your support if she made that decision.'

'Yes,' said Hazel. 'I can see it's a very serious situation and I would like to support her. And I certainly don't want to have that kind of build up of anger in my own life. I would certainly want to learn to deal with situations as they arise,' she said thoughtfully. 'That would mean telling Jacinta just how I feel when she says something hurtful. Like when she said my shoes didn't suit me and my legs were too fat. I felt really upset by that. My boyfriend Phillip has been concerned that I have been so upset by Jacinta lately. He was the one who encouraged me to come and see you. Let me think about what I might say to Jacinta in that situation. Maybe I could say something like, "When you say that, I feel unhappy and angry. I would like us to remain friends, but I can't continue to be your friend if you keep making disparaging remarks about me."'

'That would be very suitable,' said James. 'But I must warn you. Until now, you have just been ignoring Jacinta's unkind comments. When we begin to set boundaries with people, if we have not been doing that previously, they may react quite angrily. You need to be prepared for that and think how you could respond if she does react angrily.'

'I don't want to be unkind to Jacinta,' said Hazel.

'No, you wouldn't be being unkind,' explained James. 'Setting boundaries firmly and politely is the opposite of being unkind. It is actually being kind to be honest. If we decide not to be honest, we are opting for peace at any price.

And accepting unkind comments like that is a high price to pay for peace. And, as we discussed before, you are likely to become resentful if you don't say anything.'

'I wouldn't want to cave in and apologise if she became angry with me,' said Hazel. 'I would have to think beforehand what I might say. Maybe I could reiterate what I have said, without losing my cool. As I think about it, when anyone has ever got upset with me, I tend to get defensive. Later, I might blame myself assuming that I was the one in the wrong. Sometimes I might apologise even if I have not done anything wrong.'

'When we are criticised,' suggested James, 'It is a good idea to ask, "Is that criticism valid?" We might need some time to think about that. If the criticism is valid, it is appropriate to admit it, to apologise and to seek with God's help to do better. But if the criticism is not valid it is important to recognise that too. Just because we have been criticised it does not necessarily mean that we have done something wrong.'

'I feel so nervous when I think of standing up to Jacinta rather than saying nothing which is what I have been doing up till now,' exclaimed Hazel.

'It is certainly not easy to change our behaviour in that way,' agreed James. 'Practising ahead of time what you might say is one way to feel more confident. Also, we need support in situations like this. I suggest that we book another session for this time next week to see how things are progressing. And, as well, your boyfriend Phillip can be a support person for you. He sounds very much as if he's on your side.'

'Oh, he is,' said Hazel. 'We're planning our engagement very soon. We're very committed to each other. I can't wait to tell him all about our session. And maybe what we've talked about today will be able to help us in our marriage relationship, although I can't imagine Phillip ever being unkind to me.'

'Maybe in the future something of what we have discussed will be helpful,' said James smiling.

Hazel could not wait to share her counselling session with Phillip. They had arranged for him to have dinner at her place that evening, and over the meal she explained what had happened.

Phillip was interested. 'I've never been one to challenge people myself,' he said reflectively. 'But I can see your point about resentment building up if you don't say anything. Maybe there is also a difference between ignoring a single thoughtless remark and comments that have become habitual.'

'I think there is a difference,' pondered Hazel. 'And Jacinta's negative comments have definitely become habitual. At the moment, I'm feeling so discouraged about my friendship with her that I'm ready to give it up if things don't change. I think I have to say something for the sake of my own self-respect. I thought the right thing to do was to ignore her comments, but now I can see that I'm allowing her to bully me and that is wrong. James pointed out that we can have peace at any price, but in fact there can be a high price to pay for it.'

This was a new side of Hazel that Phillip had not seen before, but he was determined to support her. They role played what Jacinta might say and how Hazel might respond and when they parted for the evening, Hazel felt confident that she would be able to be honest with her friend.

Hazel did not sleep well that night. She found that possible conversations with Jacinta kept going over and over in her mind. When she got up the next morning, she felt tired but was still determined to politely confront her friend should the need arise.

She walked into the staffroom and was soon doing her final preparations for her lessons that day. Jacinta had already arrived and Hazel gave her what she hoped would be a warm smile. The dreaded conversation was not long coming. At morning recess, Jacinta came up to Hazel and told her that the cardigan she was wearing did not match her slacks. She added, 'They look terrible together, Hazel. Surely you must have known when you got dressed this morning that they weren't a match.'

Hazel swallowed hard feeling her heart beating within her like the beat of a drum. She took a deep breath, looked Jacinta in the eye and said quietly and politely, 'Jacinta, when you say things like that, I feel really upset. In fact, if the comments don't stop, I'll have to protect myself by keeping away from you. I don't want to do that because we've been such good friends in the past and I hope we can continue the friendship.'

Jacinta looked surprised. 'Oh, I didn't realise I was upsetting you,' was all she said before retreating to her desk. Hazel also sat down at her desk, her heart still pounding. What had she done? She couldn't ever remember speaking like that to anyone before and was afraid that she had done some irretrievable damage. Should she go and apologise to Jacinta? Every instinct told her that she should, but then she remembered her conversation with James and how they had discussed that she would not need to apologise for speaking the truth politely.

The two women went their separate ways without saying any more to each other that day. Hazel kept reminding herself that she could no longer have peace at any price. At lunchtime, she rang Phillip and told him what had happened. He responded, 'Hazel, I'm so proud of you. You said just the right thing with an "I" statement. Now the ball is in Jacinta's court. The best thing to happen would be that she would come to you and apologise and you could renew the friendship on a different footing. And if that were the case, I believe she would have more respect for you because you've shown respect for yourself today by giving her that feedback on her behaviour. I'm hoping that will be the case because I know how much the friendship has meant to you over the years. If she doesn't respond like that, I know it will be hard for you, but we both know that you couldn't allow things to continue as they were.'

This was just what Hazel needed to hear and she went back to her afternoon class feeling both supported and reassured. Her heart felt warm as she thought of Phillip's love for her. If Jacinta did not respond positively, it would be awkward working together in the same school, but that might just have to happen. She resolved to be friendly and polite to Jacinta but she would not back down.

Nothing at all happened for the next few days. Jacinta seemed to be avoiding Hazel, and Hazel did not go out of her way to speak to Jacinta. Hazel kept reminding herself that she had not said anything wrong and Phillip supported her.

Eventually, one lunchtime, Jacinta came to Hazel and said she would like to talk to her. They found a secluded spot in the lunchroom and Hazel waited for her friend to speak. Jacinta looked as if she was finding it difficult to find the words she needed.

Finally, she said rather hesitantly, 'Hazel, I am so sorry. I really did not realise that what I was saying would be hurtful to you. I thought I was just speaking honestly. You didn't seem hurt, but I can see now that you must have been. I hope you will forgive me and that we can still be friends. Your friendship means a lot to me and I would hate to lose it. Do you know what I think happened? I think I was jealous when you got the promotion and I didn't. It's difficult to admit it, but I was. Now, when I think of it, I should have been glad for you and that's how I'm going to be from now on.

'And do you know what? I think I was also jealous of your relationship with Phillip. I don't seem to have had much luck, in the romance department, and seeing you so happy together....' Her voice trailed off.

Jacinta looked so earnest that Hazel could tell that she really meant what she said.

'Of course, I'll forgive you,' she exclaimed. 'I want us to be friends too. Thank you for coming to me and sharing as you have. I'm sure God has good plans for your life, just as He has for mine. It's promised in the Bible you know.'

Jacinta felt relieved. She had feared that Hazel would want to reject her for her behaviour. Now she knew that Hazel would continue to be the loyal friend she had always been.

The two women embraced before going to prepare for the afternoon's teaching. Hazel smiled to herself as she realised the good news that she would now be able to share with both Phillip and James. I've learned such a valuable lesson in relationships, she thought to herself.

FOUND

Grant felt excited as he thought about the coming weekend. He was playing football with the senior team from his country town for the very first time. It was a dream come true for him. Ever since he had been very small, he had loved to kick a football. His father Ken would join him in kicking the football around the yard, but Ken was not a natural football player. He was doing it because he was a good father rather than because he enjoyed football. Even at the age of five, Grant had been very excited seeing the footballers playing on Saturday afternoons at the sports ground opposite their home. He would ask if they could go over there to watch, and either Ken or Grant's mother Mia would take him across. As he got older, he was allowed to go on his own and he never missed a match if he could help it. His younger brother Clive was not interested in football and his small sister Daisy was definitely not interested in the game.

The day came when Grant was chosen for the town's junior football team. How he loved the coaching sessions with Wayne, one of the teachers from his school who was as enthusiastic about football as he was. The whole family would come to see the matches, but it was more out of duty than it was out of interest in the game. Nevertheless, Grant loved them being there knowing that they loved him even if they did not particularly like football.

Ken and Mia had both grown up in the city. They had known each other since they were children because they had been in the same class in primary school and then again at the local high school. But what had really drawn them together was their mutual interest in art. They were both very good at this subject in high school and would often share their ideas about the picture they were painting at the time. In their final year of school, they had both got honours in Art and Ken had won the school Art prize.

After they left school, it seemed natural to continue their friendship which had slowly blossomed into love. Mia had decided to keep art as a hobby because she believed job security might be found more easily elsewhere. She had become a registered nurse. She loved her job as she was a caring person, but always found time to paint and draw and dreamed of having an exhibition of her work one day.

Ken had gone to university and had trained to be an art teacher in a secondary school. He enjoyed his job, especially encouraging the students who were not very confident. Some of them liked coming to the art classes because they struggled with the more academic subjects like maths and science.

They had had a fairy tale wedding at the local church. Initially, Ken had attended the church with his family and, as they got to know each other more, Mia had begun attending also. Like Ken, she had come to faith in Jesus as the Son of God who had died for the sins of the world.

Not long after their wedding, Ken had read an article which explained that there was a shortage of teachers in regional areas of the state. He had applied for a position as an art teacher in a country town, and, when he had been accepted for the job, they had settled happily in the town. Life in a country town was different from life in the city, but there were many aspects that they enjoyed, like having a chat to someone they would meet in the street and the sense of belonging because they felt accepted by the local people even though they were not 'locals' themselves.

Soon after they arrived, Mia was able to get a nursing job at the hospital in the town. The staff there were very pleased to have a qualified person to join their ranks. The only question Mia was asked was, 'When can you start?'

They were very happy together and life was nearly perfect. They enjoyed having friends and family visit from the city and were glad that the old house they had been able to rent was roomy and could easily accommodate their visitors. Then they were also able to explore the surrounding countryside and enjoy the beauty spots. Being artists, they had a keen sense of the natural world and would often have their art equipment in the car so that they could do a sketch of a scene which was particularly attractive.

Their happiness was nearly complete, but they dreamed of having a precious baby to share their happiness. It was frustrating for them that, as the years passed, this dream was not being fulfilled. They had fertility treatments, but to no avail. Sometimes a family member or friend would tease them about 'the patter of little feet' assuming that they were able to have children but were simply delaying having them. Then they would feel awkward and not know how to respond.

They had been married for six years when Mia broached the subject of adoption. They had enjoyed a delicious dinner together at the local hotel and had been chatting about how the week had been for them when Mia said suddenly, 'Ken, I know we've always thought we would have our own child, but have you thought about adoption?'

Ken replied that he had sometimes thought about it but was not quite sure whether it would be the right course of action for them.

'There aren't that many babies to adopt now, are there?' he said.

'No, but there are some,' explained Mia. 'The babies born out of wedlock are not being adopted as they were in past times. And that is a good thing. It was terrible the way mothers were forced to relinquish their babies when they wanted to keep them. Nowadays, they are given financial support so that they can look after them themselves.'

'Well, what babies would be available for adoption these days?' asked Ken.

'Some parents are really unable to look after their children for different reasons like mental illness or they might be taking drugs. Or some mothers are really young and it is thought by the family that adoption is the best way to go ahead. Some babies have resulted from rape and the mother and her family feel unable to keep them. Or the parents might both have died in an accident and there is no one in the extended family available to care for them. Or the child might have a disability and the parents feel unable to care for it. Then, some babies are adopted from overseas. Often the Australian babies are brought up in foster homes because they cannot be adopted out without the consent of the parents. But there are some who will allow their children to be adopted. There is a different system these days. The biological parents often have the right to have visits from their child.'

'Hmm,' said Ken. 'What are you thinking we could do?'

'Do you think we could try contacting an agency with a view to adopting? Maybe we could try fostering a child to begin with. That would be like dipping our toes in the water'.

'I certainly think we could offer a child a good home,' said Ken thoughtfully. 'Our marriage is stable and we have plenty of room to accommodate a child. And I think we have the love to give to a child. We've been trying for such a long time to have our own biological baby. It's been so discouraging, hasn't it?'

'Yes,' agreed Mia. 'It has. And another thing. We are in a good financial position now after both of us have been working for so long. We could think about putting a deposit on our own home now. And if we had a baby, I could do casual work at the weekends when you would be available to look after the little one.'

As a result of this conversation, they applied for either long term fostering or adoption to an agency run by their church denomination. There were all sorts of tests they had to go through, including referrals by responsible people, but eventually, they were deemed suitable as foster or adoptive parents.

Quite a while later, the phone rang unexpectedly one day, and they were told that a baby was available for fostering. They went to the home the next day and that was when they saw Grant for the first time. They were told his mother was very young and had various other problems and was not able to look after him. She was not ready to relinquish him for adoption, but this was a possibility in the future.

When they saw Grant, they fell in love with him. He was so small and helpless, their hearts went out to him. They were told that they would be able to take him home almost immediately with just a few days to make preparations.

The next few days passed in a whirl as they made sure that they had everything they would need to care for a tiny baby. Mia was able to take leave from her job and Ken was also able to have some time off.

It was not all easy-going as they adjusted to looking after a young baby. Later on, Mia would joke saying that biological parents had nine months to get used to the idea of being parents. They had only had a few days, although they had thought about it often and had already bought many of the items, including furniture, that they would need when caring for a young baby.

With such good care, Grant grew to be a healthy little boy who was much loved by his foster parents. They dreaded the phone call which would tell them that they needed to relinquish him, but it did not come. Instead, one day, the agency rang to say that Grant's mother was now happy for him to be adopted. She was still having problems and could not see that she would ever be able to look after her son. It was a very happy day for Grant and Mia when they signed the adoption papers and Grant was theirs permanently.

Sometimes, Mia wondered what problems that young mother had experienced which had caused her to give up her baby for adoption. She would speculate and then would think how caring this mother was to think of her son's welfare and to want a stable and loving home for him.

They were so happy to be Grant's parents, but when Grant was three, Mia was thrilled to find that she was pregnant. They thought their family was complete when Clive was born, but three years later, Daisy was born. An unexpected but great blessing!

The children grew and were fortunate to belong to such a happy family. One shadow for Grant was that he always felt a little different from the rest of his family. They tended to be artistic rather than sporty and they looked different from him too, as they were fair with blue eyes, whereas he had dark hair and brown eyes.

Ken and Mia were not required to take Grant for visits to his biological mother, but when Grant was quite young, they explained to him how he had been adopted and how thrilled they had been to receive him into their family.

Grant felt blessed to be in the family, but occasionally he would daydream about his natural parents. He would wonder what they were like and whether he would ever have the opportunity to meet them. He did not want to be disloyal to Ken and Mia, but part of him just wanted to know about his natural parents.

The years passed and Grant continued to hold the dream in his heart. He enjoyed playing football over the years, going from the junior to the senior team. He loved all kinds of sport and went on to study at the university to become a physical education teacher. Ken was very pleased to see his son following in his steps and becoming a teacher.

Grant loved teaching, and, like his father, encouraged the children who were not so confident. His first school was in the city, but he often visited the country town, where his parents still lived, to spend the weekend with the family.

On the staff at Grant's school, there was a young maths teacher called Eliza. When the teachers would get into a discussion in the staffroom, Grant loved to hear her point of view. He realised that she was a Christian and, as a result, she had a lot in common with him. One thing about her that attracted him was the way she had befriended one of the teachers whose name was Marion. Marion was a bit different from other people. She was an older woman, not very confident and sometimes was a bit awkward in the way she spoke and acted. Some of the teachers made fun of Marion behind her back, but Eliza never did. In fact, she would sit and have her lunch with Marion, draw her into conversation and listen to her intently. Grant could see how Eliza's acceptance of Marion made all the difference to the older woman who began to act more confidently with the other staff members.

It took a while, but one day, Grant asked Eliza if she would like to go out to dinner with him. The two had occasionally had conversations in the staffroom so they had got to know each other a little by then. Eliza accepted Grant's invitation and the two shared a wonderful evening getting to know each other. Soon they were going out regularly and it did not take long for them to fall deeply in love with each other. Although Eliza was teaching in the city, she too had been raised in the country as her parents had a wheat and sheep farm. As time went by, they each took the other to their parents' homes and were able to meet each other's parents and siblings.

It wasn't long before they announced their engagement and were busily involved in plans for their wedding. Both sets of parents were very happy about the match and Mia and Ken thought of themselves as welcoming another daughter into their family.

One evening, as Grant and Eliza were discussing their hopes and dreams for the future, they began to discuss how Grant had been adopted. He had mentioned it earlier to Eliza, but they had not discussed it in much detail. Grant shared with his fiancée how he would like to contact his biological parents, but that he did not want to be disloyal to his parents in doing so.

'They've always been so loving and accepting of me,' he explained. 'I'd hate them to think I was dissatisfied in any way with our relationship or that I would stop thinking of them as my real parents. Because that's what they are – my real parents. Nevertheless, I do wonder sometimes about my natural parents, what sort of people they are, or even if I look like them.'

This was the first time Grant had ever shared these feelings with anyone. It felt good to share and to know that Eliza was listening sympathetically.

Eliza was thoughtful. 'It would be understandable to want to know who your biological parents are,' she said. 'It may even be good to have a medical history which could help us when we have our children, but in other ways too of course. I wonder though if your parents might support you in your search. They're very caring people and I don't think they would feel insecure. They would feel confident enough in their relationship with you to know that nothing will change as far as that is concerned.'

Grant had not thought of that way of seeing it. He had assumed his parents would feel threatened if he were to search for his natural parents. Now he realised that this might not be the case.

Eliza continued, 'It's possible your biological parents have been looking for you. It's easier to find people nowadays. You could make a start by contacting the adoption agency.'

Grant admitted, 'I am a bit nervous. What if my biological parents can be contacted but don't want to know me? It could feel like a rejection. And you know Eliza, I'm not sure how I would react if that were to happen. At the back of my mind, there has always been that thought that I was rejected in the first place because I was not good enough.'

'How could you not have been good enough?' asked Eliza. 'I'm sure you were a perfectly beautiful baby. No, it wouldn't have been that. It would have been the circumstances your mother or parents found themselves in that would have resulted in that decision.'

'It might seem strange for me to say this,' said Grant, 'But I think I have always had that feeling that there must have been something wrong with me. Now that we're bringing it out into the open, I can see how irrational that thought is. It wouldn't have been all about me.'

'Of course it wasn't,' said Eliza smiling and tousling his hair. 'But that's what children tend to think. They are egocentric and can blame themselves for things that they were not at all responsible for. For example, when there is a marriage breakup, a child will think it must have been their fault. They don't see it as an adult problem at all. That's why they need a lot of reassurance that it was *not* their fault. And they don't only need to be told once. They might need assurance many times. Do you know, I had a girl in one of my classes who was distressed that her parents had separated? She remembered being told that she had cried a lot as a baby and she thought that might have been the reason her parents separated. I'm sure they would have had other reasons for what they did that were nothing to do with her. And I'm sure it's the same with you. It wasn't you that was the problem. It would have been their circumstances at the time.

'Anyway,' continued Eliza. 'What if they didn't want to know you? 'They would have their own reasons for doing that too, which would have nothing to do with your worth as a person and everything to do with them. It would not be easy for you, but would it be impossibly difficult? It would be very disappointing, of course, but you're a strong person. And at least you would know that you had tried to make the contact. If you don't try, you could always be thinking of what might have been. And how do any of us get a sense of our identity? It is through our parents and the way they have raised us, but ultimately, it is through our relationship with God. We know we are loved by God and are his precious children. That is our identity.'

'I think you're right,' said Grant. 'All this time I've been telling myself that it would be unbearable if I were to be rejected by them. It would be difficult, but not absolutely unbearable. I would get over it. I have my strong relationship with God, with you and my parents and siblings. And there are others who love me as well. You know what, Eliza, I'm going to make that phone call within the next few days. I'll have to talk to my parents about it first. That would be the respectful thing to do. I'll go back 'home' to see them next weekend and we'll discuss it. It may even be that they have been wondering if I would like to contact my natural parents, and it may not be such a surprise to them as I was thinking it would be.'

That weekend, Grant went alone to visit his parents. As they were all relaxing after dinner on the Saturday night, he broached the subject. To his surprise, his parents were quite happy with the idea of his trying to contact his biological parents. As Mia said, they knew that nothing would be able to disturb the lovely relationship they had with him. They would support him in his search, and, like him, would be interested in meeting his natural mother or parents if Grant's search proved to be successful. They shared what Grant had told them with Clive and Daisy and they too were interested in Grant's desire to meet his natural parents. Ken and Mia were also able to share that Grant's natural mother had been very young and had alluded to having other problems.

'Whatever the problems were, maybe they have been resolved by now,' said Mia.

'I hope so,' replied Grant. He felt hopeful and eager now to begin his search.

The next day, Grant phoned the adoption agency and explained his situation. They said they would look through their records and see what information they could glean. They also suggested that he do a DNA test as this could be instrumental in finding his biological parents. Grant was only too happy to do anything which could assist him in his search.

Grant and his family waited anxiously to hear back from the agency. It was a few weeks before he got the call that he had been anticipating. The young woman from the agency explained that they had been able to get in touch with his mother. Her name had not changed since they had first had the contact with her, but her address was different. Nevertheless, they had been able to make contact. She had been rather shocked that her son was wanting to meet her and had needed some time to think about it. Finally, she had reluctantly agreed to meet Grant. She was happy for Grant to have her phone number and said she would expect a call from him.

Grant received this call from the agency during the morning at school. At lunchtime, he was glad he could speak to Eliza about what had transpired. He was feeling nervous but also curious and excited about the prospect of actually coming face to face with his biological mother. Eliza was excited too.

'When are you going to ring her?' she asked.

'I'll bite the bullet and call her tonight,' replied Grant.

That night, Grant made the call. The phone was answered by a woman who said, 'Hello, it's Pam here.' Grant took a deep breath and began to explain who he was.

'I've often wondered about you,' said Pam after the initial shock of hearing her son's voice had subsided a bit. 'I didn't think you'd ever want to speak to me. I always imagined you happily settled with your new family and maybe angry with me for having you adopted. Then when I had the call from the agency, I wasn't sure what to think. I've been on my own for so long now and I wasn't sure whether it would be helpful for us to meet. We might have nothing in common. It's been such a long time....'

Pam explained that she lived in a suburb about half an hour from Grant's city address. She agreed to meet him for lunch at a café near her home, the following Saturday.

Grant found it difficult to concentrate on his teaching that week. He thought it might be better initially to meet Pam on her own and if all went well, he could introduce her to Eliza and his family.

That Saturday he arrived very early and sat down with trepidation as he waited for Pam to arrive. Eventually, an attractive young-looking woman arrived and asked if he were Grant.

'Yes, I am,' he replied. ' You must be Pam then'.

'That's right,' she said. Then there was quite a long silence when neither of them knew exactly what to say. Grant felt emotional. He had often thought about this moment. He could see that Pam too was fighting back tears. Then she asked if she could give him a hug and they had a long embrace.

Grant looked at her and thought, that with her brown eyes and dark hair, she certainly looked a lot more like him than any other members of his family. Pam was looking at him too and also thinking there was a resemblance there.

Ordering lunch helped them to overcome a small amount of the awkwardness they were feeling and finally Pam said, 'I imagine you would like to hear my story, how it was that you were given away for adoption.'

'I have often wondered about it,' said Grant. 'When I was young, I used to think that there must have been something wrong with me. I realise now that it was probably nothing to do with my not being good enough.'

'Of course it wasn't,' said Pam and, over lunch, she explained what had happened.

'I was so young, just in high school. Your father was my hero. He was a couple of years older than I was and he was the star of the school football team.'

'Oh!' exclaimed Grant. 'Well, that explains why I love football so much!'

'My parents thought I was too young to have a boyfriend. I was only fourteen. So I used to sneak out of my room at night to see Jack. And then I got into a wrong crowd, a group of teenagers, including Jack, who were using drugs. It wasn't long before I was using them as well. Then one thing led to another and before long I found out I was pregnant. I didn't know what to do and eventually I had to tell my parents. They were horrified and wanted me to have an abortion. I didn't want to go along that path. I knew of another girl who had had one and it had been very traumatic for her. Eventually, it was agreed between us that I would have the baby and an adoption would be organised. I didn't want to do it, but my parents were adamant that they did not want another baby in the family. I am the youngest of five, and they were just starting to feel they were regaining their freedom after many years of parenting. Besides, they were having some problems at that time in their marriage. My father had money worries and, maybe to drown his sorrows, he was drinking too heavily. I guess they felt I was enough of a handful for them, let alone a baby. I did not feel able to look after a baby properly and I was still using drugs at that stage. My schoolwork was suffering and I was not coping with normal living. When I told Jack I was pregnant, he did not want to know about it. Our relationship broke up and we went our separate ways. I have no idea where he would be now, or what became of him.

'I had been stealing money to keep up my drug habit, at times from my parents, so that did not help my relationship with them at all. I was very young and very wild and very angry. I realise now that my parents' problems were troubling me and maybe that was why I was so rebellious. They argued a lot in front of me. It was as if I were invisible. They were so consumed with their own problems that they didn't seem to think of me at all.

'Deep down, I also felt very lonely and sad. The months went by and finally I went into labour. I had just turned 15 and was not at all prepared for that experience, although the nurses were kind to me. My mother did take me to hospital and stayed with me during labour. Although I had a strong feeling of love for you when you were born, I just knew the right thing was to give permission for the adoption. I was pretty self-centred at that stage, but I did think it would be the best thing for you too. Then, after thinking about it a bit more, I had the idea that adoption was so final and I asked that you be put into permanent foster care. In my heart, I was thinking that, if my circumstances changed, I could eventually look after you myself.'

Grant pondered on what Pam was saying. He thought of her, wild and rebellious, with problems with her parents, being on drugs, then the situation of being pregnant and too young and immature to handle caring for a small baby. And then she had been abandoned by her boyfriend as well. It was not a nice feeling to think that he had been unwanted, but, as he thought about the circumstances of his birth, he could not help but agree with Pam that she had made the right decision.

'My life was still in chaos for a number of years after that,' went on Pam. 'I wanted to get off the drugs and get back to a normal life again, but, somehow, I just couldn't seem to stop taking them. Then one day, I was thinking about you and I just knew that the best thing for you would be to give permission to have you adopted. I had heard that you were with a couple who really loved you and were caring for you very well. I had not asked to have contact. I felt bad about being on the drugs and I was still so young that I didn't know how I would react when I saw you.'

'I have been very blessed to be with my parents,' said Grant. 'They have been very good and loving to me. I was special to them because they didn't think they would be able to have children naturally. Then, would you believe, they were able to have two other biological children, my brother Clive and my sister Daisy? They've always tried to treat us all the same. I knew I was adopted from quite an early age, but I never felt that I was treated differently.

'There was something, though,' he said reflectively. 'I'm quite different in my looks and my ways from the rest of the family. They all have fair hair and blue eyes, and I'm so much darker. And my parents are both really into art. My Dad teaches art. None of the rest of the family are into sport at all. I'm really the odd one out there, because I love football so much. Now I understand that I take after my biological father in that regard.'

'You certainly have taken after him,' commented Pam. 'I can see the resemblance all right, both in your looks and in your love of football.'

'Somehow, it helps me to know that I belong somewhere,' said Grant. 'Even if I never see my natural father, it helps to know that I take after him. Tell me a bit more of your story though.'

'I didn't manage to get free of those drugs until a few years after you were born,' explained Pam. 'It was the day before my twentieth birthday. I had a very bad reaction to one of the drugs and was very sick. I asked myself if I wanted to live like that for the rest of my life. One of my friends told me about an organisation called Teen Challenge which had a live-in program for drug addicts. She had been one of my drug buddies and had gone there a few months previously. I could see that there had been an amazing change in her life, and I wanted that sort of change for myself. As it turned out, Teen Challenge was a Christian organisation.

They helped me to get free of the drugs with God's help and also taught me what it means to be a Christian. My parents were not Christians, so I had never been taught about the faith. I thought being a Christian meant living a good life and I knew I certainly hadn't been doing *that*. At Teen Challenge, I learned that Jesus died in my place for my sins. He took the punishment for them all, past, present and future. I needed to receive what He had done for me as a free gift. It meant coming humbly to Him without anything to offer Him. Now I know how very much He loves me. It took a lot of hard work and determination to stop taking the drugs but I knew the Lord was with me helping me. I haven't taken any of them since that time.'

'That is so wonderful,' exclaimed Grant. He could not imagine how it must be to be in bondage to drugs, but he knew it would be very, very difficult.

'I am a Christian too,' he said. 'My parents are Christians and so is my fiancée Eliza.'

'Oh, I am so thrilled to hear that,' replied Pam. 'It was something that I was concerned about – that you might not have had the opportunity to hear the Gospel. Well, that has made my day!'

Grant was feeling a bond developing between himself and Pam. She had been so honest in sharing and he valued her strength of character in being able to get off the drugs. And as well, he was also thrilled that she too was a Christian.

'What happened after that?' he asked Pam.

'I was very immature,' said Pam. ' When you stop taking drugs, you are at a mental age of when you first started taking them. I was emotionally about 13 or 14 years of age. My parents tried to support me, but their hearts were not really into it. They were too immersed in their holidays. I guess I had given them a lot of headaches over the years and I can understand their feelings to some extent. However, my friend who had told me about Teen Challenge was a great support to me. She was a bit immature too, as you might understand. We decided to share a flat together and she took me to the church she had been attending. That was such a help to both of us. I did a course on the basics of the Christian faith and was able to join a weekly Bible study, which meant I was able to grow in the faith as well. The church also had counselling and I was able to work through a lot of issues with the counsellor. For example, that was when I realised that I probably turned to drugs in the first place because I felt a bit neglected at home. I was able to see the importance of forgiving my parents. That was a great relief. I was told that forgiveness is for our own benefit. It prevents us from being bitter. I learned that it is a decision that we make with God's help rather than a feeling. In fact, it was marvellous to know that I could live beyond my feelings. I could choose to do the right thing rather than having to be dictated to by my feelings.

'I learned that I am God's beloved child and that is my identity. What peace of mind that gave me! I did not need to be dominated by my past. I could have a totally new start. I drank in all this information like a thirsty person having a long drink of cool water.'

'I am so pleased for you,' said Grant. 'How did you support yourself during that time?'

'I was able to get a job in retail,' explained Pam. 'Then, as I matured, and was ready to go on to something else, I decided I would like to be a social worker. I wanted to help people who were in need just as I had been in need myself as a teenager. I joined a night class for mature age Year 12 students and eventually was accepted into university. I was very busy for a few years working full-time and studying part-time, but eventually I graduated with my social work degree. I was able to get a job in a Christian organisation and have been doing that ever since. I really love the work and I love helping people.

'I never married, although it is not beyond the bounds of possibility. I am 37 now. People do marry later nowadays. It would have to be the right person – the one God would show me.

'From time to time I have thought of you. I didn't know whether to contact you or not. I hoped you were having a happy and peaceful life and I was afraid that, if I contacted you, I might somehow disturb you. Maybe that's not quite rational. Then again, maybe I was simply afraid that you might be angry with me for letting you go and might reject me. I had a busy life too without a lot of time for introspection. However, every year on your birthday I would find myself pondering about you and wondering if I would ever have the courage to make contact with you.'

Grant looked at Pam thinking again how difficult it must have been for her without support as such a young teenager when she was expecting him. He felt admiration for the way she had managed to become clean from the drugs and was now working to help others. And he was especially thrilled that she was also a Christian. He said, 'I would really like us to continue having some contact with each other. And I would also like you to meet my family. Maybe when my parents next come to the city, I could let you know and we could all have a meal together. I would really like you to meet my fiancée Eliza too. I know they would all be loving and accepting of you and would enjoy meeting you.'

'I would really love that,' exclaimed Pam.

So it was arranged that they would all meet the next time that it was convenient. There was another long hug and some more tears shed before they parted.

Grant went away feeling thrilled and excited about his meeting with Pam. He reflected how comfortable they had felt with each other and how quickly they had established a bond. He thought how things could have been quite different. Pam could still have been using drugs. She might not have been at all open to the idea of having a relationship with him. It could have been very disappointing. He thanked God for the progress they had made in their relationship in such a short time.

A few weeks later, they all met together at Grant's home. At first Pam was a little shy and quiet as if she felt overwhelmed to meet so many new people at once in such circumstances. But Grant was pleased to see how Mia drew her into conversation and soon Pam was looking very relaxed and at home, as she realised no one was going to judge her and everyone just wanted to accept her as she was. Mia thanked Pam for having the courage in such difficult circumstances to refuse an abortion and shared how precious Grant had been to them. As they sat at the meal table, different family members shared anecdotes of Grant as he was growing up and there was a lot of fun and laughter. Pam felt as if she were being drawn into a loving circle of people where she felt safe. Pam and Eliza also enjoyed sharing together. It was agreed that they would have regular get-togethers when Grant's family were in the city and that Grant and Eliza would also go out for a meal with Pam on a regular basis.

When Pam had gone home and the rest of the family had gone to bed, Grant and Eliza went for a walk sharing together about the evening.

'I am so glad you encouraged me to look for my birth mother,' said Grant. Otherwise, it would all have been a mystery. I always wondered about my biological parents. Now I have such a lot of information. It really is like putting some pieces into a jigsaw puzzle. And just as that gives a sense of satisfaction, I have such a sense of satisfaction after talking to Pam.'

'She's such a lovely person,' added Eliza. 'I'm hoping she will remain a friend of both of us for life.'

'Yes, and my parents feel the same way,' commented Grant. 'It certainly helps that we are all Christians. We immediately have something in common then.'

'Indeed,' said Eliza. 'How do you feel now about your birth father?'

'I felt sad to think that he had abandoned Pam the way he did,' said Grant reflectively. 'I guess he was young and immature and didn't know what to do. I will probably never meet him, but I hope and pray that he will have matured and have had a fulfilling life of his own – perhaps with a wife and family. It would be wonderful too if he could have a Christian faith as well. I don't hold anything against him. The teenage years can be tumultuous, and teenagers can make wrong decisions which they might regret later.'

'Part of me is glad that he did,' said Eliza, snuggling up to him. 'Otherwise, I wouldn't have had you. And I can't imagine life without you!'

'And I'm glad to be here too, of course,' said Grant laughing. 'And I know that whatever the circumstances of our birth, it is important to remember that, first and foremost, we are God's children. Our parents may not have wanted us to be born, but God wanted us and welcomes us. I did not always understand that, but now that I do, I feel that my identity is secure. I don't have the identity of an unwanted child, but I have the identity of God's beloved child. And that makes all the difference to the way I see myself. Remember Psalm 139. That Psalm certainly reminds us of how God tenderly made each one of us and also loves us totally.'

'There are plenty of children who were born *in* wedlock who were not wanted for many different reasons,' said Eliza. 'That Psalm applies to them too, doesn't it?'

'Of course,' said Grant. 'But you know, one of the best things about talking to Pam was to find out that my natural father was a footballer! That's such a great gift he's given me. You know how much I enjoy football and I am grateful to him for that.'

'Yes,' agreed Eliza. 'We have many things to be grateful for and that is certainly one of them. It's in the future, but I wonder if our children will be sporty like you are.'

'It would be great, but I'll love them whatever they are like,' said Grant, 'Just as my parents loved me, even though I was different from them in so many ways. I certainly will want to love any child of yours,' he added with a smile.

They continued walking on in the darkness, unwilling for this special time to come to a close. Secure in God's love and in their love for each other, they felt invincible, believing that they would be able to meet anything that came to them in life, and Grant felt especially grateful and at peace that the story of his birth, unknown for so long, had finally been revealed.

ABLE TO TRUST AGAIN

'Julian,' called Anna. 'I've just had a phone call from Mum. She's not coping very well and I need to go there and check on how she is going. I think I'll go over on Saturday and stay overnight.'

Anna's mother Ida lived in a country town three hour's drive away. She had lived alone since she had been widowed twelve months previously. She had many health problems and was also inclined to feel overwhelmed and depressed at times. Anna's brother was living overseas in London and he was her only sibling. As a result, Anna felt the responsibility quite heavily. Ida was 82 years old and Anna had sometimes mentioned the possibility of her going into care. However, her mother had resisted that idea strenuously. Anna had spoken of the benefits of having people on hand to care for Ida and that she might enjoy the activities and opportunities to chat with other residents, but Ida would have none of it.

Then Anna had thought that they could build a granny flat on to their home and bring her mother over to live there, but again, Ida was not happy. She wanted to stay in her own home.

Anna sighed as she thought of her mother's needs. But she also had Julian to think about. Julian hated her going away anywhere, even to visit her mother. It was not that he disliked Ida. In fact, he was very fond of her and thought of her as the mother he had not had.

Julian's problem was that he had been abandoned by his own mother at a very early age and in very challenging circumstances. His parents had split up when he was only a toddler and he had remained with his mother. When he was only seven years old, she too had abandoned him in a very cruel way. They had been shopping in a supermarket and she had simply disappeared. It was only later, that Julian had come to understand why she would have done this to him. He remembered that she had had a new man in her life and speculated that she had decided to abandon him to go away with this new partner. Julian knew that this man did not like him. He never spoke to Julian unless it was to tell him off and once Julian heard this man telling his mother that he wanted her to go off and live with him. Both of these adults were no doubt immature and unable to see how their actions would affect Julian.

Julian would always shudder when he remembered what it had felt like that day. He had been looking at a display of children's toys and turned to show one of them to his mother. She was not there. He thought she must have gone into another aisle to find something on her list. He began to look in each aisle and his panic mounted as he realised he could not find her. After about ten minutes he started to run through the aisles again in a desperate attempt to find his mother. He began to cry and sob and eventually one of the other shoppers had tried to calm him down and find out what was the matter. He was still sobbing so convulsively that he could hardly get any words out.

'I've, I've…lost my mother,' he was finally able to get out between sobs. The woman who had stopped to help him had tried to reassure him.

'She can't be far away,' she said soothingly, with her arm around Julian. 'Let's go to the office and they will make an announcement over the loudspeaker.'

The announcement was made but there was no sign of Julian's mother. After another ten minutes or so, it was decided that the police would be called. The other customer stayed with Julian until the police arrived. She did her best to comfort him, but he was inconsolable.

Julian was taken to the police station and a search was put in place to find his mother. It seemed she had disappeared without a trace. She was not at home and the family and friends they contacted, after they found an address book, did not have any idea where she was either. No one knew that his mother had any plans other than to stay in her home caring for her son.

Julian was put into short-term foster care. He had felt very distressed and found it very hard to settle in care. Every day, he hoped his mother would come back and take him home again. He pondered on why she might have just abandoned him in that way. Was it because he had not tidied his room when asked to a couple of days before his mother had disappeared? Was it because he had got into an argument with another boy at school, a week or so before that and his mother had been called up to the school to see the principal? Julian would go over and over what it could be. He knew for sure that his mother had left him because of something wrong that he had done, but he was not sure what it was.

It was not until years later that Julian recalled the conversation between his mother and her new partner, when the man had tried to persuade her to go away with him. They had not realised that Julian was listening. But even so, the young boy still thought they were taking that action because he had failed in some way.

Days and months followed and nothing was heard of his mother. Julian was now permanently in foster care and he went from one foster home to another. Distressed by the way he had been abandoned, he knew of no other way of expressing his feelings except by misbehaving. His foster parents tried to help him as much as they could, but to no avail. And then he would be sent on to another home and the same scenario would be repeated. Julian did not hear about either of his parents and he not only hated them for abandoning him, but he also hated himself, believing he was the cause of their leaving him.

In school, he acted no differently from the way he behaved in the foster homes and was the despair of his teachers. He did not learn much but somehow managed to get into a higher grade each year, in spite of his poor results.

By the time he got to Year 11, his life had very poor prospects. However, one of his teachers, Colin Hamilton, was a steadying influence on him. Colin himself was rough and ready. Like Julian, he had had a rough beginning, but had managed to turn himself around. He had a wonderful acceptance of the teenagers in his charge and just seemed to be able to talk the language of boys like Julian. For the first time in many years, Julian felt comfortable, loved and accepted when he was with Mr. Hamilton. A group of boys would meet with their teacher at lunchtime and sometimes at other times for activities, and they felt safe sharing their lives in this way with him.

Julian was very much helped by this relationship, but he still had many problems. He still felt very angry with his parents, with God and with anyone else with whom he came in contact. He could flare up in anger at the slightest thing and afterwards would feel miserable and hopeless.

At the age of 17, he left school and, through a contact of Colin Hamilton, was able to get an apprenticeship in carpentry. His boss Brian knew that he'd had problems but was tough enough to handle him. He would take no nonsense from Julian and, in his heart of hearts, Julian felt secure with him — like a child who knows his limits. Brian was also patient teaching him the trade and Julian became quite skilled and even proud of his achievements. It felt really good after years of struggling at school. At the end of his apprenticeship, Brian asked Julian to continue working with him and the two continued to work well together.

By now, Julian had his life largely in order. His self-esteem had improved and he felt confident in his job. He had learned from Brian to be steadier emotionally, and his temper was less likely to flare up over something small. But deep down, there was that niggling feeling that there were unresolved issues in his life, particularly the feelings of abandonment.

At the age of 18, Julian had been required to leave the foster care system and be independent. Many young people found this transition difficult, but Julian here was fortunate because Brian had a small unit at the back of his house. It had been occupied by his mother-in-law until she had died and was now vacant. Julian moved in and was under the watchful eye not only of Brian but of his wife Noelene. Noelene sometimes helped Julian with cooking and would often pass on a recipe that she thought Julian would like. Julian was able to keep his home reasonably clean and tidy because he'd always had to do domestic chores when he was in the foster care system.

Noelene and Brian asked Julian if he would like to come to church with them. At first Julian had refused. He didn't know anything about church and if God was anything like his father, he certainly did not want to have anything to do with Him. One Sunday, however, there was a special service with a visiting preacher and the congregation were to enjoy a meal afterwards. Noelene had described the pot-luck meals they sometimes had at church to Julian. Everyone would bring something to share and the result would be a real feast. Julian did not have anything particular to do on that Sunday and the thought of the meal was attractive to him.

He sat in church with Brian and Noelene feeling rather uncomfortable, like a fish out of water. The preacher spoke about Jesus and His love for everyone, but Julian found that difficult to understand. However, he did reflect on how kind Brian and Noelene had been to him. He knew that a lot of people, particularly his parents – the most significant ones in his life - had been the opposite of kind and loving and had told himself that no-one would really care for him. It had taken him quite a while to appreciate Brian and Noelene's care for him and also that of his teacher Colin Hamilton. In his relationship with them, he had initially tended to rebuff their kindness as if he were expecting them to reject him. They might be kind for a short while but, in his heart of hearts, he knew that they would not be able to keep it up, especially when he was surly or his temper would flare up, as happened quite often. It had surprised him that they did not react angrily to his behaviour. They had continued to show patience and kindness until, eventually, he had begun to feel safe with them. This was a new feeling for him. He could not remember feeling really safe with anyone in his life! Nevertheless, the thought would often pop into his mind that if they *really* knew what he was like, they would certainly despise and reject him. But the thought also came to him that if they could show continuing love and kindness to him, maybe Jesus too could love him as the preacher had said. But he did not take this thought too seriously.

As they were eating lunch at church that day, Julian was surprised that quite a few people came up to him and chatted to him. He began to feel more relaxed and comfortable. He resolved that he might come to church again, if not every week, maybe when there was a special service and another meal like the one he was enjoying. A couple of months later, he went again to church. Again, the sermon did not make a lot of sense, but he felt warmed by the people who made him feel welcome. And it was on this occasion that he had met Anna. She had seen him sitting by himself and had sat down beside him to have a chat.

Julian had got into conversation with Anna quite quickly and he was surprised at how relaxed he felt chatting to her. She explained that she had been coming to the church for a number of years, since she had moved into the area to work at the local library. They had gone on to share about their lives and their families and Anna had been moved to hear Julian's story and how he had been abandoned. As they were discussing how it had been for him, Julian was touched to see a tear glistening on her cheek.

After working up the courage for a few days, Julian asked Anna if she would like to go out to dinner with him and she had accepted. Again, they conversed effortlessly and very soon they were going out regularly.

One thing that concerned Anna was that Julian was not a Christian. She prayed that God would reveal Himself to Julian but did not want to put too much pressure on him. One evening, he asked her to explain her faith to him and she had told him the story of Jesus, the Lord of glory, choosing to come from heaven to earth and be born as a helpless baby. She explained how He, as the sinless Son of God, had chosen to die on the cross taking the penalty for all of our sins or wrongdoing and how He invites each one of us to accept His gift of salvation. He does not force His way into our lives, and we have the free will to accept or reject the gift He offers.

It was on this night that Julian said he would like to accept the gift Jesus was offering and Anna led him in a simple prayer to confess his sins, receive Jesus Christ as his Saviour and to receive the gift of the Holy Spirit. Julian felt lighter as if a burden had been lifted from his shoulders. He was eager to learn more about the faith and Anna had invited him to join a class at the church for new Christians so that he could understand the step he had taken.

Julian and Anna got into the habit of praying together and reading the Bible using some study notes. Julian drank it all in, getting a glimpse for the first time how much God really loved him.

It wasn't long before they announced their engagement and they were married the following year. They were happy together, although Julian had yet to learn to communicate some of his deep feelings to Anna and he also needed to learn how to deal with problems and challenges by talking about them and working out what was the best way forward. Anna had always had a good example of problem solving in this way from her parents Gordon and Ida and hoped that she and Julian would be able to communicate in a similar way.

The years passed and they were blessed with two beautiful daughters, Judy and Kay. The girls had grown up and left home to live their own lives with their own families and Julian and Anna had been delighted to welcome four beautiful grandchildren, two from each family. Gordon had passed away, and Anna had been very sad going through the mourning process and trying to support Ida as much as possible.

As Julian looked back over his lifetime, he could see that he had been very blessed. Colin Hamilton and Brian and Noelene had believed in him and been patient with him and, through knowing them, he had learned not to react angrily at the smallest thing. Through their love and care and through the love of Anna, he had begun to see that God loved him too. Being a Christian had been such a stabilising influence and reading the Bible had also been a big factor in his personal growth. Anna had been a stable and happy person when they were married so she had been able to support him in his growth to maturity. They had learned to talk through problems with each other so that they could reach a solution together. He sometimes thought that, without Anna, his life could have been very different.

There was one thing, however, that remained a problem for them both and that was Julian's irrational fear of abandonment. When Anna went away anywhere or even out for a while on a shopping trip, Julian could still become quite anxious and afraid that she would not return. No matter, how much Anna tried to reassure him, Julian could not stop the dread and fears flooding into his mind. For a while, Anna had tried leaving him as little as possible. They would do things like shopping together. But then Anna came to believe that this behaviour was not helping Julian. She also needed to be free to do such things as visit her mother overnight.

As they sat down and talked about Anna's trip to visit Ida, Anna felt frustrated and defeated. Would Julian ever be able to be free of his problem? She could not think what they could do about it.

But Julian had also been thinking of his problem and wondering if he could overcome it after all these years. He had decided that he needed some professional help. A friend at work had told him about a psychologist he had visited and how the sessions had helped him. Julian decided that he too would take advantage of some psychological help. He told Anna he was booked in to see the psychologist Barbara the following week.

Meanwhile, Anna made the trip to see Ida. She and Julian kept in touch by phone, but she could tell that he was anxious. However, she knew it was important to be with Ida and felt reassured that Julian was having the appointment with Barbara the following week.

In the days before he was to see Barbara, Julian had mixed feelings. Part of him felt hopeful and optimistic that something could be done for him. Another part felt wary and reluctant to hope in case those hopes would be dashed. Finally, the time arrived, and he was ushered into Barbara's room. She asked how she could help him and slowly and a little awkwardly, he began to tell his story. Encouraged by the understanding he could see in her eyes, and her attentiveness, he continued. Over a number of sessions, he poured out his whole story. As he talked, he began to feel less oppressed as if he were being released from a heavy burden that he had been carrying. Then he shared the ways that he had been helped by his friends and Anna and the difference that that had made. Finally, he explained how he would still have feelings of abandonment whenever Anna left him even for a short time and how it was causing problems for them both.

Barbara explained to Julian that he was dealing here with an irrational thought. We often have these irrational thoughts and need to recognise them for what they are — irrational. She explained to Julian that they are sometimes called automatic thoughts, because they come into our minds quite quickly and we can mistake them for the truth. She asked Julian if Anna had ever abandoned him. Had she ever disappeared without explaining where she was going and when she would return? Julian had to admit that this had never happened. 'Then,' said Barbara, 'There is no basis for this thought. Where is there any evidence for it?' Again, Julian had to admit that there was no evidence.

Barbara suggested that, when he became anxious that Anna would not return, he needed to acknowledge his feelings but also challenge the thought that was driving them. She explained that we cannot change our feelings, but we can change our thoughts and, when we do that, our feelings will often come into line. She suggested that Julian say the following to himself when Anna was going somewhere and when the strong feeling that he would be abandoned overwhelmed him: Right now, I am scared and anxious. I am afraid that Anna will go away and not come back. But there is no evidence for that thought. I know how much Anna loves me and that she would never treat me like that. I am feeling as I do because my parents abandoned me, and I felt especially distressed to be left as I was in the supermarket. My mother is not Anna. That was then and this is now. To think that Anna would treat me like that is an irrational thought and I recognise it as such and choose to challenge it. I choose to believe the best of Anna and, when she goes away, I will quietly go on with my life, reminding myself that there is no reason to be concerned.

Barbara said that Julian might need to remind himself many times that all would be well. He wrote out the words that she had suggested so that he could have them on hand when needed. She also told him not to take too much notice of his feelings. Even if he felt overwhelmed by feelings of fear, he must still make the choice to affirm that Anna would return. Eventually, his feelings would come into line with the thought that he could trust Anna.

'And it is important that Anna comes and goes as she needs to,' explained Barbara. 'She should not stay away from visiting her mother or from any other legitimate activity because of your fears. That will not help either of you. Married couples need to trust each other and to give each other the freedom to do their own thing at times.'

'I understand,' said Julian, 'and I can see now that not to trust each other could damage the relationship. In fact, I can see that Anna has been very patient with me because all this time I have been acting as if she were untrustworthy. That has certainly not been very complimentary to her.'

'No, indeed!' said Barbara. 'She sounds like a treasure and, from now on, I'm sure you're going to appreciate her more.'

'I'm starting to see that it isn't all about me,' said Julian rather sheepishly. 'When we have a problem, it's difficult to see it from the other person's point of view. I've been very egocentric.'

'People often are egocentric when they are immersed in their own problems,' commented Barbara. 'That's the time when we need to make an extra effort to see the situation from the other person's point of view. We can always learn something that can improve our relationships,' she added.

Julian went home determined to put Barbara's recommendations into practice. He explained to Anna what Barbara had said and she was thrilled that her husband might be making progress with such a long-standing problem. She began to feel freer to leave the home to go shopping or on other errands or to go out for lunch with her friends. Julian resolutely challenged his irrational thoughts. A few weeks later, Anna accepted an invitation to visit a friend and stay overnight so that they could go to a concert together. She and her friend had often discussed such visits, but Anna had wistfully thought that she could not leave Julian unless it were absolutely necessary as was the case with her visits to her mother. She knew Julian was nervous about being left alone, but she also realised she was not helping him by giving in to his fears.

On this occasion, Julian followed Barbara's advice to the letter. He was still afraid of being abandoned, but believed that if he persisted, the feelings would begin to fade. He felt proud of his progress and knew that it had been right for Anna to visit her friend.

Not long after this weekend, Julian had some unexpected help from his church pastor who preached on a verse from the Old Testament:

> Can a woman forget her nursing child,
> Or show no compassion to the child of her womb?
> Even these may forget,
> Yet I will not forget you (Isaiah 49:15).

The pastor explained that, while the context of this verse was God's care for His people in exile, it also showed God's loving care for each one of us individually. We would not expect a mother to neglect or abuse her young child, but this can happen. In contrast, God will never neglect us or fail to show love. Showing love is His very nature.

At the end of the sermon, those who wanted prayer were invited to go to the front of the church to be prayed for. Julian went and explained a little of his story to Bill, an elder who was assigned to pray for him. Bill grasped Julian's hand firmly and prayed a beautiful prayer that God's love would fill all the empty places in Julian's heart. He also prayed that Julian would be able to forgive his parents for forsaking him, explaining that this was a decision, rather than a feeling.

Julian went back to his seat feeling relaxed and peaceful. It was as if God had been speaking directly to him that day. Anna too could see that God had blessed him.

Weeks and months followed. Anna was now feeling free to leave the home either for shorter visits or overnight. It had been a process, but each time she was away, Julian had felt more and more confident.

The time came when he felt completely free of the feelings that had dogged him for so long. He had memorised the verse from Isaiah and would repeat it along with Barbara's helpful challenges to his thoughts whenever Anna left the house. He knew that God loved him and was looking after him whatever happened and felt so grateful to be released from the bondage he had carried for so long. He now felt free to take up other interests and hobbies and use his time productively when he was on his own.

He and Anna also had a fresh love for each other as he had learned to appreciate her more and she had responded. They knew that they could now go forward together with confidence.

TO LOVE AGAIN

Paul felt a stab of pain in his heart. He was sitting in his chair. What had he been thinking of? Then it came to him. He had been thinking of the delicious pancakes that Audrey would make. He could almost smell the aroma. And then came the sudden realisation. Audrey was gone. He would not see her again – at least not in this life. For a moment it felt unbearable. He just wanted her to be there, sitting in the other chair, or maybe walking through the door asking how his day had been, or perhaps cooking in the kitchen, an activity she had always enjoyed so much.

It had been 18 months since Audrey had gone, and he could still have those sudden triggers of grief. He might be driving the car and suddenly think how the seat next to him was now empty. He might be watching a program on television and think sadly how much he would have liked to share it with Audrey. He thought of a program about the seaside resort of Seaport where they had enjoyed so many happy holidays. They would have enjoyed discussing it so much. As he read a Christian book, he thought how he would like to get Audrey's opinion about it. He remembered how they would pray together and read the Bible each morning and evening. There were so many things they had enjoyed doing together and, as a result, there were so many triggers to his grief.

Certain times of the day were harder than others. He missed her in the morning as he ate his solitary breakfast. Then he missed her company in the evening. Saturdays and Sundays also tended to be lonely as he thought of the times they would enjoy together. Perhaps he missed most of all the caravan holidays they had enjoyed over the years, sometimes with friends. They had enjoyed many holidays in different parts of Australia. As they had travelled in the car, the time had rarely seemed to drag. There was always something to talk about. Or maybe they might listen to a talking book and discuss that. Then they had loved exploring the beautiful countryside or tourist attractions. Maybe they would go out for an evening meal and have a laugh about something that had happened or sometimes have a more serious discussion. They were mates. There was no doubt about it.

Paul would sometimes think about how he had met Audrey. They worked together in an office. He had been quietly sitting at his desk when he heard a peal of laughter as she stood nearby having a quick exchange with one of the other workers. Suddenly, it was as if he saw her for the very first time, as if he had been looking through binoculars which had suddenly come into focus. He remembered the beautiful cherry red blouse she had on and how suddenly he wanted to know more about her.

He thought about Audrey for a few days before plucking up the courage to ask her out. Finally, one day, he asked if she would like to go to a concert with him the following Friday night. A friend of his was singing in the choir and he thought she might enjoy it. He was delighted when she agreed to come, and she invited him back to her house for supper afterwards.

They had enjoyed each other's company so much that it seemed natural for them to go out again and they soon got into the habit of going out every Saturday night. After only a couple of months, they had fallen deeply in love and, a few weeks later, they became engaged, to the delight of all the others who worked in the office with them.

They planned their wedding for six months later and all went well. They moved into a rented unit, grateful for all the beautiful wedding presents they had received and eager to begin their life together. Audrey had worked for a couple of years before leaving in preparation for the birth of their daughter Jane. Two more children, Carmel and Donald completed their family.

They had been able to put a deposit on their own home and it had been an exciting day when they finally moved in. As Paul thought back, he smiled a little sadly to himself as he thought of that happy time.

Of course, it was not all like a fairy tale. They were very different people and had to learn to get on together. Paul smiled again as he remembered how Audrey had been so exuberant and spontaneous in her personality, while he had been steadier and more methodical. They had needed to learn to appreciate their differences and value each other's gifts. It had helped that they were both Christians. A series of meetings at the church had helped them to be more accepting of each other, to share feelings and also to work on solving problems. They had learned to discuss issues together, to brainstorm possible ways of approaching these issues and to make decisions about the best way forward.

The children had all grown and left the nest. All had married and Paul and Audrey were delighted to welcome their grandchildren. There were seven of them and they tried to take an interest in each one. These years also gave them the opportunity to take up different interests and activities. Audrey enjoyed teaching a Bible study at church and Paul would help out in the church office, having developed excellent computer skills.

Their life seemed peaceful and happy and then, like a bolt out of the blue, came the news that Audrey was suffering from cancer. She had undergone surgery and chemotherapy and they had all hoped that would be the end of it. But 12 months later, they got the terrible news that the cancer had spread, and Audrey would probably have only a few months to live.

As Paul thought about it looking back, he could feel something of the anguish of that time. The family had gathered around to help. Audrey had been peaceful, confident of her Christian faith and he had been indeed grateful for that. She had spent the last few weeks in hospital and one evening she had slipped quietly away with the family gathered around her, praying and singing hymns. Paul had been grateful that the hospital staff had called them when Audrey's passing was imminent.

The weeks after the Audrey's passing had been a very sad time for the whole family. They had got through the funeral, and neighbours and friends had brought food and loving cards which expressed their sympathy. Then things had settled down and everyone had got back to their own lives and Paul was left on his own. He was grateful that the children continued to visit him and include him in their family activities. However, it was at this stage that Paul had felt particularly lonely. It was as if the reality had final hit him. Audrey was gone.

Difficult weeks and months followed. Paul tried to keep himself occupied as much as possible. He had prayer times and exercised each day to keep himself fit. He continued to work in the church office and tried to keep in touch with family and friends as much as possible. He tried not to suppress his feelings of grief, but to allow himself to feel them. He knew that suppressing these feelings was not healthy and he did not want to get stuck in his grief. It had been helpful to go to some grief management sessions provided by his local council.

By the time Audrey had been gone for 18 months, he could still experience feelings of quite intense grief, but these feelings were less common than in the early months after her passing. He could now think about her with less anguish and could be grateful that they'd enjoyed every one of their 40 years together. The feelings of grief, although they could be strong, were usually less intense. He still felt quite lonely at times and sometimes he thought about the possibility of remarriage. He had learned in his grief management classes that, when you are bereaved, especially after losing a spouse of many years, you are needy. A needy person may get into another relationship too quickly because of that need. They may not make a good choice. This was exactly what Paul's friend Len had done. He had been widowed and remarried within six months. It was as if he were trying to get things to come back to 'normal' again as soon as possible. He had been blind to the failings in his new wife and had not allowed enough time for them to get to know each other properly. It turned out that she was really only interested in his money. He had done well over the years and was comfortable, but it became painfully obvious within just weeks of the wedding that his wife was not really interested in Len as a person. She just enjoyed spending the money. She became very critical of her new husband and was not interested in sharing the housework. Len had stayed with her but often reflected that he would have been happier if he had remained on his own.

As Paul thought about Len's story, he thought that it would be better to remain single than to remarry and be unhappy. He thought about the possibility and decided that he would be happy to be single unless he found a suitable person to marry. He pondered that he was not desperate, but it would be nice to have someone to share his day with, to chat to over meals and, especially, to enjoy holidays with him. Then he thought how it would require a reorganisation of his life and compromises. Where would they live? He was happy in the area where he was at the moment. He was close to his children. What if his hypothetical wife wanted just as badly to live somewhere else?

Then he would have to be careful that he did not compare his new wife unfavourably with Audrey. He would have to accept that she was different and to value her personality and strengths for what they were. To accept her weaknesses for what they were too.

Over the years, he and Audrey had discussed the possibility of remarriage should one of them be widowed. They had agreed that the other person would be free to remarry and Audrey had reiterated this thought to him in the months before she passed away. He knew she only wanted what was best for him and felt grateful for her thoughtfulness.

What if he could not find anyone suitable? Paul resolved that that situation would not be the end of the world. He would still have a good life with his family, church, friends and his interests which included gardening and golf.

Paul went to a gardening club and loved discussing anything to do with plants with the other club members. One day, there was a new member called Janice. The two of them got talking and seemed to have a lot in common. Janice lived near him and, one day, he plucked up the courage to ask her out for coffee. They got on well and continued to go on outings together. They had been together for six months and Paul was nearly ready to suggest that they might get engaged. Then there was a bombshell. June, one of the other women at the garden club drew Paul aside one evening and had a quiet chat with him.

'Paul,' she said. 'There is something that we should talk about.' June went on to explain that she had a sister in a nursing home. One day, when she was visiting her sister, she had seen Janice there too. She was surprised, wondering whom Janice was visiting. She did not have to wonder for long. A carer came up to Janice and said, 'Your husband is ready for you to see him now.' June was shocked. It turned out that Janice was married although she had told the members of the gardening club that she was a widow. Her husband was very disabled, and Janice had decided to have a life of her own without him, although she still visited him from time to time.

As June shared this information with Paul, he felt himself trembling and needed to find a chair to sit down on. It was such a shock! And he had not had any idea about Janice's deception. He thought of the hopes and dreams he had entertained as he had thought of having a new companion in his life. He felt shattered. You can think you know someone, and you do not know them at all.

When he confronted Janice, she looked threatened, like a child caught stealing a cake from the pantry. 'I was just enjoying having the friendship with you,' she explained. It seemed she had not been thinking about marriage. She simply wanted the companionship. It sounded innocent, but Paul had the feeling that she had not been sensitive to his feelings at all.

For a while, Paul did not go to Garden Club. He stayed home and nursed his wounded feelings. If he went out, he tried to enjoy his golf games. One day, in his enthusiasm to get the perfect shot, his body twisted, and he fell down heavily. He put out his right hand to protect himself and then realised he could not get up. An ambulance was called, and it transpired that he had a broken wrist. He had surgery to correct the break and his family made sure that, when he got home, he had meals and home help which helped him with his basic housework.

His neighbour Maisie also came in each day to see how he was going. She had been a good neighbour to Paul and Audrey over the years. If they saw each other in the garden, they might have a short chat. Like Paul, Maisie loved her garden, and quite often, they would discuss the plants they were going to buy, fertilisers, weeds and anything else there was to discuss about the garden. Maisie had been supportive of Audrey when she had become ill too, often bringing in a meal for them to heat up or asking if she could help with shopping. Maisie had been widowed many years before and she did not have any children. Audrey had sometimes said that Maisie needed a little extra care from her neighbours because she did not have close family. A few years previously, Audrey had invited Maisie to attend a women's group at church and it was not long before Maisie had become a Christian, enthusiastically attending church meetings and reaching out to people in the community.

One day, Paul's daughter Carmel was visiting Paul as she did regularly, especially during the time of his recovery from the broken wrist. There was a knock at the door and Maisie came in with some fresh scones that she had just taken out of the oven. Paul invited her to have morning tea with them and they all had a good chat. After Maisie had gone, Carmel commented on what a kind person Maisie was, and Paul agreed that she was indeed a wonderful neighbour.

When Carmel too had left for her home, Paul thought about what she had said about Maisie. She was very kind and thoughtful, and he had a lot in common with her, especially their interest in gardening. He had never thought of her as a possible marriage partner. Maybe because she was always there and, in his heart, he had been looking for someone more, well….exotic or exciting. Had he been overlooking the most obvious person? He knew Audrey would approve. He started to think about going on holidays again, this time with Maisie. He believed they would get on very well and enjoy many places together, especially the gardens!

But where would he begin? Maybe he could suggest having afternoon tea or lunch in the local café. Maybe they could enjoy a day trip together when he would be able to drive again. Or what about going to the cinema? They could take things slowly and see what happened.

Paul looked up Maisie's phone number and keyed it into his phone.

THE VALUE OF A LIFE

'No one will criticise you if you have a termination. It is entirely your decision. I advise you not to tell anyone about this just yet. You need some time to think about it.' Estelle and Jason were sitting in the room of their genetic counsellor. The last few days had passed in a flurry of anxiety and apprehension. They were the parents of two beautiful daughters and two much loved sons. Life was rich and full, and they enjoyed being parents although their lives were busy. Annie and Isobel were 16 and 14. Jake and Garry were eleven and seven. Jason worked in a real estate business and, when she had the time, Estelle was a writer. She had already had two novels published. Sometimes, she reflected, being a Mum was full-time work in itself. There was always something to do – homework to supervise, a child needing to be taken to sport or some other activity, meals to prepare as well as washing and cleaning, teaching the children how to do jobs and then making sure that they did them regularly. Just taking an interest in each child and having some quality time with each one was a challenge.

Jason was a good father and did his share of the housework and was also good in the garden. He was particularly good at helping with the many trips each week to get the children to school or other activities. Estelle often reflected that they worked well together as a team.

The years had gone by and sometimes Estelle could not believe how quickly they had gone. Annie at 16 was almost grown up, and Isobel not far behind her. Thoughtful Jake was fast approaching adolescence and sometimes Garry seemed seven going on 27. Estelle and Garry sometimes thought about what they would do when the children were grown up. When things in the household were particularly busy, they might dream of an overseas holiday, or maybe one in their home country Australia. They might brainstorm about new hobbies or interests they could have. Or maybe they could do some Christian work in outback Australia.

Estelle and Jason were both 45 years old. They had been in the same class at school so had known each other for 40 years. Estelle had been not been feeling well for a while and one day decided to visit the doctor. He had suggested they do a number of tests to investigate the nausea she had been having, including a pregnancy test.

'I don't think that would be the case at my age,' said Estelle. She had been thinking it might be something more sinister like cancer.

But it had turned out that she was indeed pregnant. Initially, they kept the news to themselves in case there was a miscarriage. They had not even told the children. However, they talked about it between themselves, and over the weeks they began to joyfully anticipate the new addition to their family.

Then Estelle had undergone further tests and the doctor had called both of them back to the surgery. He had explained that those tests had shown that there was a high probability of the baby having Down's Syndrome. Estelle and Jason were shocked not knowing how to react. They were silent for a minute or two as the information sank in. Then Jason asked, 'What does that mean?' The doctor had explained that Down's was a genetic disorder associated with developmental delays and intellectual disability. There was a distinct facial appearance with almond shaped eyes and sometimes there could be heart or thyroid disease.

Estelle felt crushed as if a huge weight was on her shoulders pushing her down. As if from a distance, she heard the doctor say that he would refer them to a genetic counsellor. That appointment was made for the following week.

It was difficult for them to go home and act normally with the children, but somehow that routine of getting the evening meal and the activities of family life helped them to keep going. When they were alone, the baby was all they could think about and some tears were shed. Whatever they were doing, the news they had heard was on their minds and it was a relief when they finally found themselves in the room with the genetic counsellor.

This was when he had suggested the idea of termination. He had explained that over 90 percent of foetuses with Down's Syndrome were aborted. They were both shocked to hear this, but Jason, as he pondered the situation later, remembered having a feeling that this could solve the problem. They could then go on with their lives as if nothing had happened.

But something would have happened. That's how Jason felt. It wasn't that simple. He looked at Estelle. She looked totally miserable. But then she said suddenly, 'I cannot just decide to do that to our baby. I already feel as if I love this little one. I want to keep him or her. Whatever happens, we will take one day at a time and do what we can. I think we have enough love in our family to share with this little one.' As soon as Estelle said these words, Jason immediately knew that he felt the same way. A feeling of protection towards their baby flooded through his heart.

The counsellor suggested they have a few more days to think the situation over. 'Don't make a hasty decision,' he said. 'Don't tell anyone about the baby just yet. I'll call you next week and we'll discuss it again.'

Over the next few days, they remained firm in their decision to keep the baby. 'God will give us the strength that we need for each situation,' said Jason and Estelle agreed with him wholeheartedly. When the counsellor rang, they were able to tell him that their decision was definite.

It was then that they shared the news with their children and felt both humbled and delighted to know how excited they all were about the thought of a new little sibling. They wanted to support their parents in caring for this precious new life.

The months passed. Estelle and Jason prepared themselves in every way they could. They bought a cot and other baby furniture and all the little baby clothes that they knew would be needed. Estelle kept herself healthy and they read up as much as they could about Down's Syndrome. They had a room that they had been using as a study which they set up as the baby's new bedroom. It was next door to their own room, so it seemed the most appropriate place. They moved the contents of the study into a corner of the lounge room, which fortunately was large enough to accommodate the extra furniture.

Finally, after months of anticipation by the whole family, Estelle went into labour one evening. They knew their girls were mature enough to look after the boys while they were away and soon set off for the hospital.

It was quite a long labour and Estelle was exhausted when finally, their little boy arrived. She was so glad that Jason had been by her side. As she saw this tiny new baby, a strong feeling of love surged through her. He looked perfect and she was certain that they would love him very dearly.

Some tests were done, and they showed that little Kenneth had a heart defect that would need surgery in the next few days. It was an anxious time and they all prayed that everything would go well. And everything did go well with the surgery. Estelle had been trying to breast-feed Kenneth as she had her other babies. It was difficult getting the feeding established after the surgery, but she found invaluable help from the Breastfeeding Association. She had valued their help with her other babies and, this time, was especially grateful as she realised the time and care that the association devoted to babies with problems in feeding, including the Down's Syndrome babies.

Eventually, it was time for them to take their precious little baby home. The homecoming was very heart-warming as all their other children were so thrilled to have little Kenneth at home with them. They couldn't wait to hold him and were all eager to help care for him. The girls became very expert at changing nappies and all would enjoy finding little ways to distract him. If he were crying, there was always a pair of hands to pick him up and comfort him. Estelle pondered that he had been her easiest baby. The other children were also old enough to help with the household chores and that made a considerable difference to her workload. When Kenneth smiled for the first time, they were all so excited that they felt they had to do something special to celebrate. So they went out to the local hotel for a meal. The people dining at the nearby tables tended to smile as they saw this family so obviously enjoying themselves and with such a loved little baby.

The weeks, months and years went by. Kenneth was a little slow in meeting his milestones, but he did eventually meet them. He was slow to walk, but when he did, it seemed nothing could stop him. He was slow to talk, but Estelle sometimes thought that that was because all his needs were met before he needed to ask for anything. But when he did start talking, like the walking, nothing could stop him. He was such a little chatterbox.

As Jason watched Kenneth playing with his toys and enjoying time with his siblings, he shuddered as he thought that he had even entertained for a moment the idea of termination of the pregnancy. Kenneth was now so much part of their lives that none of them could imagine life without him. Jason knew he would not judge anyone else for the decisions they made. Some of the situations people faced were not easy. There were babies much more disabled than Kenneth had been and the quality of their life would have been severely compromised. These situations were extremely complex and heart-breaking for many couples.

Jason turned his attention again to his youngest son. He had such a beautiful nature, and, just as he was so loved by the family, so he loved them in return. They had received some help from the government providing extra help for Kenneth with his speech and physical training and they knew he had benefitted from this support. Jason reflected that this little boy was really just an ordinary little boy who had just as much right to live as any other child. What value do you put on a life? Jason thought how all people are made in God's image and are therefore special. He drew his beloved little son up on to his lap to give him a long and loving cuddle.

LIVING IN HARMONY

Eileen turned her face to the wall and a shed a tear or two. She knew she would have to get up and attend to her baby, Rose, in a minute. It was almost time for her feed. How could her husband Les have gone out to the football with his friend Jordan when he knew she was not well? She had a bad cold and it had not improved by having to get up to feed Rose during the night. She felt neglected like a child whose mother had been too busy to hear how she had been mistreated in the schoolyard.

Rose's crying interrupted her thoughts and she got up and changed and fed her, still feeling very unhappy. She wondered what she would get for dinner. Would that leftover casserole from last night be enough for them? Or maybe they could have scrambled eggs with baked beans. She tried to think of something easy.

Les arrived home near dinner time, happy with his afternoon with his friend. His team had won the football and he was feeling very contented about that too. He did not even seem to notice that Eileen was unhappy and enjoyed the scrambled eggs she had prepared for him.

Eileen did not say anything to him about how she was feeling. However, she was annoyed that he seemed to take her for granted so much. The evening passed and, at one, stage, Les asked her if she was all right. She replied that she was, inwardly thinking how insensitive he was not to notice that she needed more help and that her cold was troubling her so much.

The following day, they went to church and then Les busied himself with the computer while Eileen felt more and more angry and miserable. Late in the afternoon, her friend Pauline rang to see how she was going and to have a chat. Eileen had not meant to, but she found herself pouring out her troubles to her friend and sharing how sad and neglected she felt.

Pauline had known Les before he had married Eileen. Her parents and Les's parents had been friends so she and Les had grown up together almost like cousins. Pauline and Eileen had been in the same netball team and it was through Pauline that Eileen had met Les. Pauline had been going out with Frank, who was later to become her husband. One day she suggested a double date. She and Frank could go out with Eileen and her friend Les. Eileen and Les had both been agreeable to the idea and they had all enjoyed a pleasant evening together. Eileen wondered if that would be the end of it and was surprised and pleased when Les asked her out on her own a week or so later. Their relationship had moved on quite quickly and, before a few months had passed, they were making plans for the wedding. Pauline had been their maid of honour as she and Frank were married by then. Eileen had previously been Pauline's bridesmaid.

The two couples had remained close, often having a meal together in one of their homes or going out to a restaurant. Pauline and Eileen would often have chats over the phone or go out together for coffee. Pauline and Frank soon had two little boys and not long after the second one, Travis, was born, Eileen had found out that she was expecting Rose.

Now, as Eileen poured out her heart to her friend, Pauline found herself feeling a little surprised. She had always thought what a thoughtful young man Les was. In fact, they had often agreed how kind he was and shared examples of his kindness. Les would think of small presents to surprise Eileen with when they were courting. She knew that if she needed help with anything, he would not mind helping. If she asked him to help clean up the kitchen when she was preparing for visitors, he would come in and have everything sparkling and in order in no time. He was kind to other people too. He would often be at the church helping at a working bee and would be the first to stop and help someone in need.

Over the next week, Pauline continued to ponder what Eileen had told her. It did not fit in with her idea of Les at all. The following weekend, she went to visit Les's parents, Noel and Dot, as she did from time to time. As they sat over their afternoon tea and cake, Pauline's mind continued to work to solve the puzzle. Dot's phone rang and she excused herself saying that she needed to take the call. Noel's voice broke through Pauline's preoccupation.

'I'm worried about Dot,' he explained. 'She's having stomach pains and they're quite severe at times, but she won't go to see a doctor. She's like that. She doesn't want a fuss made when she's got anything wrong with her. It's almost as if she thinks, if she ignores it, it will go away. I'm going to sit down with her tonight and tell her how worried I am, and maybe then, she will go to the doctor and get it checked out. Why, I remember when she had the flu a few months ago, how she just kept going and didn't want anyone to mention it.'

Pauline agreed that it could be difficult if Dot did not want to see a doctor even when it was important to do so. When Dot came back, they shared some more time chatting together before Pauline set out for home. Later, she and Frank were sitting together over their evening meal, when she heard Frank's voice saying, 'A penny for your thoughts.'

'Oh,' said Pauline, 'I was just thinking about Eileen and Les – how Eileen thought Les was so selfish recently, when he went to the football and she wasn't feeling well. I've never thought of him as being a selfish person at all. I just can't understand it.'

And then, as she thought a bit more she gasped and said, 'I think I understand what's going on. You know what Dot's like? How she doesn't want a fuss made if she's unwell? Les has learned to ignore her aches and pains, and that's what he's doing to Eileen too.'

'And Eileen doesn't like it,' said Frank. 'She interprets it as selfishness. I think you're going to have to have a word about it to Eileen.'

The next day, Pauline rang her friend and shared the revelation she had had. 'He probably thinks you're the same as his mother and would prefer it if he ignored it when you're sick as well.'

There was a pause at the other end of the phone as Eileen digested what Pauline had told her. Finally she said, 'You know you may be right. Les isn't selfish in other ways. This could be what's happening. Another thing is that I've never actually told him how I want him to act when I get sick. I've just expected him to know. But I can see that he doesn't know and I need to tell him what I need.'

'Do you remember that marriage course that we did at the church last year?' asked Pauline. 'We were told that our spouses are not mind-readers and we can't expect them to be. We need to explain things to them.'

'I do remember that now,' said Eileen. 'Looks like I've got some explaining to do.'

'Remember how they told us to use "I" statements rather than "you" statements reminded Pauline. 'You might need to say something like, "When you ignore it when I'm not feeling well, I feel upset and start thinking that you don't really care for me." That's being responsible for your own feelings rather than suggesting Les is responsible for how you feel. If you say, "You never look after me when I'm ill. You're just selfish," that's accusing him of mistreating you, when he may not be intending to do that at all.'

'You've got a good handle on it,' exclaimed Eileen.

'Frank and I have made a conscious effort to use "I" statements when talking about sensitive subjects,' explained Pauline. 'And we've found it helps us a lot. Another good idea is to choose the time when you approach the subject. It wouldn't be the right thing to start talking about it when you're both busy or anxious about something. Choose a time when you're both relaxed. We find that works well for us.'

'Good idea,' said Eileen. 'It's common sense really, isn't it?'

Eileen thought about what she would say to Les, and she did not think she could improve on what Pauline had suggested. She waited and prayed for the right time to speak to Les and, in the few days she was waiting, another thought came to her. She remembered her own mother Gwen. When Gwen was sick, she wanted to be pampered. How she loved it if someone would get her a cup of tea or a meal, or maybe make up her bed with fresh sheets. If Eileen came in and tidied up her room a little or put some fresh flowers on the dressing table, Gwen would express her gratitude. Eileen thought about it further. Her father Edwin had not been good at looking after his wife in these situations. He tended to be immature and selfish and, rather than caring for his wife when she was sick, he would be more likely to go out and spend some time with a friend or even to go to the local restaurant and get a meal for himself there. He did not like Gwen being sick, because then she was not able to care for him in the way he wanted. He had acted in this way when Gwen had needed surgery, and although Eileen was only young at the time, she had been the one who had tried to care for her mother, making meals, washing up and even doing the washing. Her older brother Dean had been studying at the time and had tended to hide away in his room. Now, as she thought about Dean's behaviour, Eileen could see that he was just following his father's example. And she could see that Les too was simply following the example set by *his* father.

Eileen also recalled how her mother would feel really neglected when she could see that she was being ignored. These feelings of neglect could easily fester and become resentment and bitterness.

Eileen even remembered how her father would insist on her mother getting up from her sick bed to go to a meeting or some other planned activity. Rather than remonstrating with Edwin, Gwen would meekly get up and go with him however she was feeling. Now, as Eileen thought about it, she could see that it would have been better for their relationship if Gwen had been more assertive. It would have been difficult to be assertive with a volatile man like Edwin, especially in those days when women were generally expected to be submissive to their husbands, but being assertive may have borne fruit. Eileen could see that there was a point when it was important not to allow someone to mistreat you. We can lose self-respect if that happens, especially if it has become a habit. Submitting to one another was important of course in a marriage in certain situations. Eileen thought how, when she and Les needed to make a decision, they would discuss it together, trying to work out what was the best way forward. They would try to be respectful of each other's opinions and each would try not to insist on their opinions being implemented at any cost, just because it was their opinion and they needed to be right.

Gwen had tended not to share her feelings with Edwin. She simply expected him to know the right thing to do. It was possible too, thought Eileen, that he might not have listened to his wife either if she did try to explain what she needed. He might have thought that he was being criticised, felt threatened and reacted angrily. Edwin tended to be an angry man and the family had reacted accordingly, trying to keep out of his way, even to be 'invisible' or maybe they would try to placate him. It was certainly 'peace at any price' reflected Eileen.

But what about Les? He was not at all like her father. Could he have simply been responding to her as he had been taught to respond to his mother? And could she, Eileen, have been following her mother's example becoming angry and resentful, when explaining how she felt could have made all the difference to the situation.

One Friday evening, when they were both feeling relaxed with the week's work finished and Rose had been lovingly tucked into bed, Eileen broached the subject as they enjoyed a cup of coffee after their evening meal. She shared about her own mother first, how neglected and resentful Gwen had felt when her husband would ignore her aches and pains. She explained how she too would appreciate some pampering when she was not feeling well and how she had felt disappointed when Les had gone to the football with his friend leaving her to cope alone with Rose.

'Oh, I had no idea you felt like that,' exclaimed Les. 'I thought you would want to go on as usual as if there was nothing wrong.'

This gave Eileen the opportunity to explain how he would have got that idea from his mother, Dot. 'We are all different,' she went on, and I am not like your mother in that way at all. My role model has been my own mother and she is the opposite of yours in that respect. But, you know, Les,' she continued, 'I was at fault, because I did not explain to you what I needed. I expected you to be a mind-reader and that was not being fair to you.'

Les thought about what Eileen was saying. 'I am so sorry,' he said. 'I realise now that I was in automatic mode. It did not even occur to me that you would be different from Mum. When I think of it, her behaviour is a bit extreme. Dad's worried at the moment because he thinks she should see a doctor and she doesn't want to go. You're not like that at all. But I want you to let me know what you need from me in future so that I can look after you properly.'

Eileen agreed that she would do that in future. 'I was just following my mother's example blindly,' she admitted. 'I can see now that I need to take responsibility for my own feelings and to share them with you.'

'I hope you'll be patient with me if I take a while to learn,' said Les. 'Maybe write out a list of instructions for me!' They both laughed.

'I will indeed. What a good idea!' responded Eileen. 'Thank you so much for listening to me tonight. I really appreciate your willingness to do things differently.'

'I think we need to celebrate with another cup of coffee and another slice of that delicious cake you made,' said Les. 'You just stay there and let me pamper you a little.'

Left on her own, Eileen thought how kind Les was to her and how fortunate she was to have him as her husband. She knew now that sharing her feelings was a key to having her needs met and resolved that, in future, she would encourage Les to share his feelings too and she would make a genuine attempt to listen to them. A problem that had seemed too difficult to solve had now been resolved like thick fog disappearing in the morning sunshine.

GRANDPARENTS

'And this is my grandson Billy,' said Beryl and she showed Shirley and Tom another photo. They were all for out for lunch together and Beryl had been proudly showing them photos of each of her grandchildren. In all, there were eight of them, so it had taken Beryl quite a while to show the photos and describe the achievements of each one. They ranged from her oldest grandchild at university to her youngest who was just two years old, getting into all kinds of trouble as he explored his world, not realising for example that it may not be the best thing to upend a full, opened jar of honey on to the carpet.

As they drove home, Shirley sighed as she thought about their own family. She and Tom had two daughters. Lilly, their older daughter was 39 and very involved with her career. She was a nurse educator and loved her job. She had not ever said that she would not get married and have children, but somehow her career had always come first. Shirley would never have put any pressure on her daughter of course. She just wanted Lilly to be happy.

Life was so different from when she and Tom had been young. Then it seemed that couples would meet and marry in their early twenties, sometimes even earlier, and by the time they were 30, they might have two or three children. Women were not encouraged to continue their career after they had children and there was no childcare. Shirley had enjoyed being at home with her preschool children, something that modern mothers did not have the luxury to do. After the girls went to school, she had found part-time work in a local shop and had enjoyed being with the customers, but she sometimes wondered what her life would have been like if she had been able to go to university and have a 'real career'.

Then there was their daughter Denise. Denise was married to Laurie. She was a kindergarten teacher and was now aged 36. Unlike Lilly, Denise was very eager to have children but so far, even with IVF, she and Laurie had been unsuccessful. Shirley sometimes felt very sad as she thought about their situation and realised how fortunate she and Tom had been to have their own children without any major problems.

'Shirley!' Tom's voice sounded a long way away. Shirley gave a little start and looked at Tom. 'Where were you, just then?' he asked.

Shirley explained what she had been thinking about and added, 'When Beryl was showing us all those photos of her grandchildren, I felt so sad that we don't have any. Most of our friends have grandchildren now, and sometimes I just long to have a grandchild in my arms.'

'It would be nice,' agreed Tom. 'I feel the same way. But there's nothing we can do about it.'

'No', said Shirley. 'I must decide to be happy for Beryl and our other friends with grandchildren. None of us has everything in this life. But sometimes I feel a bit sad.'

'That's natural,' said Tom. 'You can allow yourself to feel sad sometimes and still be happy for our friends. Hey! Why don't we do something special tonight just to celebrate us, grandchildren or no grandchildren. I know we've been out for lunch, but just for once, why don't we go out for dinner as well?'

'Lovely,' said Shirley, thinking how fortunate she was to have Tom as her husband. She looked forward to spending a pleasant evening with him.

The following week, Shirley noticed that there was a removalist's van at the house next door. This house had been vacant for a few weeks and they were wondering who their new neighbours would be. Shirley decided she would make a quiche and take it in for the new family. She thought how moving house can be so hectic and how wonderful it can be to be given some freshly prepared food.

When she delivered the quiche she met a harassed looking mother with her three children. Katrina, the mother, introduced the children, Will aged 12, Belinda aged ten and Kate aged six. Shirley asked if there was anything she could do to help and Katrina thanked her and said she could manage. 'You've already done so much for us by bringing us this quiche,' she added. 'That is a real life saver.'

'Do you have cutlery and crockery to eat it with and what about sheets and bedding?' enquired Shirley.

'Oh, yes! I made sure those things were packed where we could find them easily when we got here,' explained Katrina.

'I'll leave you to it,' said Shirley, 'but do let me know if there is anything I can do to help. And my husband Tom is very practical. He is one of those people who can "do anything". Don't hesitate to call on him if you need anything done. He would be very willing to help in any way he can. And maybe when everything settles down for you, you might like to come into my place and have morning tea with us.'

'Thank you for thinking of me,' said Katrina. But Shirley could see that her neighbour looked a bit guarded as if she didn't think it would be such a good idea.

'What if I call you next week to see how you are getting on?' said Shirley 'But, in the meantime, don't hesitate to call us if there is anything either of us can do to help you.'

Later that evening, Shirley and Tom decided to go on a walk together. It was a beautiful summer evening and they often took advantage of that extra summer light to enjoy some time walking and talking over the events of the day. They were both retired but still found at times that the days could be busy, so they appreciated the times when they could simply relax and share together.

Tom shared about his men's group. A group of men from the church, retired like Tom, would meet together for afternoon tea in the local shopping centre each Thursday at three o'clock. Tom would sometimes recount some of their conversations to Shirley. He would say with a laugh, 'We try to solve the world's problems.'

Shirley went on to explain about her visit to Katrina. She continued, 'It's so sad to see a young Mum like Katrina having to bring up the children on her own. I'm so glad I had you to support me when we were bringing up our girls.'

'It's sad to think of all the broken marriages these days,' said Tom. 'When we were young, it was more difficult to get a divorce and people tended to stay together.'

'Our generation was encouraged to stay in their marriages, but there were some people who suffered, like victims of domestic violence. It's difficult for them to leave a marriage where there is violence nowadays. It must have seemed impossible in earlier times. And then, women were expected to work at home and not have outside work when their children were small, so it was difficult if not impossible for many women to leave a marriage for their own protection. They couldn't afford it.'

'Yes it was difficult for those caught in domestic violence,' agreed Tom. 'Nevertheless, I sometimes wonder if it's too easy nowadays. Sometimes couples think that when that romantic glow dies down, that means they are not in love anymore and should separate. I worry about the children.'

'Yes, so do I,' exclaimed Shirley. 'You know, we are trained how to do so many things nowadays, but people can go into marriage without any training. I'm so grateful for the weekends we did, when we learned how to relate to each other.'

'What a key it was to know that we did not have to base our lives on our feelings,' said Tom. 'We could decide to love. We learned to share feelings with each other too and that has brought us closer together. Then we have learned to solve problems together. We are such different people, aren't we? We've had quite a few issues to work on in our marriage. But to have tools and techniques to use in that process makes all the difference.'

Shirley remembered how, when they were first married, that they did not have those skills and how they would often end up fighting and disillusioned with each other. She felt relieved that now, when an issue arose, they could simply talk it through. 'There are still often times when we have to submit to each other,' she said. 'We always have to be aware that there are occasions when we can't both have our way.

'We don't know Katrina's story,' she went on. 'I hope we'll be able to support her. I told her how practical you are and that she can always ask you for help in that way.'

'And I'd be glad to help her if I can,' said Tom.

Shirley explained how she had also said that she would ring Katrina in a few days and see if she could have morning tea with them and Tom replied that he would look forward to meeting her.

Shirley gave Katrina a few days to get settled in her new home and then rang to invite her over for morning tea. To her surprise, Katrina was a little offhand and rejected the invitation. She explained that she was doing well with her unpacking and the children were adjusting well but she did not want to socialise just then.

'What about in a week or so?' asked Shirley.

'No, not even then,' responded Katrina and Shirley ended the conversation feeling rather puzzled.

Later, Shirley explained what had happened to Tom. He thought about it and commented, 'Well you've offered friendship and hospitality. That's all you can do. Maybe Katrina will change her mind. In the meantime, we'll be friendly and polite and respect what she wants.'

'She just seemed to be different the day they moved in,' mused Shirley. 'I'm wondering what happened to make her change her mind.'

The weeks went by and Shirley and Tom kept busy as usual with their own family and activities. Then one evening at about 5pm, there was a call from Katrina. She sounded frantic. Her six year old daughter Kate had become really ill quite suddenly and she needed to get her to hospital urgently. The ambulance was on its way. She asked if Shirley and Tom could look after her other children Will and Belinda while she was at the hospital with Kate.

'Of course,' said Shirley. 'Tell them to come in here and we'll give them some dinner. Then we can take them back home when they need to get ready for bed and we'll stay with them until you come home. Don't worry about them. You've got enough on your mind with Kate.'

After the ambulance had taken Kate to the hospital, Katrina had quickly said goodbye to her other children and sent them in to Tom and Shirley's house, before going in her car to the hospital.

Will and Belinda were also feeling panicky about the situation and Shirley and Tom did their best to reassure them, talking calmly to them and trying to keep the routine as normal as possible. When they went back home and got ready for bed, Shirley stayed with them. They were able to ring Katrina before they went to sleep and she assured them that Kate's condition was stable and everything possible was being done for her.

Just before midnight, Katrina finally arrived back home. She looked exhausted. Shirley made her a cup of tea and they talked quietly for a while.

'The doctors said she's got sepsis,' she explained. 'They think she will pull through, but it was touch and go for a while. I am so grateful to you for caring for the children. I just knew they would be safe with you. And I am so sorry I rejected your offer to have coffee with you. It's just that….'

Shirley could see that Katrina was on the point of tears. 'It's been a very stressful night for you,' she said. 'I hope you can sleep well now so that you can take care of everything tomorrow. I've been praying for you and the children during the evening.'

'Thank you,' said Katrina, 'and I think I can feel the effect of those prayers because I'm feeling a lot more peaceful than I was. It has been very stressful but there's something more and I'd just like to explain now why I didn't come to your place when you asked me.

'It's only a few months since I lost my husband. We were so happy together and then he became ill with cancer. When you asked me over, I really wanted to come, but part of me was afraid. I didn't want to get involved with anyone again just yet, not even on a friendship level. It was so traumatic losing Brett and I didn't want to become too close to anyone because I did not want to experience that terrible feeling of loss again.'

Shirley's heart went out to her young neighbour. She and Tom had been speaking of marriage breakups and had not even thought that Katrina could have been widowed.

'And then, when Kate got so sick so suddenly, I was afraid I might lose her,' went on Katrina. 'That really made me panic. But as I was sitting by her bed in the hospital this evening, I realised that I can't just cut myself off from everyone. As a mother, I need to love my children and be vulnerable, and of course I do love them. We need to love even if we know we would go through tremendous grief if we were to lose them. And I need to open my heart to other people as well. I can't just shut myself off from everybody to avoid being hurt. I need to make friends and be open to love again. Living in fear like I was doing is not really living.'

Shirley did not say anything, but reached out to take Katrina's hand.

'You must have wondered what was going on when I rejected your kindness,' continued Katrina. 'I just thought that if I shut myself up in a bubble, I wouldn't ever be hurt again in the way that I was.'

'You must have really loved Brett,' said Shirley.

'He was so kind and good to me,' answered Katrina. 'I do feel so lost on my own.'

'You must allow yourself to grieve and give yourself time too,' said Shirley. 'That's how we eventually get through grief, by allowing ourselves to feel those painful feelings. You've been through such a lot not only losing Brett, but also going though his illness with him, and trying to do your best by the children during all that time as well.'

'Yes. Maybe I have to give myself time,' responded Katrina. 'You've been so kind to me. I really would like to come to your place some time soon and have that coffee you mentioned.'

'That would be really lovely, and maybe some time you and the children can come to our place for an evening meal. We would love to have you all. It's a while since we had children in the house. But now, I think it's time for you to go to bed. I know how early children can wake up in the morning, and you've had a harrowing evening as well. But do let me know if there is anything we can do to help.'

'Thank you so much for talking with me just now,' said Katrina. 'I feel much better somehow just to have talked with you.'

'I'll ring you in the morning to find out how things are going,' said Shirley as they said goodnight.

The two parted and both were glad to crawl into bed as soon as possible.

The following morning, Shirley rang Katrina who explained that she had taken the other children to school and would shortly be going in to the hospital.

'Would you like me to come with you?' asked Shirley.

'That's very kind, but I will be all right thank you,' said Katrina.

It was arranged that Shirley would look after the other children when they came home from school and that she would take in a casserole for the family to have for dinner.

The days went by and Shirley continued to care for the family as much as possible. They began to feel more and more comfortable with each other and Tom also got involved playing board games with the children. When Kate came home from hospital, she still looked pale and weak, but with good care at home, she improved and was eventually back to her normal self.

Shirley and Tom had their neighbours in quite often for a meal and enjoyed seeing the family looking so relaxed and happy when they visited. Sometimes the adults would have morning tea together, either at one of their homes or at a nearby café while the children were at school. Katrina had been able to get a part-time job but, when she was available, she would enjoy the times with Tom and Shirley.

Katrina's in-laws were interstate and her parents lived in the country. Her parents visited as often as they could, but were limited because her father was not well.

One evening, when the families had enjoyed a barbecue together, Kate looked at Tom and Shirley and said, 'I feel that you are like grandparents to us.' The other children agreed.

Shirley glanced across at Tom as she suddenly thought of their conversation when she had felt so sad about their not being grandparents. There was a tear in her eye as she remembered. 'I think it feels like that to us too,' she said softly. 'No one can replace your own dear grandparents but we do love having the time with you so much. I think God has brought us all together because He knew we needed each other. God is so special and I love the way He has done this.'

Tom's loving smile showed that he agreed with her and Katrina and her family were nodding in agreement too.

CHANGES

Marissa sighed as she got her solitary meal and prepared to eat it alone. It had been six months since she and Guy had agreed to split up. They were both 30 years old and had been married for eight years. She still missed Guy.

In the beginning of their relationship, everything had been so wonderful. They had been neighbours and would often meet when walking their dogs in the nearby park. One day, they had sat down on the park bench and started chatting. Both were living alone. Guy was a real estate agent and Marissa worked in the local bank. They talked about their dogs and their work and a small bond developed between them. From that time on, they would always stop and chat when they saw each other, and eventually, they started going out together regularly. They soon realised they were in love and became engaged and then, within another nine months, they were married.

As she looked back on their marriage now, Marissa could see that she had created a lot of the problems. She had come from a very unhappy home with a violent and abusive father. She and her siblings, and also her mother, lived in fear of him. Her mother would always be trying to placate their father, usually unsuccessfully. Her mother never stood up to her husband; she was passive and afraid and that was how Marissa had learned to be too. Anything to stop her father going into one of his violent rages. But deep within, she felt broken and worthless. As a teenager, she had wanted her mother to leave her father, but in her heart, she knew her mother would never have the courage. She was afraid of what her husband might do if she attempted to leave with the children, and he would have made sure that she had very little money to play around with too.

As soon as she was old enough, Marissa had left home. She had managed to get a job in the bank and was able to rent a small unit. She had left the family home, but she had not left behind all her fears and insecurities. Her self-esteem was very low, and she was fearful of trusting anyone. When she had first met Guy, she did not really believe he could be interested in her. She continually needed reassurance which must have been exhausting for Guy. In contrast, he was a relaxed, contented person. If he complimented her for doing something well, it seemed that she would always be self-critical rather than simply accepting the compliment with a smile and a polite thank you. She would often say to Guy, 'If you really knew what I was like, you wouldn't like me.'

If Guy did something kind for her, like bringing her breakfast in bed, she would doubt his motives. She could not believe he was simply being kind. She thought he might be doing it to get something in return. One day they were in conversation with some friends and she saw Guy looking at her intently. She immediately doubted herself and thought he was being critical of her. It did not occur to her that he was just interested in what she was saying. Her father had always been so critical of her and had also ridiculed her when she made mistakes, and she somehow assumed all men would be like that.

Marissa could also be very touchy, flying off the handle at the least provocation. There was the time when Guy had inadvertently walked into the house with a small amount of mud on his shoe. Rather than quietly pointing it out to him or even asking him politely to clean it up, Marissa had taken it very personally, acting as if he had done it on purpose to upset her. When he accidentally broke a plate, she berated his for his carelessness and lack of thoughtfulness towards her. She took everything very personally.

If something upset Marissa, she might go for days without speaking to Guy. She would expect him to know what was wrong without being told. This way of behaving was the way her mother had been with her and she had copied it in her relationship with Guy.

At first, Guy had been loving and sympathetic. But, over the years, he had felt worn down and exhausted. He felt threatened as if he were always walking on eggshells, never knowing when there would be an outburst about his so-called bad behaviour or a long period of silence, when he would try desperately to work out what he had done that was wrong. The truth was that Marissa did not like herself and, as a result, it was impossible to really love another person. Guy hoped that maybe his love towards her would soften her heart, and there were moments when this seemed to be happening, but then something small would happen and there would be another outburst or week of silence.

Eventually, Guy became depressed and felt his health was suffering, so, very reluctantly, he suggested a separation. In Marissa's mind at the time, the problems were all his fault. At that time, she seemed unable to see her own faults in the breakdown of their marriage. It may have been that she had been used to seeing her father as the perpetrator of violence and abuse, which he was, and herself as an innocent victim, and had carried this black and white way of seeing things into their marriage.

Now she was back on her own and had time to reflect on their relationship. With the benefit of hindsight, she was beginning to recognise that maybe it was not a black and white situation, but she did not know what to do about it. She knew that she felt very bad about herself. Her self-esteem was very low and she wished for a better life.

Marissa did not have many friends. She did not trust people and had not developed social skills which could help her to make friendships. However, there was an older woman at work who took an interest in her and seemed to accept her as she was. This was Tessie. One day, Tessie, noticing that Marissa had been looking sad and exhausted, quietly asked her how she was feeling. Marissa was at first wary of trusting Tessie, but the kindness of the older woman touched her and soon she was pouring out her story. Tessie listened sympathetically, not interrupting, until Marissa brought her story to a tearful conclusion.

Tessie was concerned for Marissa and resolved to give her as much love and care as she could in order to support her as she went through her crisis. She would sit with Marissa during lunchtime or sometimes they would go for a short walk, which gave the older woman the opportunity to speak in private to her young fellow worker. One day, she asked Marissa to go to her home for the evening meal and it gave the two women the opportunity to have a longer, uninterrupted conversation.

On this occasion, Marissa shared with her friend how she had been thinking about the situation and had come to realise that the problems in her marriage were not all Guy's fault, although initially, she had tended to put the blame upon him. 'But I don't know what to do about it,' she confided. On impulse, she shared also the situation she had had while growing up, her father's violence and abuse, her mother's passivity and her own feelings of worthlessness. She rarely shared these things with anyone, as she had a sense of shame about them and feared people would judge her.

Tessie was thoughtful as she listened carefully to what Marissa was saying. Finally, she said, 'Marissa, your story reminds me of my own story. I also grew up in an unhappy and violent home. My mother was similar to yours, always trying to placate my father. If she could, I think she would have preferred to be invisible. I certainly learned to hide from my father when he was in one of his rages. I hated the way he spoke about us all. He would ridicule us and call us stupid if we made even the slightest mistake.' She gave a rueful laugh. 'I was always trying to be perfect because I thought then that I could escape criticism. I don't know if that would have worked either! I really felt totally worthless and thought I would never achieve anything worthwhile in my life at all.'

Marissa stared at her friend. 'But you seem so confident and stable,' she exclaimed. 'What happened to change things?'

'It was a long process' said Tessie. 'As a young person, I just wanted to get away from home and begin afresh on my own. I became friendly with a young man from my workplace and we were married quite quickly. I did not realise until after we were married that he had a very bad temper. In fact, he reminded me of my father. I became like my mother, always trying to please him, but, as was the case with my parents, nothing worked. I felt very angry and resentful, judging myself to be a victim. In the end, I knew I needed to leave the marriage for my own health and safety. I left feeling totally shattered and fearing that I would never be able to find happiness.

'Two or three years later, I met another young man. I was very wary. I had started attending a local church and we were in a home group or Bible study group together. While I was at the church, I made a decision to accept Jesus Christ as my Lord and Saviour. The minister explained one day how Jesus died to take the punishment for our sins and we could receive what He had done for us as a free gift.' She laughed again as she remembered. 'It took me a couple of years before I could accept that God loved me. I thought I was totally unlovable. But the people in the church loved me and accepted me, and through their love, I was finally able to believe that God loved me.'

'That's exactly how I feel,' said Marissa. 'If there is a God, I can't believe that he would love me. I feel so bad about myself. And anyway, why has He allowed all those horrible things to happen to me?'

'It's hard to explain,' went on Tessie. 'I guess a short answer is to say that God made the world perfect, but our ancestors rebelled against God's way and, through that rebellion, sin or wrongdoing came into the world and it still affects every one of us. The Bible explains how it all happened.'

'That sounds like a very gloomy picture,' exclaimed Marissa. 'It seems hopeless.'

'Yes. It was a hopeless situation,' went on Tessie. 'But there is hope after all. God wanted to bring us back to Himself and sent His only Son, Jesus Christ to come to earth to die and take the punishment for all the wrong things we had done. Jesus is also God, as is the Holy Spirit. Jesus was sinless and God the Father accepted His death on the cross as payment for our sins. And another thing, God did this because He loved us. He loves each of us totally and unconditionally and has a home in heaven for those who accept Jesus as their Saviour. But it's important to remember that Jesus will not force His way into our lives. We can accept or reject the gift of salvation that He offers. I'm so glad I accepted that gift.'

'I've never heard about that before,' returned Marissa slowly. 'I'd have to think about it.'

'Well, in the meantime, would you like to come to church with me next Sunday?' asked her friend. We're having a guest speaker and then we're all having lunch together. You would be most welcome. What if I pick you up at 9.40? The service starts at ten.'

And so it was agreed. During the week, Marissa wondered if she had done the right thing in accepting. She doubted that anyone would take any interest in her, but then she thought how kind Tessie had been to her and deep down she was thinking how wonderful it would be if there was a God who loved her.

Tessie picked her up promptly at 9.40. Marissa was feeling nervous, but Tessie's kind and friendly manner calmed her feelings. When they arrived at the church, they were greeted lovingly and sat down for the service. It felt strange to Marissa. She was not used to hymns and did not understand the Bible readings very well. When the guest speaker got up, she heard the same message that Tessie had given her earlier in the week. Could it be possible that God loved her? She was still not sure. She was however touched by a Bible verse quoted by the preacher, 'For God loved the world so much that he gave His only Son.' She thought wistfully that it would indeed be wonderful if God really did love her.

At the lunch, she was made to feel really welcome and quite a number of people came up and spoke to her. She felt loved, accepted and at home in spite of her misgivings.

During the week, Marissa shared these feelings with Tessie and Tessie suggested that she come to church with her the following week. And so it was that Marissa got into the habit of going to church each Sunday. It wasn't long before she was asked to join a home group. This was a small group of eight people who met during the week for prayer and Bible study as well as sharing their lives with each other. Marissa came to love the time spent in the home group every Wednesday night. The older women acted towards her in a motherly way and one night she felt able to share the story of her unhappy childhood and her marriage breakup. The other women assured her that they would be praying for her. It was about this time, that Marissa prayed in the group one night to receive the Lord Jesus Christ as her Saviour and Lord. She asked Him to forgive her sins and to come into her life through the Holy Spirit.

When she prayed this prayer, Marissa felt relaxed as if a load had been lifted from her shoulders. But she still felt in need of emotional healing. Kathryn, one of the women in the group suggested that she have prayer ministry. Kathryn was part of a prayer ministry team. A couple of people would pray for the person who needed healing and another group of people would be praying in the next room while the session was going on.

Marissa felt nervous of going to prayer ministry, but she knew she needed emotional healing and she remembered how much she had been loved and accepted by the Christians with whom she had come in contact.

Over a period of months, Marissa went to prayer ministry and God moved powerfully in her life. She was able to picture Jesus holding her as the vulnerable little child she had been and to see her true worth and value in His sight. She was able to see that her parents had their own unresolved problems which had played out in their behaviour towards her. She had always assumed that she deserved their treatment of her and that she had been somehow responsible for the family situation - that she had been the cause of the problems in the family. She was able to see herself as a helpless little girl who did not deserve the treatment she had received. It was suggested that she forgive her parents. At first, she thought that was impossible, but the prayer ministers explained that it was a decision she could make with God's help. She was not to worry about her feelings. Whenever she felt angry and resentful, she could simple affirm forgiveness and focus on something else. It took a while, but eventually, Marissa began to see her parents in a different light. She began to feel compassion for them and even to be thankful for any good qualities she could see in their lives. She prayed that God would give her the ability to love her parents and began to pray for them regularly. She had only visited them occasionally since she had left home, but now she hoped to visit them more often. She realised too that she would need to cut the visit short if her father became abusive to her. She would need to protect herself.

The prayer ministers prayed for emotional healing of all that Marissa had gone through as a child and encouraged her to read and ponder on verses in the Bible which would remind her of God's love and His desire for her healing. It was a process, but, gradually, she began to see herself as a whole person rather than someone wounded and broken.

Marissa could see that her relationships were improving, especially as she had been learning to manage her anger. She could see now that it was understandable that she would have been angry for the way she had been treated as a child. She had a session where she poured out her anger to God and asked Him to take that anger from her and to fill all the places where it had been with His love and grace. She also learned ways of managing her anger which she could now see as a gift from God to tell her that something was wrong – that someone was taking advantage of her. She pondered on the Bible verse, 'Be angry but sin not', and learned that anger itself was not wrong, but what she did with it could be wrong. When she felt angry with someone, she learned to take a step backward and not to react immediately. She would ask herself if her anger was justified and learn to respond in a loving way. For example, when her fellow worker in the bank, Loris, kept taking the pens off her desk, she felt angry. She realised that her anger was justified and decided to tell Loris that she needed the pens and it was frustrating when they disappeared from her desk. She spoke in a calm, respectful voice and, to her surprise, Loris apologised and said she would not do it again. She had been thoughtless and had not realised how annoying her actions were.

In the past, Marissa would have felt resentful towards Loris but would not have said anything. She might have acted in a passive-aggressive way by taking something off Loris's desk. She realised that, when she bottled up her anger, it could accumulate within her until she might explode with anger about some small thing. She knew too that not everyone would respond as Loris had done. There could be times when someone might become angry with her for being assertive. As Marissa thought about that, she recalled a conversation she had had with Tessie. They had discussed how we cannot please everybody, but it is not the end of the world if someone does not like us or if they respond in a negative way when we are assertive. That conversation had been a revelation for Marissa. She had always thought it would be a disaster if someone did not like her. Now she saw it was inevitable occasionally, and she devised a plan to deal with this situation when it might occur in the future. She would pray for that person, make a decision to forgive them and ask for healing of any hurts she had felt as a result of the interaction.

In all the discussions about anger and how to manage it, Marissa found herself thinking increasingly about Guy and their relationship. She was beginning to see more and more how she had often taken offence when none was intended. She had flared up or spent days not speaking to her husband. As she tried to put herself into her husband's shoes, she thought how very frustrating it must have been for him. No wonder he had made the decision to leave her.

He had become depressed and concerned for his health. She wondered what he was doing now.

One morning, Marissa woke up with an overwhelming feeling that she needed to apologise unreservedly to Guy for the way she had treated him. She'd had no contact with him since the divorce a couple of years previously. Maybe he had another partner by then. She did not even know if he were still working with the same real estate agent. She thought carefully about what she might do. An email or text might make her apology seem too trivial. But if he had another partner, she did not want to cause problems between them. She thought and prayed about it for a couple of days and finally decided that she would ring him on his mobile and ask if they could meet.

Guy answered the mobile and she explained that she wanted to speak to him. She could hear from his tone of voice that he felt cautious about the whole idea. It was not surprising considering what had occurred in their marriage. However, he agreed to meet her after work at a local coffee shop. Marissa hoped she would be able to explain everything to him and that he would accept her apology.

The day came. Marissa had asked her church group to pray for her. She and Guy met at the shop and each ordered coffee. Marissa thanked Guy for coming and began to explain all the changes that had taken place in her life since their divorce. At first it felt awkward, but, as Guy realised Marissa was not going to attack him, he felt more comfortable and was able to listen.

As far as she could, Marissa explained the whole story, beginning with her friendship with Tessie, her going to the church, her decision to become a Christian and all that she had learned from the prayer ministry. Finally, she explained how she wanted to apologise for the way she had treated him in the marriage.

'I was only thinking about myself and my knee jerk reactions,' she explained. 'I see now that I was all wrapped up in myself and wasn't thinking about you at all. It must have been very difficult for you and I can understand that you must have felt hopeless about our relationship. I just want to say how sorry I am that I put you through such a lot of pain. I see myself differently now. I understand how much God loves me and I value myself now. And that helps me to value other people. I'm learning to see things from the point of view of the other person. I do hope you can forgive me.'

Guy hesitated and looked serious. 'I need some time to think this through,' he said. 'I can see that you have changed a lot and I am grateful for that. However, you did hurt me a lot, and it is difficult to forgive. Give me some time to think about it and I will get back to you.'

With that, Marissa had to be content. She reminded herself that she had done all that she could in apologising and Guy's reaction was his responsibility.

A few weeks went by and Marissa immersed herself in her work and church activities. She hoped that Guy would get back to her, but she could understand how forgiveness could be difficult.

Then, one evening her phone rang and it was Guy. He asked her to meet at the same coffee shop the following day so that they could continue their discussion.

After ordering their coffee, Guy immediately plunged into serious discussion. He explained how surprised he had been that they'd had their previous conversation. He had not been expecting it at all. He could see even from talking to her that evening that her whole manner was different, and he had marvelled that such a change could have taken place. He was interested in the church she had described and the small group and the prayer ministry she had received. He even said that, although he had never had a church background, he would be interested in attending the church, just to check out if it were really as good as Marissa had described it. As they continued to talk, Marissa felt more comfortable with Guy who also asked her to forgive any wrong behaviour on his part.

'It always takes two,' he said. 'My reactions were not always good. I hope you will forgive me for the part I played in our marriage.'

Marissa had not been expecting this and felt immediately able to assure Guy of her forgiveness. She added, 'Maybe you might like to come to the church on Sunday.'

'I think I will,' said Guy. Marissa gave him the details and they parted amicably.

On the Sunday, Marissa was pleased to see that Guy did come, and just as she had been welcomed so warmly, so she could see that he also was warmly welcomed. She spoke to him only briefly and hoped he would continue coming to church.

As it turned out, Guy did continue to come to church and, like Marissa, was also welcomed into a small group. And also like Marissa, it was not long before he too made a commitment to Jesus as his Lord and Saviour.

 A few months later, Marissa was surprised to get another call from Guy. She had only had minimal contact with him at church. Once again, they met after work at the coffee shop.

After they had relaxed for a while and discussed how their day's work had been for them, Guy said, 'I suppose you're wondering why I've asked you to come here this evening. I've been thinking about it for a while now, and I'm wondering if we could try getting back together. I don't mean immediately,' he added quickly. 'We've probably got a lot of issues to discuss and work through, so we would need to take it very slowly.'

Guy went on to explain that after he and Marissa had been divorced, he'd had a brief relationship with another young woman. 'It was too soon after the breakup of our relationship,' he continued. 'I wasn't ready for another relationship but somehow it seemed the right thing because it felt good just to have a partner again and I hoped it would make me feel less lonely. It wasn't fair to her just as it wasn't right for me. Since then, I haven't had any relationships, and now I feel ready to at least consider that you and I might have another try at being together.'

Marissa was surprised. She had thought their relationship was over. 'We…ell,' she said thoughtfully, 'Let's take it very slowly and see what happens. I know I'm a very different person now from what I was. I do like the idea of talking to someone, maybe a counsellor about our issues.'

'Why don't we?' said Guy. 'Actually, I believe Don Brown does very good pre-marriage preparation. Why don't we try that?' Don was one of the ministers from their church.

'I do know I'm a different person from when we were married,' said Marissa. 'I almost think we could manage on our own. But let's have a few sessions with Don as well. Maybe we could also have a regular date night when we go out to dinner.'

Marissa and Guy enjoyed their marriage preparation classes. It was like starting all over again. They found it helpful to discuss many topics with Don, beginning with their families of origin and their resulting expectations. Then they worked on communication and sharing feelings in a loving way. Among other things, they discussed how they would deal with stress, with their in-laws, money, their sexual relationship, their relationship with God and home maintenance. They felt they had been given keys to help them to deal with difficult situations. Don explained that it was inevitable that they would disagree about some issues and how to communicate in a positive and loving way when this would happen.

On their weekly nights out, Marissa and Guy would discuss what they had been learning together. Marissa knew she would now be much more able to share her feelings if she were hurt about something. There would now be no need to attack Guy or give him the silent treatment as before. And Guy recognised too that there were times when he would need to be more assertive, rather than silently putting up with bad behaviour. That unfinished business had led to him being depressed and he was determined that this would not happen again. Gradually too, the feelings of love that they had once had for each other were coming back as they were able to begin to trust each other again.

Time went by and eventually they both knew that they were ready to make the big step of recommitting to each other. They were remarried in a quiet ceremony with just their immediate family present. Don officiated at the wedding.

On their wedding morning, Marissa thought about their previous wedding day. Their hopes had been so high, but she now realised how unprepared they had been. They had both changed so much since then, that they seemed like different people. She had a momentary feeling of fear. What if things did not work out this second time around? But then she knew that with God's help, and the help they had received from Don, they would be able to weather any problems and conflicts.

She took a deep breath and went quietly and confidently out to the car which was waiting to take her to the church.

SHARING THE LOAD

Catherine heard the boys screaming in the other room. Oh, no! What was it this time? She ran to see what was happening. Shawn and Timothy were fighting over a toy while baby Jonathan cried loudly in a corner.

'Stop it boys,' shouted Catherine trying to restore order. 'Take turns. You go first Shawn and then it will be your turn in a minute, Timothy.' Timothy reluctantly let go and order was restored for at least the time being.

Catherine sighed. She loved being a Mum, but she had to admit it was, well, constant. The boys were so close in age too. She and her husband Justin had initially thought this would be a good idea. Having their children close together would mean they would play well together. Now Shawn was four, Timothy was three and Jonathan was just 18 months old.

Catherine and Justin had decided that she would stay home with the boys while they were pre-schoolers. She was able to do that because she worked in the family business. Justin was a motor mechanic. He had his own business and Catherine had worked there doing the office work until not long before Shawn was born. As it turned out, Justin's sister Julia was looking for work at that time. Her youngest child had just started school and she was glad to be able to do the work until Catherine was ready to return.

Justin and Julia's parents had worked very long hours as owners of a restaurant when their children were little. The children had sometimes felt neglected and, when they had become parents themselves, had both resolved that it was important, if possible, to have one parent at home before the children went to school. Catherine had been happy to fit in with this plan. She knew the time would pass quickly enough and that she would be able to go back to work again when the boys were all in school.

But sometimes, the time did not seem to be passing that quickly. Catherine would chide herself as she thought how fortunate they were to have three healthy boys. She remembered her school friend Carry who had tried so hard on the IVF program and yet was still childless. What right did she have to complain when she was blessed with three beautiful boys? Nevertheless, there were times when she felt completely overwhelmed and would wonder how she would be able to keep going.

Catherine had tried to share her feelings with Justin, but he did not seem to understand. They had made the agreement and he expected her to stick with it. It was not that he was harsh. He just saw things through the lens of his own childhood.

Then one day, Catherine got a call from her mother to say that she was going to visit them. Catherine was thrilled. Her mother lived in another capital city, so they did not get together very often. Her mother Angeline explained that this time, Catherine's father Ed would not be able to come with her. He was very busy with a new project at work, but Angeline had some time off and was glad of the opportunity to visit Catherine and the family. She was always glad to see the boys who were growing up so fast.

Catherine really looked forward to Angeline's visit. She had always valued the support her parents gave her and knew this visit would not be an exception. The days went by and it was not long before they were picking Angeline up from the airport. The boys were excited to see Nanna again and Justin always appreciated his mother-in-law's visits too.

After they had had a meal together and Angeline had spent time with the children before they went to bed, Justin needed to make some phone calls and Catherine and Angeline sat down together over a cup of tea and a chat.

'You look a bit tired, Catherine,' said her mother. 'It's a very busy time of your life isn't it with three pre-schoolers? And the boys are so active. You must feel as if you are on the go most of the time.'

Her mother's sympathy touched Catherine's heart. It seemed so long since someone had been so concerned about her. Tears sprang to her eyes as she tried to explain her feelings to Angeline.

'It's not that I'm not grateful for having the boys and I should be grateful for having the opportunity to look after them full-time during these important years. When I think of Carrie and her struggles with IVF, I feel really guilty. I'm the fortunate one. But, sometimes, well, it does seem to get a bit overwhelming. I feel I'm working all the time and it's so hard to keep the house tidy. There doesn't seem to be much to show for all the work I've done at the end of the day. And then, I can't expect Justin to help too much. He's working so hard in the business. You know how important it is for us to have a parent full-time with the boys during their pre-school years.'

Angeline was thoughtful. 'Nevertheless, it does sound overwhelming for you,' she said. 'I'm glad I'm here because I think we need to think this situation through. And Justin needs to be involved in that process, too. For a start, Carrie's problems with IVF, while it's been very sad for them, do not invalidate the way you feel. It's important that you recognise that you are finding things difficult so that we can all work out the way ahead.'

Catherine looked gratefully at her mother. It was so good to have another person's perspective on the way she was feeling, and to know that she did not need to feel guilty because she was feeling overwhelmed.

'And another thing,' said her mother. 'I think you need to go to the doctor and have a thorough medical check-up. You need to be super fit for the job you are doing at present. She may be able to suggest something which can help.'

Catherine agreed, pondering that she had been putting her own needs last when the needs of the rest of the family were so pressing.

'We need to think things through,' continued Angeline. 'When was the last time you played the recorder? You used to love being in your recorder group, didn't you?'

Catherine confessed that she had totally given up playing the recorder. 'I know I used to love it so much, and it was a bonus to have the group. We weren't wonderful players, but we enjoyed playing the pieces so much together. It was such fun.'

'Are the other girls still involved in that group?' enquired her mother.

'Oh yes. They still meet every Tuesday night,' replied Catherine wistfully. 'I would love to rejoin the group and I know they would love to have me. It's just....' Her voice trailed away.

'What?' enquired Angeline.

'I gave up the group when Jonathan was born,' confessed Catherine. 'I was so busy and somehow it seemed a bit selfish to continue to go to the group when there was so much to do at home.'

'It sounds as if you didn't think you had the right to have an interest of your own. But Catherine, you need to have your own interests and not feel guilty. You need to have something to look forward to during your week. When you feel bogged down with children and the household chores, you need to smile to yourself and picture yourself in the group having fun with the other girls. That will help to keep you going in the difficult times.'

'It does sound wonderful,' agreed her daughter. 'Maybe we could have an earlier dinner on Tuesday nights and Justin could babysit the children.'

'No, he would not be babysitting,' said Angeline smiling. 'That would be when he was looking after someone else's children. Looking after the boys, he would just be doing his duty as a father.'

'I hadn't thought of it like that,' exclaimed Catherine.

'He needs time with them to bond with them,' went on Angeline. 'I bet the boys would love to have him spending that time with them and putting them to bed. Does he put them to bed sometimes?'

'Only very occasionally,' explained Catherine. 'I don't like to burden him as he is so busy with the business.'

'No wonder you're exhausted,' said Angeline. 'Remember that you've been working very hard on a very difficult job all day yourself. Many mothers are working nowadays outside the home, and I've heard more than one say that the days they are home with the children are more tiring than the ones they spend at work.

'I've got an idea,' said Angeline suddenly. 'What if I look after the boys one evening and you and Justin can go out to dinner and you can discuss what we've been talking about with him. I even think you need some time out during the day occasionally – maybe once a week. And you and Justin need to have a regular date night as well. You need that for your own relationship to thrive. And that's very good for the boys as well. They need to see their parents making time for each other. You are role models for them after all. Now, I don't want to be too bossy, but I am concerned for you, and think a few changes could make all the difference to your life.'

Catherine thanked her mother. Already she was beginning to feel hopeful that things could change so that her burden could be lightened.

Angeline was as good as her word and a few days later, she was looking after the boys as Catherine and Justin prepared for their night out.

'How long has it been since we've done this?' asked Justin as they drove to the restaurant.

'I can't remember,' admitted Catherine, 'But I think we need to do it more often. Our lives are so busy, that it's easy to lose touch with each other. It feels so good to be going out with you. I feel like a teenager on a date.'

Justin agreed. As they relaxed over their meal, Catherine was able to share how she had been feeling and the suggestions her mother had made.

'How would you feel about having an earlier meal on Tuesday nights and then you could look after the boys while I go to my recorder group?' she said.

Justin pondered what Catherine had said. 'I agree with your mother that you need to have an interest of your own,' he replied. 'Yes, I am very busy with the business but give me some time to think about that. And I agree that it would be good for you to have some time off during the day once a week too – maybe to meet a friend for coffee. And I certainly think we have been neglecting our own relationship. We need a date night and I think once a week would be a good idea. I've been working so hard to build up the business that I'm afraid I haven't been thinking about what it's been like for you. If I had the boys full-time, I would definitely need a break sometime!'

Catherine felt relieved that Justin understood. She had feared that he would have found it difficult to see her point of view.

As they drank their hot chocolate, Justin said suddenly, 'I think I know what we might be able to do. Do you remember my old schoolmate Peter? I met him recently at the shops. His father was a motor mechanic and he retired recently. Peter said it's been a bit difficult for him going from full-time work to retirement and his father's really missing the work. But he's not missing all that owning his own business entails! I wonder if he might like to work for me for one or two days a week. That would mean I wouldn't be so busy. It would free up my time to look after the boys during the day while you had your time out and I could come home earlier on Tuesday nights. And earlier on our date night too,' he added.

'We'll have to find a babysitter for that night,' said Catherine. 'What if I ask at church if there's a young girl who would sit for us once a week? I used to enjoy babysitting when I was a teenager. I'm sure we could find someone reliable.'

'All this will cost some money, of course,' remarked Justin. 'But we must remember that the business is doing well at the moment.'

'That's because you're so good at your job,' interposed Catherine.

'Yes, God has been good to me in giving me the skills and I try to be conscientious.'

'Of course, you are,' exclaimed Catherine. 'People know they can trust you to do a good job and that's why they keep coming back.'

'So, I think we need to trust God that He will provide for everything we need. God is our source of supply rather than our job or business or bank balance. But we need to do our part and be good stewards of the money He has given us and that includes giving generously. I want to be generous too in paying Peter's father, that's if he can do the job. Otherwise, we'll have to look for someone else. And God will guide us in that too.'

'I'm so glad we've had this discussion,' said Catherine. 'I felt so overwhelmed and didn't know what to do about everything. It's been wonderful tonight to talk things over and to be reminded of just how much you care for me. I think I was losing sight of it because I felt so burdened with the responsibility of the boys. I'm so glad you've been so understanding.'

'We can always work things out together,' said her husband gently. 'We are a team, remember. I'm just sorry I neglected you. Your mother said you needed to have a medical check-up, didn't she? That's important too.'

'Yes, I've got an appointment tomorrow,' explained Catherine.

The medical tests showed that all was well physically with Catherine. She had just been under too much strain. The couple were able to get a young woman from the church to babysit for their date nights and Peter's father gladly accepted the job of working two days a week for Justin. Catherine enjoyed going to her recorder group and Justin was pleased to have some extra time with the boys during those evenings.

As Catherine looked at her boys happily playing together one day, she thought how things had changed so much for her. She was now coping much better than previously, and the times of respite that she was now enjoying helped her in the times when the boys were boisterous. She knew that she could now look forward to having some time out and, consequently, she felt more relaxed with the boys and able to enjoy them more. She realised how we need to share our problems with those we love rather than keeping them to ourselves. Sometimes we just need the perspective and support of someone we can trust.

GAMBLING

Esther felt her excitement levels rising. It was payday and at last she would be able to play the pokies again. The noises of the machines and the bright lights gave her a sense of anticipation that she was addicted to. Wasting no time, she sat down at a machine and got out the cash she had just withdrawn from the bank.

Esther went to play the machines at every opportunity. In her more sober moments, she knew it was foolish. She had now used up all of her savings and had even been forced to leave her house because she had not been able to keep up the payments. If her son and daughter-in-law had not taken her in, she would have been out on the street. Rod and Felicity had hoped that it would be a short-term arrangement, that soon Esther would be able to stop the habit and have enough money to rent a unit.

But she had not stopped the habit. If anything, things had got worse. Esther still had her office job, but, every payday, she would be down at the hotel playing the pokies until all her money was used up. She might arrive back home at three or four in the morning, exhausted and repentant, yet knowing that she would be there again the following week.

Esther had stopped paying any money to Rod and Felicity for expenses. They had all agreed on a certain amount when Esther came into their home. They knew it was wrong to allow Esther to continue as she did, but they felt reluctant to enforce the consequence of insisting that she leave the home. Where would she go? Sometimes they felt at their wits end as they thought about Esther and her problems. They knew that she was deeply in debt with her credit cards. The situation was too difficult for them and they had run out of answers. If they mentioned the problems to Esther, she could easily become unreasonably angry with them as if she thought they were attacking her rather than trying to help her.

Esther had been in a very unhappy marriage. Her husband Ryan had been a very heavy drinker, and when drunk, could become very violent. Many times, Esther and Rod had been forced to flee from the house to a sympathetic neighbour who would shelter them until things settled down. Sometimes they had stayed all night at the neighbour's, Esther sleeping on the couch and Rod in the room of Peter, one of the neighbour's children. Esther had felt deeply humiliated by these events. She longed to leave Ryan, but she was afraid of what he might do if she attempted to leave him and take Rod with her. As well, at the time, she only had a part-time job, and she did not think she could survive financially on her own.

Ryan was an unhappy man who often put Esther down. It seemed nothing she could do was right. She tried to keep the peace as much as possible, but that was a difficult if not impossible task.

Then, one evening, as he was coming home drunk from the hotel, Ryan had inadvertently stepped in front of a moving car. He was taken to hospital critically injured and had only lived for another 24 hours. Esther had all sorts of feelings, but the strongest one was that of relief, that she no longer had to put up with Ryan's cruelty.

Esther and Rod had settled down to a new life together, which of course was much more peaceful. Esther was grateful that her brother Albie had taken an interest in Rod, especially after his father's death. They would ride their bikes together and, as time went by, Rod felt able to share with Albie some of the strong feelings that he had had about his father, his fear, his shame, his concern that he had been unable to protect his mother, his relief when his father had died, his feelings of guilt about that relief and his wistfulness that he had not had a father who truly loved him. Albie was a good listener and would draw out Rod's feelings and validate them. He became like a father figure to Rod and eventually the conversation turned to what Rod would do in the future. His schoolwork was gradually improving as he felt increasingly settled. He hoped he could study social work, as he wanted to help young people who were in difficult plights as he had been. With Albie's encouragement, he was eventually accepted by the university to do social work. It was there that he met Felicity who was studying for a nursing degree. The two had met at the Christian group at the university where they had both become Christians. After they had finished their courses, they had been able to find jobs and they were soon married and enjoying setting up their first home together.

Unlike Rod, Esther had not had anyone to lean on during the years following her husband's death. She had tended to keep to herself, a habit she had formed during her marriage when she had felt she needed to pretend that everything was all right, even when it was definitely *not* all right. She had led an isolated life with Ryan who had discouraged her from seeing her friends and even her family. Her self-esteem was low because of all the verbal abuse she had suffered. Unlike her son, she had kept her feelings bottled up inside her and she sometimes suffered from nightmares at night and intrusive thoughts during the daytime as memories of her husband's cruelty came into her mind. She felt her whole life had been ruined and it could never be repaired.

One evening, she was walking home from work and went past the very hotel that Ryan had frequented so much. It was not far from her home. Feeling lonely, she thought wistfully of the people inside who seemed to be enjoying themselves. On impulse, she walked into the room where the pokies were. She got out her money and one of the attendants gave her a quick lesson in how to use the machines. She played the machines until she had run out of money, but was soon able to get more money from a nearby automatic teller.

After a number of hours, all her money was gone. But she reflected that, while she was playing the machines, she had felt released from all the feelings of sadness that had pursued her so constantly. She had been totally distracted.

As she thought of all the money she had gone through, Esther came to her senses. What had she done? She resolved that she would not spend an evening like that again. Her money was precious and not to be frittered away like that. After Ryan had died, she had managed to change her job from part-time to full-time. She had been able to keep her head above water financially and wanted to stay that way.

But, the following payday, it was unfortunately the same story. Esther found herself anticipating her visit to the hotel and, as soon as work was over, she was there going through the same routine. Once again, she resolved that this would be the last time she would do it, but each payday, found her at the pokies working the machines. She had gradually got more and more into debt until her credit cards were at their limit and Rod and Felicity had taken her into their home. They hoped it would be temporary, but now they feared that they were enabling Esther and did not know what to do about it. Tension was high in the home.

Whenever Rod tried to speak with his mother about her problems, she became very defensive and Rod would retreat thinking ruefully that it was much easier dealing with one of his clients than with his own mother.

And Esther really wanted to change but she felt trapped. Besides making full use of her credit cards, she had also at times borrowed money from her friends until they eventually refused to lend her money anymore, realising that they were not going to get it back. Her friend Ivy seemed especially angry about the money Esther owed her. Esther had gone to her literally crying that she could not pay her car registration and Ivy had loaned her five hundred dollars. Of course, Esther had promised to pay it back, and maybe at the time she made the promise, she had really thought that she would do so. But many months had gone by, and Ivy was becoming increasingly angry with her friend. Ivy herself was not well off financially and she simply did not understand how her friend could be so inconsiderate.

Then, one day, Ivy had met Rod in the supermarket. Although usually circumspect about his mother's problems, he had his own frustrations about the situation, and he had shared those frustrations with Ivy. At first, he had just hinted that his mother was having problems, but soon the whole story had come pouring out. Ivy was incensed. She rang Esther that night and demanded that her money be returned immediately. Of course, Esther was unable to pay back the debt and the two friends had become enemies.

The following day, however, was even more traumatic for Esther. Ivy had arrived at her workplace and, in a loud voice, because she was still seething with anger, had loudly denounced Esther in front of her colleagues. Esther had felt humiliated, wishing that she could become invisible. She had felt like resigning on the spot, but did not know how she would get another job.

After Ivy had gone, Esther had imagined that all her workmates were talking about her behind her back. She dreaded the thought of having to go back to work, day after day, knowing that those she worked with now knew her shameful secret.

At the end of the workday, she gathered her belongings and crept out of the office feeling that all eyes were upon her. At dinner that night, she found it hard to eat her meal. Felicity enquired what was wrong and then Esther, at her wit's end, told her son and his wife the sorry story. She began to cry and was unable to stop. After the meal was over, the three sat down together to talk.

Esther explained how humiliated she had felt and how Ivy's coming to her workplace had been a wakeup call to her. She felt that she had to do something about it, but did not know how she could stop her gambling habit.

Felicity put her arm around her mother-in-law. Although she had felt at times totally exasperated with Esther, she had a kind heart and really wanted her to get some help for her own sake, as well as for theirs. Esther felt encouraged by the love of her daughter-in-law, but it made her cry harder. She had put walls around her heart to stop others getting in. She had been hurt so much by Ryan, that she had vowed inwardly that no one would ever hurt her like that again. Now she had a feeling that almost felt like peace as she realised that she was still loved in spite of all that she had done wrong. This was amazing as she really did not feel that she could love herself or that she was at all loveable.

Rod too spoke encouragingly to his mother. He felt slightly guilty that he had been the one to share Esther's problems with Ivy. Nevertheless, he also believed that it was good that these problems had come out into the open. Esther could no longer pretend that all was well. He could see that she had come to the place of recognising that there were problems that needed to be dealt with urgently. For a while, Rod was silent, not knowing exactly what to say to has mother. Finally, he said, 'Mum, this is more than a gambling problem, isn't it? People get into addictions like this because they are hurting. And you had a lot of hurt from Dad. I did too, and I've been able to work through it. There are times when I'm still confronted by our past, but I do have some tools now which help me when that happens. It's not easy and I think you could definitely use some help to work through those issues. I have a colleague called Dawn who is very loving and compassionate. She is a very good counsellor and I believe you would benefit from some sessions with her. I know you already owe us a lot of money, but I would like to loan you the money for these sessions. I really believe that this could be a new beginning for you, and we will work out a payment plan for you to pay us back. I think that is important as part of your rehabilitation. It is fortunate that you still have your job. I know it will be difficult for you to face your colleagues, but that could also be important for you. Those who really care about you will support you and the others, well, hold your head high and try not to worry about what they think.' Felicity nodded in agreement with Rod. They had spoken previously about Esther's problems and agreed together that they would like to support her as much as possible when she was ready to seek help.

'I really feel that this is a turning point for me,' said Esther, still struggling with her tears. 'I can see now that I do need help and it is more than a gambling problem. It's all about the way I've been treated and how I've reacted in a way that was toxic rather than dealing with the underlying issues. Now, I really do want to do things differently and I will gladly accept your offer of help.'

'Mum, that's wonderful,' continued Rod, relieved that his mother had not acted angrily to his comments, but, for once was being honest with them. 'It's not going to be easy for you. There will be times when you don't want to deal with those issues and will have a strong desire to go back to gambling again. I suggest that I go with you to the hotel and that you tell the staff that you have made the decision to stop the pokies and that you will not be going there any longer. They are to take you off that list of people who receive free offers, and if you go there and they recognise you, they are to tell you to go home.'

Esther agreed that they should go to the hotel together the very next day and that is what they did. Rod also gave his mother Dawn's number and she agreed to ring her the following day as well. An appointment was made for the next week.

Esther felt apprehensive about sharing her relationship problems with Dawn. She had felt they were so shameful that she had kept them hidden. Her tendency to push her problems down had also extended to her gambling addiction and this was why it had been so painful when Ivy had exposed her problems in front of the other staff members. Previously, Esther had not even admitted to herself that she had a problem in this area. She had tended to see it as her hobby. Now, she could see clearly that she had a problem that she was not able to resolve herself. She needed to be vulnerable and accept help from others.

Esther left work early on the day of her appointment with Dawn. She had felt tempted throughout the day to cancel, but she kept reminding herself that she did need help and had promised Rod and Felicity that she would see Dawn at least once.

Soon she was in Dawn's room and the session began. Dawn was a pleasant woman with a warm smile and for the first time that day, Esther began to feel at ease. When Dawn asked why she was there, she found herself telling her story, how she had the problem with gambling and how she could now see that it was related to her unresolved issues from the past.

Dawn encouraged Esther to tell her story fully. She said it did not matter how many sessions it took; it was important to share the story. She explained to Esther that when we share a story like this and allow ourselves to feel the strong feelings our story generates, even though those feelings can be painful, it begins to free us from the power of what has happened to us.

Over a number of sessions, Esther shared her story, often with tears. Dawn listened intently, sometimes giving a brief summary of what Esther had said, and showing also with body language and verbal affirmations that she was listening and understood what her client was saying. Eventually, Esther felt that she had shared all that she could. She felt relieved as if a weight had been lifted off her shoulders.

Esther realised that she had been very angry with her husband Ryan. She knew he had taken a lot away from her as far as quality of life was concerned. Because of the anger she felt, she had developed a sense of entitlement as if the world owed her something. Because of this sense of entitlement, she had been vulnerable to using the pokies. She was also quick to get angry at times with those around her and sometimes Rod and Felicity had been targets of her anger.

Dawn had some suggestions for Esther. She spoke about anger management. Esther had previously bottled up her feelings of anger, not knowing what to do with them. Dawn explained that anger was usually a secondary emotion. Behind the anger there might be fear, sadness or frustration. It was important to identify the emotion behind the anger rather than just dealing with the anger itself. For example, if there is sadness behind an outburst of anger, it is important to recognise that sadness and allow oneself to feel it. Sometimes something further can be done to help. If Esther felt sad because of the way Rod had been treated by his father, she might talk with her son about it and ask how he was managing. If Esther felt frustrated when her boss at work was unrealistic about how much she could achieve in a day, she could explain her feelings to the boss rather than erupting with anger at someone else in the workplace. If she felt afraid because of the future, she could talk about those fears with a trusted friend and make some plans for the future, rather than reacting in anger with a family member or friend who just happened to be nearby at the time. Esther also came to see that the sense of entitlement that she had developed was also a dysfunctional way of dealing with her problems.

As they spoke further, Dawn realised that Esther had been, of necessity so preoccupied with keeping herself and Rod safe, when they were living with Ryan, that she'd had little time or thought for anything else. Now she tried to help Esther develop her sense of self and identity. She asked Esther what hopes and dreams she had once had for her life. What dreams were deeply buried that Esther could bring forth and maybe begin to work towards? Esther explained how she had always wanted to work with children, but had never had the opportunity. Dawn gently probed. What could Esther see herself doing? Esther explained that she had always wanted to be a primary school teacher. As they talked further, she decided that she would explore the possibility of doing a course in teaching, or maybe she could become a teacher's aide so that she could work with children one-to-one. She decided that if she went ahead with this plan of action, she would study part-time and continue with her job so that she would be able to pay for her study.

'There's another problem, though,' she explained ruefully. 'I owe such a lot of money. I think I would have to pay off at least some of my debts before I could begin to pay for a course. I feel overwhelmed when I think of the credit cards, not to speak of the money I owe to Rod and Felicity. They have been so good to me and I have taken advantage of them so much.'

Dawn agreed that she Esther would need to address this issue. She suggested that Esther could see a colleague of hers who specialised in financial counselling. Then she could make arrangements to pay back the money she owed at a rate that she could manage. Although Esther did not want to spend more money in further counselling, she recognised that it would be a good investment for her, and in fact could not believe how helpful it was. Doug, the financial counsellor, had her affairs sorted out quite quickly and she was able to plan for her course which would train her to become a teacher's aide.

'I'll be so busy with my work and the course that I won't have any time for gambling now,' she said one day to Dawn.

'That's what I'm hoping,' commented Dawn. 'When people stop an activity like gambling or taking drugs, there is usually an empty space in their lives, and they don't know what to do with it. The temptation can be to go back to that unhelpful activity. Sometimes people have to learn to do normal everyday activities like going out for lunch and catching up with friends. It may be just to catch up with things in the house that have been neglected. It's as if you have to learn to live a normal life again and that can take practice. I'm glad you're going into the course of study because that will fill the void nicely. What do you think you will do if the temptation comes to go back to gambling?'

'I hope I never will,' said Esther. 'It was ruining my life. But, somehow, I didn't realise it until I had the wake-up call with Ivy coming into the office. Maybe just remembering that would deter me.'

'There will be times when you will be tempted to go back to the pokies. It might be when you are feeling stressed or troubled about something,' explained Dawn. 'How do you think you would handle that situation?'

'The clue might be to think what I am feeling stressed about and then work out a better way to deal with it rather than going to the pokies. Maybe talking it out with someone might help,' said Esther thoughtfully.

'Yes, if you have a plan, maybe to immediately contact Rod or Felicity, that could be helpful', said Dawn.

Esther felt very supported in her new life away from gambling. She knew however, that temptation could come at any time. Dawn had recommended that she go regularly to Gamblers Anonymous meetings as an extra means of support, and Esther found the love and acceptance of the other members helped her to be more determined to continue with her new life.

One thing that she found helpful was to work on forgiving Ryan. This did not mean that he had not wronged her. But she had come to realise that the feelings of unforgiveness that she had harboured for so long were doing harm to her. It was helpful to know that forgiveness was a choice rather than a feeling. When the feelings of bitterness returned, Esther would say quietly, 'I choose to forgive him' and eventually, she found that she was feeling less bitter and resentful. She was seeing more clearly than before that Ryan had been the victim of an unhappy home and, just as she had not known what to do with her strong feelings, so Ryan had not known what to do with his feelings. He had turned to drink, just as she had sought solace in the pokies. She began to feel compassion for him and found that she was also feeling more compassionate and less condemning of herself. She began going to church with Rod and Felicity and was able to accept God's love for her and to receive His gift of forgiveness and new life.

Twelve months later, Esther had not paid off all her debts, but they were under control. She had begun a part-time course as a teacher aide and was really looking forward to working with children who needed that bit of extra assistance for the classroom. She was learning to deal with problems and stress in a more positive way and to share some of those problems with the Gamblers' Anonymous participants and a new friend at church, rather than bottling up everything inside herself and sometimes lashing out in anger. She knew that she could still call on Dawn if she needed to talk something over. She felt humbled as she realised how much others had helped her and that she did not need to hide her problems from everyone. She hoped that she could help others by being a good listener, and, indeed she often now found herself lending a sympathetic ear to someone else who needed to share a problem. She had been able to move out of Rod and Felicity's house into a small unit and treasured her independence, but also valued the times she could spend with her loving family. Her life now could not have been more different from what it had been such a short time before, and, as Esther looked back to those turbulent times, she knew she would never go back to her old life. She felt a profound sense of gratitude towards God and to all who had helped her in the changes she had made. It was like being rescued from drowning and she knew that her life was now abundant and full.

STEP MUM

'You can't make me' screamed Angie.

Michelle sighed. Life as a stepmother was a lot more difficult than she had imagined would be. It was two years since she had married Angie's father Patrick. Patrick, at 36 was twelve years older than Michelle. His two daughters, Angie aged thirteen and Trudy who was eight, were naturally part of the arrangement.

In fact, Trudy had settled in well into the new family. She had missed her mother who had been tragically killed in a car crash a few years earlier. Michelle had been loving and affectionate to Trudy and Trudy had responded lovingly to her stepmother. She loved to sit in Michelle's lap and have a cuddle. When they walked along the street together, she would hold Michelle's hand and chat about the events of the day.

But Angie was another story. She had been deeply shocked by her mother's death and, when Patrick and Michelle had got married, she resented Patrick having a new woman in his life. She had felt as if her mother were being replaced and believed her father had less time for her now that he was married to Michelle.

Angie was now 15 and Trudy had just had her tenth birthday. On this occasion, Angie was reacting simply because Michelle had suggested she put on her jacket. A cold wind had sprung up and all Michelle had said was, 'Angie, you might need to put your coat on.' Angie had definitely over-reacted but that was typical thought Michelle. Why hadn't she just kept quiet and allowed Angie to put the coat on or leave it off as she wished? She pondered that, with Angie, she was always walking on eggshells, having to be careful what she said all the time.

'You're right,' she said to Angie. 'Of course, I can't make you put your coat on. Only you can decide that. I shouldn't have said anything.'

One of the hardest things about the whole situation was the fact that Patrick would sometimes take his daughter's side against her. On this occasion, he had said to her, 'Can't you leave her alone? She's old enough to make her own decisions about things like that.'

Michelle felt hurt and bit back the angry words she felt like saying. The worst thing was that he had made this comment in front of Angie, and Michelle could see that Angie got a certain satisfaction in her father's words. When Patrick made comments like that, Michelle felt sad and alienated from him. She felt afraid even to talk to him about it, fearing he might react rather than listening and responding in a positive way. The truth was that Patrick felt out of his depth with the whole situation and this feeling was reflected in the comments that he would make to Michelle from time to time. Michelle thought that if they could only present a united front to the girls, it would be better for everyone.

Another situation that Michelle found difficult was getting the girls organised for school and then doing the school drop-off each weekday morning. Angie could be particularly difficult at these times, dawdling and reacting angrily if Michelle gently attempted to get her to hurry. Michelle would feel at her wits end sometimes and come home in tears. Sometimes the tears persisted until lunchtime.

Michelle ran a small business from home selling baby clothes. It was often a relief to go into her office where she could just be herself and quietly do her work without any strife or criticism. Angie was not only touchy when Michelle tried to help her and guide her. Lately, she had become very critical of Michelle in all sorts of other ways. She would make unkind comments about Michelle's clothes or her hairstyle or the way she tackled a problem. Her driving was also criticised and Michelle was beginning to feel that she could not do anything right. Patrick would either ignore Angie's comments to her stepmother or take his daughter's part. It was becoming unbearable for Michelle and she did not know what to do about it. At times she fantasised about leaving Patrick and letting him manage the situation on his own, but then she would remember her marriage vows and feel that she should stay and do the best that she could.

One day Patrick had a phone call to say that his brother Declan and his wife Sally were coming to stay with them. This happened from time to time and both Patrick and Michelle looked forward to their visits as they were good company. Trudy and Angie also enjoyed having the visitors whom they had known all their lives.

The day came when Declan and Sally arrived. They did not have children, so they always looked forward to catching up with their nieces. The couple had come from interstate, so they were tired after their long car journey when they arrived just in time for the evening meal.

Michelle was busy in the kitchen preparing for dinner when Sally came in to have a chat. There would once have been a time when Patrick would have been in the kitchen working alongside her, but today he was not there. Michelle thought with a sigh how the relationship had become so strained. It was almost as if he were avoiding her. However, she was glad Sally was there and the two women chatted as they set the table and did the final preparations for the meal.

Meanwhile, Patrick and Declan had settled down with a pre-dinner drink in Patrick's study – the one place they could count on to be quiet. The girls were in their bedroom finishing off their homework.

'Well, how are things going for you all?' enquired Declan.

Patrick's face changed. His brother noticed. 'Why what's the matter?' he asked.

Patrick had not meant to tell his brother everything that was going on, but now he couldn't seem to help himself and the story came spilling out. He explained how Michelle and Angie were not getting on at all, and he could not understand how Michelle, who was the adult in the situation, could not be more patient and handle things better. He gave example after example of the fights between the two of them and explained that he was at his wits end.

Declan listened carefully, not sure how to respond. And then they were called as dinner was ready.

Angie became aggressive with Michelle almost immediately. Why had Michelle put pumpkin on her plate? She knew Angie did not like it. Michelle responded that in the flurry of getting the meal ready for everyone, she had temporarily forgotten. This was not good enough for Angie who went on and on reciting a list of things she was aggrieved about. It certainly made the meal most unpleasant, and it was made worse for Michelle when Patrick turned to her and said, 'Why did you put the pumpkin on her plate? You know she doesn't like it'.

That was enough for Michelle. She ran out of the room to their bedroom and threw herself on to the bed sobbing loudly. It was just too much! Why did Patrick always have to blame her? And why had he not helped her with the dinner? Then she might not have been so flustered and might have remembered that Angie did not like pumpkin.

After a few minutes, there was a gentle knock on the door and Sally came in. Michelle poured out her heart to her sister-in-law explaining how miserable she was, and how she would just like to leave the family to manage on their own.

Sally listened patiently, realising that Michelle needed to get everything off her chest. She was fond of Michelle although she had not known her for very long. Finally, she said, 'Michelle, this needs to be sorted out. It was not right the way that Patrick spoke to you in front of the girls. I wonder if it would help to have a meeting with the four of us to talk it through. I know Declan is very good at mediation. Sometimes he does it in his job. There are a number of issues here and I think one of them is that Patrick has not really grieved properly for Charmaine. It was such a shock when she was killed. And maybe that is Angie's problem too. She may not have grieved properly for her mother. And then you have come into such a difficult situation. It's an impossible situation for you.'

'I came into the marriage with such high hopes,' explained Michelle. 'I really wanted to be a blessing to the girls. I know I could never replace Charmaine, but I wanted to be there for them. Trudy has accepted me, but Angie…. There are times when I think I have made a big mistake and I just want to get out of the whole situation. And Patrick's been so distant.' She started to cry again as she thought of it. 'We seemed to be so much in love and I really thought everything would have to go smoothly.'

Meanwhile, the rest of the family had finished dinner and after Patrick had supervised the girls to do the dishes, he sat down again in his study with Declan. For a while the two brothers sat in silence until Patrick suddenly sat up straight in his chair.

'I've had enough!' he exclaimed. 'Angie and Michelle are fighting all the time and I really don't know what to do about it. Michelle keeps doing silly things which annoy Angie and off they go again. I really have had enough of it. I'm thinking I did the wrong thing getting married again.'

Declan wanted to say that Patrick should not be taking Angie's side against Michelle, but instead he kept quiet and eventually the two moved on to less volatile topics.

Later that night, Sally told Declan about her conversation with Michelle and suggested that the four of them get together and talk things out. 'It's easier for us to see what's happening,' she commented. We've come in as observers, but they're all in the middle of it and it's difficult for them to be objective. We'll have to be careful what we say, though as everyone's feeling so tense. I don't think Patrick has any idea how much he is favouring Angie. Maybe he's feeling bad about remarrying and the effect it's having on her. Maybe he feels he's got to somehow make it up to her for Charmaine's death. I hope we'll find out anyway and that the situation can improve.'

It was arranged that the four would meet together to discuss the situation on the Saturday night after Trudy had gone to bed. Angie was going to a friend's for a sleepover that night, so they knew that it would be a good night for them to talk.

After Trudy had gone to bed, the four adults sat down in the loungeroom with their coffee and nibbles. For a while there was small talk and then Declan introduced the more serious topic by asking Patrick to share how he was feeling about the family situation. Declan explained that he also wanted Michelle to have her turn in describing her feelings, but he asked her to listen carefully to Patrick first without making any comment.

Patrick began speaking carefully as if afraid of giving offence, but, as he continued speaking, he gained momentum like a steam train taking off from the station. He shared how frustrated he was that Michelle was always arguing and fighting with Angie, and, as he had previously shared with Declan, he named incident after incident. Michelle sat quietly sobbing while this tirade proceeded. Finally, Patrick had said all that he could think of, and he lapsed into silence.

'Michelle,' said Declan, 'Have you heard what Patrick is saying?'

'Yes,' replied Michelle. 'He thinks I am too quick to argue and fight with Angie.'

'What would you say in response to Patrick?' asked Declan. 'And Patrick, while Michelle is speaking, I want you to listen with both your head and your heart. We won't interrupt Michelle but let her speak her mind just as you did.'

Still shedding tears, Michelle shared how much she had loved Patrick, and how very much she had wanted to look after the girls, how sad she had felt for them in losing their mother so tragically, how she had not meant to cause problems, but that Angie had taken offence at all her attempts to be a loving stepmother. Even innocent remarks, like the suggestion that Angie put her coat on or her mistakenly putting the pumpkin on Angie's plate, were blown up to be much bigger than they should have been. It was as if Angie was always looking for something to complain about.

Then Michelle, between sobs, shared how crushed she felt when Patrick corrected her in front of the girls and how she felt it reinforced Angie in her opposition to her stepmother.

'It feels like you're always on Angie's side against me,' she said finally, her voice quivering.

Patrick thought about what Michelle had said before responding. Was he really as insensitive to Michelle as she was saying? Was he taking Angie's side against her? In his mind, he had simply been caring for his daughter whom he knew had suffered such a devastating loss in the death of her mother.

After a minute or two of silence, Patrick spoke to his brother and sister-in-law, asking how they saw the situation. Declan replied that of course, they had not been in the house for very long, but the incident of the pumpkin on Angie's plate certainly seemed to suggest that Patrick was taking Angie's side against Michelle.

'And you know Patrick,' continued Declan. 'That is not good for Angie. She needs to know that the two of you are united. As it is, she's able at present to manipulate you both. I suspect she will keep trying to manipulate things just to see how far she can go.'

'It's possible,' commented Sally, 'that Angie is thinking that you haven't got as much time for her now that you and Michelle are married, and that is why she is misbehaving. She could be feeling quite insecure, feeling that she's lost her mother, and now she might think she's losing her father.'

'I wonder what I can do about that,' pondered Patrick. 'My marrying Michelle does not mean that I love the girls any the less.'

'No, but that might be her perception,' said Sally. 'I've got an idea about that. I remember how I once felt insecure as a teenager. My best friend, whom I had known for years, went to live interstate. My father knew how sad I was feeling and suggested that every week, he and I could have some time together – just the two of us. Sometimes we went for a long walk. Sometimes we would go out for a meal together. Or we might go to the cinema together and discuss the film over supper in a café. It gave me the time to share my sadness at losing my friend and helped me to begin my life afresh.'

'Maybe I could do that with Angie,' said Patrick.

'It would be important to have that special time with Trudy, too,' said Sally. 'She's been very good and compliant, but maybe that's her way of dealing with her mother's passing. She needs to have time alone with you too and know that she is free to express her feelings of grief. It may even be that the girls don't want to express their grief because they don't want to upset you.'

'Yes,' agreed Patrick. 'I can also see that even that might be the case. I'll have to rearrange my timetable to fit everything in,' added Patrick thoughtfully. 'I can see now that I've been spending a bit too much time at work because things were difficult at home, and that hasn't helped the situation at all. It's made it worse in fact.' He looked across at Michelle. 'I can also see that even my being absent so often like that has put a heavier burden on you and I am really sorry about that. In fact, as I see it now, I've been selfish, thinking only of my grief about Charmaine and not thinking about what the whole situation has been like for you.' He got up and went across to the couch where Michelle was sitting and put his arm around her. 'You've been so good and kind to us all and we haven't treated you well at all.'

Michelle leaned into him. She really did love him and had been prepared to make allowances, but the situation with Angie had left her feeling in despair and she had not known how to address the problem.

'I know it's been difficult for all of us,' she said. 'I'm hopeful now that we can make a fresh start. I think you and I need to have more time together too, just the two of us. We had lovely times together when we first met, but we don't make time to be alone together anymore.'

'We'll fix that!' exclaimed Patrick.

'Patrick, I wonder if you got married again a little too quickly,' said Declan. 'That can happen so easily. People lose a partner and just want everything to get back to "normal" again, so they can go too quickly into another relationship. I think it would be helpful for you to have some grief counselling. Charmaine will always be part of your life and I'm sure Michelle understands that. Grief counselling will help you express some of the strong feelings of grief rather than having them bottled up inside of you. People sometimes bottle up the feelings because giving themselves permission to feel them is so painful. But giving ourselves permission to feel them helps us to get through our grief. Trying not to feel those strong feelings causes some people to get stuck in their grief.'

'Yes,' admitted Patrick. 'I think I have been a bit stuck in my grief and I didn't want to burden Michelle with it either. I thought I could just deal with it myself. But doing that hasn't been the answer. It's made me act selfishly.'

'Of course, I want to support you in every way that I can,' commented Michelle. 'My relationship with you will be different from the one you had with Charmaine, because we are different people. We will be a new family unit and will probably develop new traditions and customs. Things will never be the same for you as they were, but I'm sure we have the potential to be a happy family. And remember, whatever we do as a family, you will always have Charmaine in your heart, so don't be afraid to move on with your life. Charmaine would want you to be happy.'

'I'm sure she would,' said Patrick. 'One day we talked together about the possibility of the other being left alone and we agreed together that the one left would be free to remarry.'

'There's just one other thing I'm thinking about,' added Sally. 'Michelle, I don't think it's your role to discipline the girls. That should be Patrick's job. You were saying that you were having trouble with Angie getting ready for school. Maybe Patrick, you need to take over in that area, at least for a while until Angie settles down and can take on the responsibility for getting herself organised. I think you should step back from that role, Michelle.'

'You can't think how glad I would be to have a break from disciplining the girls and getting them ready for school,' said Michelle. 'Sometimes I come home and cry all morning. It's been so discouraging and exhausting.'

Patrick looked up quickly. 'I had no idea it has been so difficult for you,' he exclaimed. 'Why didn't you tell me?'

'I thought it was my job to get them organised and didn't know if you would understand about the problems I've been having,' admitted Michelle. 'Part of it was pride. I didn't want to admit I was struggling.'

'Well, from now on, it's my job to supervise them getting ready for school and to take them there as well,' said Patrick. 'I can see so clearly now what I need to do. In my grief, it was as if I was asleep and couldn't see things properly. Now it's as if I've woken up!'

'How are you going to manage these extra commitments with your job?' asked Michelle.

'I'm going to sit down with my boss and explain the whole situation,' said Patrick. 'He's been very sympathetic already. I'll ask him if I can be flexible in my work hours, and, if necessary, I know he will be willing to reduce the hours that I work. I can see now that the family is more important. If we have to cut down on some expenses, it will be a small sacrifice and worth it to get things sorted out in the family.

We've got the money coming in from your business and that will help to keep things stable as well.'

'Thank you so much Patrick,' said Michelle. 'I'm really beginning to feel more hopeful now for us as a family. Thank you for listening.'

Patrick's reply was to tighten his arm around her.

The weeks and months passed. One day, Michelle was sitting in her office ostensibly working on her business but with her mind drifting. She thought with joy about how much everything had changed since the evening they had discussed the problems with Sally and Declan.

Patrick had been true to his word in everything. He had gone to sessions on grief counselling and was working through his grief. He had taken on the discipline of the girls and getting them organised for school. He had a time each week separately with both Trudy and Angie and both girls were showing the benefit of this one-on-one time with their father. He had also had a date night with Michelle each week and, for them both, it felt like the times when they had been first getting to know each other. Patrick now came home from work promptly rather than lingering on unnecessarily. He was careful now not to take Angie's side against Michelle, so that Angie had come to realise that she could not now manipulate her father against her stepmother. In fact, Angie was becoming much more friendly towards Michelle. The other day, she had asked Michelle's advice about the outfit she should wear to the school social.

Patrick had shared with Michelle how he had become stuck in his grief and as a result had become passive. He now played a much more active role within the family and everyone was benefiting. It had not all gone totally smoothly. Sometimes it is difficult to get out of bad habits, but Patrick had been determined to keep working on changing and was willing to apologise when he fell back into his old ways.

Sally and Declan were due to arrive within the next fortnight to spend Christmas with the family. Michelle smiled to herself as she thought how pleased they would be to see the wonderful changes within the family.

A TANGLED WEB

Shayne was driving home from work. He felt bored, bored with his marriage. He and Kerryn had been married for ten years and had two children, Lucille who was six and Anthony who was four. Shayne reflected that there were a lot of good things that had happened. He had a good job as an interstate truck driver and Kerryn was a dental nurse. She had been very good at saving money and, three years previously, they had been able to put a deposit on a home in a suitable location, near Kerryn's job and also close to the school that Lucille was now attending. The couple had good friends and they enjoyed visiting each other's houses to enjoy meals together. Yet Shayne felt restless and dissatisfied. He and Kerryn always seemed so busy with work or children. They were like ships passing in the night. Where was the excitement they had experienced when they first met each other and would talk together for hours on end? Sometimes Shayne felt flat like a deflated balloon.

One day, while out on a job he had met by chance a man he knew from work, Larry, who was also a truck driver and had stopped at the servo for a meal, just as Shayne had. The two sat talking over their meal. Larry was single and he explained to Shayne that he had put his details on an internet dating site.

'I'm really hoping something will come of it,' he explained. 'I've been single long enough and I'm really hopeful I will meet someone. I've had a few nibbles and I'm meeting a girl at a café on Saturday. Looking at her profile, she sounds like she could be just the right person for me. I'll know more on Saturday anyway.'

Shayne wished Larry well and the two had parted. As he drove the long road home, Shayne found himself wishing that he could meet someone like that. How wonderful it would be to have some excitement in his life. By the time he had reached home, he had convinced himself that it would be a good idea to put his own profile on to the dating site. I'll just see what happens, he had said to himself. I'll do it as a fun thing. It won't cause any harm. It will be like an experiment.

And within the next few days, he had put his profile on to the dating site. He had thought quite a bit about how he would describe himself and eventually he found himself saying that he was a single father with two children looking for friendship, with a view to having 'something more.'

Within a week, three women had responded to him. He spoke to each of them and could not really decide which one he would be interested in. So, in turn, he dated each of them. He did start to feel he was going in too deep, but it was as if he were drunk on the attention he was getting. It was easy to persuade Kerryn that he had been given extra work to do. He was often away from home, for quite long periods of time with his work.

One of the women was Julianne. She had never married and was looking for love. Shayne liked her blond hair and her beautiful smile as well as the fact that she doted on his every word. Within three weeks, they were discussing the possibility of getting engaged.

Then there was Rena. She was short and dark and divorced from her husband whom she described as being abusive.

She had two sons aged nine and six. She perceived Shayne as being very kind, in stark contrast to the way her husband had treated her. It was not long before they too were discussing getting engaged.

The third woman was Anna. She was very quiet and more reticent about a committed relationship than the other women. She'd had a couple of relationships that had not worked out. She had been cheated on, so she was wary. Nevertheless, it was obvious that after a few weeks she was beginning to trust Shayne and he drank in her liking for him.

Shayne felt quite busy as he tried to do his job, have time with the family and spend time with each of the women. But somehow it seemed worth it. He had not come from a happy home. He had been an only child and his parents had regarded him as something of a nuisance. He had craved attention from them but never seemed to get it. They were too busy with their own busy social lives to pay much attention to him. Then they had sent him to boarding school. He still remembered how sad he had felt there and how difficult it had been for him to make friends. He had been teased and bullied because his distress had been so obvious to the other boys. Coming home for the holidays had not been much better. It was as if he were invisible to his parents, and he often found himself trying to amuse himself in a sad and solitary way.

When he had met Kerryn, he had thought things would be different. They had fallen for each other quite deeply. Kerryn had come from a happier home and was more well-adjusted. She had a group of friends with whom she was close. However, as time went on, Shayne's neediness had become a problem for her. He always needed to be complimented for anything he did. He obsessed about his appearance. Because he was needy himself, he found it difficult to give Kerryn the love and attention that she needed. It was as if everything revolved around him. Shayne also found it was difficult to be a good and loving father and Kerryn had done much of the work as far as bringing up the children was concerned. Gradually he and Kerryn had drifted apart and tended to live their own separate lives.

Whenever he had a date with one of the women, Shayne found himself extremely excited as he anticipated being with her. It was like a drug. Things continued in this way for three or four months and then, suddenly, everything went wrong. He had been having dinner with Rena at a local restaurant when Beck, one of Kerryn's friends had seen them together. She had not spoken to Shayne, but he had seen her on the other side of the restaurant and knew that she had seen him with Rena. He wondered if she would report what she had seen to Kerryn or would she think it was harmless, maybe an innocent chat with an acquaintance or even a relative?

As it turned out, Beck did talk to Kerryn about seeing Shayne with Rena, but he was able to convince her that he and Rena had met by chance and had begun chatting while they waited to be served at the café. Shayne knew he had to be more careful, but it was so intoxicating to be with women that he could not seem to help himself.

Then Laura, another of Kerryn's friends, happened to see Shayne out walking with Julianne and realised that something was going on as Shayne had his arm around her. She messaged what she had seen to Kerryn on Facebook and this alarmed Beck who was also a Facebook friend. The two friends both warned Kerryn that something strange was going on and she needed to investigate it. After that, Kerryn really did become suspicious and, when Shayne was not looking, she checked his mobile phone for the messages on it. She found suspicious messages that Shayne had made to all three women and confronted him with them.

Shayne at first had blustered that what he had on his phone was no business of hers. He tried to make out that she was the one in the wrong. But really, he had been caught red-handed and finally had to admit to all that he had done.

For Kerryn, it was a real abuse of trust and her first inclination had been to suggest that they separate, and this would be the end of the marriage. However, she did not want to be hasty, and knew they had the children to consider. She thought about it carefully over the next week and then presented a plan to Shayne.

He was to leave the home at least temporarily while they tried to sort out what they were to do. She did not want him to come back until he could guarantee that he would not repeat his behaviour. She told him that, if he were serious about saving their marriage, he was to break off all the relationships with the women immediately. He would need to apologise to them for misleading them and to realise how hurtful his behaviour would have been for each of them. Then he needed to have counselling to work out why he had acted in that way and to try to remedy the situation. Kerryn also realised that they needed to have couple counselling to work on their marriage. She was aware how much they had drifted apart and wondered if that situation might have contributed to Shayne's behaviour.

If Shayne were not willing to follow that plan, Kerryn told him that they were to separate and that would be final. As it turned out, Shayne had not really been interested in breaking up their marriage. All he had wanted was the feeling of intoxication that he experienced when the women showed an interest in him. Now, as he experienced more of the reality of what he had done, he thought how inconvenient it would be to have the marriage break up. It would be messy trying to work out arrangements with the children and he did not want to leave the house which had become so comfortable for him. Then again, he still had feelings for Kerryn and did not want them to separate. He decided to follow the plan that she had set out for them.

For a few days, he went to his parents' home. He explained that he and Kerryn were sorting out a few problems and Kerryn needed some space. He felt relieved that his parents did not ask many questions and reflected that, as usual, they were too involved with their own lives to take much interest in him. Then he was able to organise a short-term rental unit. That felt better than being with his parents, but he missed the hustle and bustle of family life.

It took quite a lot of courage to speak to the women and confess what he had done. He spoke to Julianne first. She was totally crushed. She had trusted him completely and had been looking forward to a future as his wife and the mother of his children. In her late thirties, she had feared that she would get too old to have children before she met someone suitable. He had met her in the café where they had been accustomed to see each other and, when she heard what he had to say, she could not stop crying. Although Shayne was self-centred, even he was shocked at the impact of his revelation upon her. It was as if he had realised for the first time his potential to hurt the women. In the end, she left him still crying and he had felt miserable and guilty.

He was not looking forward to seeing Rena, but he made an appointment to see her soon afterwards. She too was shocked and also angry. Her former husband had been abusive, and she had seen Shayne as the answer to her hopes and dreams for a better life. She had bitterly denounced him and when they parted, he had felt relieved but also miserable and guilty as he had felt following the conversation with Julianne.

Finally, he made a time to see Anna. She had taken a while to trust him as she had been cheated on in the past. But she had begun to trust him and now she was shocked and horrified. She commented bitterly that she did not think she would ever be able to trust anyone ever again. As he watched her walk away from him, Shayne felt despicable and hated what he had done to her as well as to the other women.

Then he knew he needed to find a counsellor. Part of him shrank from laying bare what he had done to anyone. It had been a very private part of him. For a couple of weeks, he fought the idea, but finally he looked up a counselling service in his area on the internet. An appointment was made for the following Tuesday. During that day, he thought of all the excuses he could think of not to turn up, but finally, he found himself in the waiting-room. His main motivation was that he knew he could not go back to Kerryn without having counselling. He did not have a good relationship with his parents and really did not have friends, just the occasional acquaintance with whom he would have a chat sometimes. He missed Kerryn and the children and the unit he had rented felt very quiet and lonely.

He was deep in thought when the counsellor called him into the counselling room and introduced himself as Hugh. After Hugh had got Shayne to fill in a form and explained about confidentiality, he asked Shayne why he had come for counselling. In a faltering voice, Shayne explained the whole situation, the dating service, the three women, how Kerryn had found out and the stipulations she had made to him. Hugh listened carefully, occasionally nodding or showing in other ways that he understood and was listening. Shayne was relieved to see that Hugh did not seem judgmental. He had feared being criticised, but Hugh was acting as if he was used to hearing stories like Shayne's.

It felt such a relief to unburden himself. For many years, Shayne had not had anyone to talk to like this. Even with

Kerryn, he had tended not to share deeply. His feelings had been deep within him and sometimes his heart had felt very heavy.

Hugh asked Shayne about the family he had grown up in and Shayne shared with tears how he had been an only child and how left out he had felt by his parents, who had been too busy with their own concerns to take much notice of him. He had rarely shared these feelings with anyone, and again he felt relieved to share the burden with Hugh who listened with compassion in his eyes.

Hugh asked him if he could see a connection between his upbringing and the way he had related to the women. Shayne had not been aware of a connection between these things, so Hugh went on to explain that the behaviour with the women was addictive behaviour. People seek solace in addictions when they have been hurt in some way. Shayne had been hurt by his parents' neglect and was trying to compensate himself with the highs he would get in the relationships with the women. An addiction is not a good way to deal with something painful. It is dysfunctional but somehow it distracts from the hurt the person is feeling. Hugh explained that there are all sorts of addictions that people can have – alcohol, drugs, gambling, excessive shopping, to name a few, and there are sexual addictions when a person might go from one relationship to another always wanting to get a 'high'. When that feeling of intoxication or infatuation wears off, another person might be found to fill the gap. In a similar way, a person on drugs, alcohol or gambling might continually seek that high feeling of excitement that the addiction would bring. With drugs and alcohol, their body would begin to crave the substance they were addicted to, and they would feel no relief until they could have more of it. A person with a shopping addiction might feel intense excitement when they bought a garment. However, the feeling would wear off and they might feel the need to go out the following day to repeat the process and get another intense, high feeling. Similarly, Shayne was addicted to the feelings of excitement that he experienced when with the women.

Hugh discussed with Shayne the harm an addiction can do to the relatives and even the friends of the addicted person. Not to speak of people like the women Shayne had deceived. Kerryn and also the children were suffering from Shayne's behaviour. Shayne was beginning to see that the sense of excitement he had sought so much from the attention of the women had a high cost. Somehow, in the intensity of the moment, he had discounted this cost. He had known that paedophilia was a very strong addiction which caused much suffering to children and their families, but somehow had managed to see himself as reasonably blameless in comparison. Now he could see that he too had caused considerable suffering.

Shayne continued to see Hugh over a number of weeks. They discussed in detail Shayne's experiences as a small child when he had felt neglected by his parents. Shayne felt a sense of release as he shared deep feelings he had never shared before, not even with Kerryn. What was particularly helpful was the insight that he was not the one who had caused his parents' rejection. He had always thought that there must have been something wrong with him which had caused his parents to reject him. Now Hugh explained that children are egocentric and often think they are the cause of their parent's behaviour. It is typical for small children to blame themselves for their parents' marriage breakup, for example. If a parent is in a bad mood, a child might believe he has caused it, even if he has been an innocent bystander. Parents can also blame the child when that child has done nothing wrong. Children often see the adults as being right and even all powerful so they can easily feel guilty even if they have done nothing wrong at all.

'Your parents were probably immature and a bit selfish,' commented Hugh. 'It's not easy to be a parent and not all parents learn to be unselfish. They might have found it inconvenient to have a small child to look after. Not all people are natural parents. It sounds as if they prioritised their own interests and naturally, you assumed there was something wrong with you.'

Shayne could see it quite clearly now. He knew his parents were selfish by the way they had sometimes argued with each other. And, all the time, he had thought it was his fault.

'Where do I go from here?' he asked Hugh.

Hugh suggested that he needed to keep reminding himself that he was not responsible for his parents' behaviour. That belief had been a significant part of Shayne's identity. Now Hugh suggested that Shayne think of the positive things that were part of his identity. What did he like doing? What interests and hobbies did he have? Shayne explained that he was an interstate truck driver, and he was proud of his ability to drive the truck and provide for his family in this way. He also enjoyed photography. He would sometimes take photos of the scenery as he crossed the country and he also enjoyed taking photos of his children. He had even won a couple of photographic competitions.

'I've always been a bit of a loner,' he explained to Hugh. 'And photography has been something I can do on my own.'

'Tell me about being a loner,' said Hugh. 'Would you like to have more contact with people?'

'I would like to,' commented Shayne, 'But somehow, I've always thought of myself as flawed and that hasn't given me much confidence in relationships. I don't really have any friends. Occasionally, our next-door neighbour Wally has asked us if we would like to go to their church. He is very friendly and helpful. He helped me to sort things out when a tree fell down in that recent storm. He says there is a small men's group. They meet in a café on Saturday mornings. There are just a few of them. Of course, I'm not always available on Saturday mornings, but I am available sometimes. Maybe I could accept his invitation. I'm not so sure about going to a church service, though.'

'Why don't you accept his invitation and go along one Saturday and see how you go?' suggested Hugh. 'If you don't like it, you could try something else – maybe a photography club.'

So Shayne did have a chat to his neighbour Wally, and arranged that he would go with him to the café the following Saturday. The men did not know about his history, although Wally must have realised that Shayne was not living at the family home. However, he did not comment on that and introduced Shayne to the other men who welcomed him warmly. In spite of his apprehensions, he began to feel comfortable quite quickly. The men asked some questions about his job, and he was able to tell them about some of his adventures on the road. For much of the time, he was content to sit and listen and he was struck by the kindness of the men for each other and for himself. He resolved that he would go each week when he was available and soon the group was part of his life and something that he looked forward to going to. Once while travelling, he thought about the group and pondered that he was getting the love and acceptance from these men that he had craved all his life. It was this desire for acceptance that had led him into the dysfunctional relationships with the women. Now he realised he could have acceptance in a legitimate way rather than using other people for his own purposes, as he had done previously.

He continued seeing Hugh each week and this also was a support to him. He realised his life was changing, and for the better. Hugh's unconditional acceptance of him, like the acceptance of the men, was causing a change in his life. He knew he was gradually becoming less self-centred and more able to see things from the point of view of the other person. He began to see how he had been selfish in his relationship with Kerryn and hoped that he would be different if they could get back together. He hoped too that he would be able to play a bigger part in his children's lives too. He remembered times when he had been abrupt with them, seeing their desire to have time with him as an interruption rather than an opportunity to bond with them. As he pondered his behaviour, it reminded him of the way his parents had treated him when he was a child. Since he had left the family home, he was having phone contact with the children and having them at his unit every second weekend. Now he found himself looking forward to the times he had with them, asking them about what was happening in their lives and affirming them.

Occasionally, the men in the group would speak about God's love for each one and, at first, Shayne had felt a bit uncomfortable. He was not sure that there was a God and he could not imagine that this God would be able to love him. He thought about all the wrong things he had done and believed in his heart that, if there were a God, he would be totally unacceptable to Him. He expressed this belief to the other men who reassured him that God did indeed love everyone, that Jesus, perfect man and perfect God, had died so that the sins or wrongdoing of everyone could be forgiven. Jesus offers forgiveness or salvation as a gift but would not force this gift on anyone. Each one must receive it. In doing so, they would eventually have a wonderful home in heaven.

It took a while for Shayne to understand this message. One day, Wally gave him a pamphlet which explained what the men had been talking about. For a while, Shayne did not read it but thrust it into his pocket. There it stayed for two or three weeks, until one evening, while having a solitary meal at a truck stop, he got it out and read through it. For the first time, the message made sense to him. Tears came to his eyes as he thought of God's love for him and the sacrifice that Jesus had made in dying for him. At the end of the pamphlet there was a short prayer that he could pray if he wanted to receive Jesus as his Saviour. He prayed it immediately and, although he did not feel any different, he knew in his heart that he was now a member of God's family, that his sins were forgiven, and he could begin life afresh. He could not wait until the next time he would be together with the men and could share the step that he had taken.

Meanwhile, Hugh came into the counselling session one day and explained that he had been to some in-service training and had heard about men's groups which were specifically for men who had sexual addictions. He wondered if Shayne would find a group like this helpful. At first Shayne was doubtful, but he resolved to go one week to see how it was, just as he had gone to the men's group from the church.

This group were held on a Wednesday evening, and although Shayne did not have any particular commitment on that evening, he knew he would sometimes be unable to attend because of his work. He realised that this had not been a problem for the Saturday group, so one evening, he plucked up his courage and drove out to the hall where the men were meeting. He felt very nervous but made himself go into the hall. He was immediately made welcome by a man called Jerry. He talked for a few minutes with Jerry before being assigned to a group. As with the Saturday group, he was warmly welcomed. For that first session, he just sat there listening to the other men sharing. One thing he learned was that all of them had found going to the group in the first place, a very difficult thing to do. It had been difficult to admit that they had a problem with sexual addiction. Shayne attended the group for a few weeks before he hesitatingly shared his own story. He felt shame as he recounted it, but somehow it felt good to be able to talk about it. Getting out in the open what had been a shameful secret made him feel more accountable for his actions, and the other men in the group were not judgmental. They too knew the struggles of a person with these addictions. Shayne valued the way they supported each other in doing the right thing and in healthy relationships. They each had a buddy and, if they were feeling tempted to do the wrong thing, they could ring the buddy and support each other in not giving way to the temptation.

The men also discussed their lives as children and young people and the circumstances which had led them on to a wrong pathway. While they could see that, as in Shayne's case, they had often not been given the love they should have been given, they were encouraged to be responsible for their own lives, rather than blaming others like their parents. Jerry the leader, would go from group to group, listening to the discussion, occasionally adding a helpful comment. Shayne could see that the support the men gave each other could often compensate for parents who had been unloving. It felt so encouraging to belong to the group and to feel so affirmed and accepted by the members. He pondered that these relationships were so much better than the ones he'd had with the three women. He no longer felt the need to have the attention they gave him at any cost. However, he decided that he would still benefit from coming to the men's group.

Within a few weeks, Hugh felt that Shayne was ready to stop the counselling sessions. He was very pleased with the progress Shayne was making. He told Shayne that he could always come back for more sessions if he felt the need.

It was then that Hugh suggested that Shayne was ready for marriage counselling. Although Hugh counselled couples, he thought it would be better if Shayne and Kerryn began afresh with a new counsellor who would be more impartial than he would be after all the sessions he'd had with Shayne. Hugh recommended his colleague Noel to take on the couple counselling.

When Shayne rang Kerryn and explained something of the process he had gone through and that he was ready to do the couple counselling which she had originally specified as a condition of their getting back together, she was willing to go with him, but he sensed a hesitation in her voice as if she were not quite convinced that everything would work out well. Nevertheless, she agreed to the counselling, and they arranged for a time to meet together with Noel.

They explained the story to Noel briefly and he suggested they both tell their stories individually before they tried to work out some strategies with him about the best way to proceed forward. He suggested that Kerryn share her story first. Shayne listened carefully to what Kerryn was saying. Noel had warned him against becoming defensive. He was simply to listen without correcting Kerryn. At times he struggled to do that, but he reminded himself that he had put Kerryn through a lot, and now was not the time to argue with her.

Kerryn shared tearfully how they had drifted apart and how shocked she had been to find out about the women Shayne had brought into his life. She had believed it was the end of their marriage but had resolved to give it one more chance.

As he listened to Kerryn sharing her feelings, Shayne felt sad to think of the ordeal he had put her through because of his selfishness. He felt ashamed and, when she had finished sharing, he apologised sincerely for his bad behaviour and promised that he would never act like that again. He then went on to share his own story, his distant relationship with his parents, his falling in love with Kerryn and the sadness he felt at the way they had drifted apart, the intoxicating feelings he had felt when with the women, when reason had flown out the window and he lived only for the infatuation he had felt. He went on to explain how he was now deeply sorry for the hurt he had caused them as well as the pain he had given Kerryn and the children. He explained how his counselling with Hugh had helped him to see the situation from the point of view of those he had hurt, rather than from his own selfish point of view. Then he explained about the two men's groups and how he believed they were making him more accountable.

He could see the hope in Kerryn's eyes as he spoke, but he could also see that she was cautious. She did not want to be hurt again. Noel suggested that Shayne continue with the men's groups and, if Kerryn agreed, they could get back together again. They could have a trial period of three months and then review the situation. He suggested that one thing they could do was to arrange a babysitter and have a date night each week. He explained that having time together like this could help with their rebonding process, and suggested they make it a regular part of their lives in the future as well.

One thing Kerryn had said was that she would like Shayne to become more involved with the children and in the household work. Knowing his neglect of these duties in the past, Shayne agreed to be more available to help in these areas. In one of the sessions, they discussed specific household tasks that would need doing and who would be responsible for each one. He agreed that he would take equal share in getting the children to bed each night, when he was not working, and they both agreed that one adult and one child would also have a time together each week.

This could be as simple as going for a walk together or having a snack at the local café.

All these details were written down in a contract, so that there could be no misunderstanding about who was responsible for each task. Shayne and Kerryn agreed also to meet once a month to discuss how things were going and to make any amendments to the contract.

They'd had a number of sessions with Noel in order to work on all these details. Finally, Noel suggested it was time for Shayne to return to the family home so that they could put everything they had decided upon into practice.

Shayne felt strange as he packed his bags and prepared to leave the unit he had been living in, but he felt reassured when he was greeted with shouts of happiness by his children Lucille and Anthony. As he put his arms around them, he thought that anything which could take him away from them again was too, too costly. He shivered as he thought how very nearly his marriage had been broken up and the impact this would have had on the children.

Kerryn was businesslike, but he could understand why. She was learning to trust him again. They had agreed that he would sleep in the spare room until they both felt comfortable about sharing a bed again. Shayne refreshed his memory by looking at the contract they had made and made a point of fulfilling all his duties to the letter. As the weeks went by, he sensed a softening in Kerryn's attitude. On their weekly dates, he was kind and courteous, listening carefully to Kerryn and assuring her of his love for her. He even began to bring her flowers, something he had never done before. He had told himself he was not a romantic at heart, but now he remembered how Hugh had said that he could decide to give Kerryn flowers and care for her in other ways too. He did not have to feel like it. It was a decision. But, as time went by, he began to feel more loving towards his wife and he could see that she was reciprocating. Occasionally, he would slip back into bad habits, and they would get into an argument. Then he would remind himself, as Hugh had said, that he did not always have to be right. He could apologise when he was wrong and stop the argument then and there. If it were something they needed to discuss, they could agree to talk about it at another time, either when they were relaxed on their date night or at the monthly meeting, which had proved to be very successful. If either of them had a grievance, that one would share it using the 'I' statements that Noel had taught them. The person sharing would have the floor and the other would listen respectfully. Then they would discuss different ways to solve the problem and usually would find a solution that suited both of them. They had practised this procedure in their sessions with Noel and he would give them feedback about how well they were listening to each other. Shayne was working very hard on their marriage and he realised that Kerryn too was making a big effort.

The times with the children were also a blessing to Shayne. How he valued their unconditional love. While he had been away from the home, Kerryn had been careful not to criticise him to them and he was very grateful for that. Now he could feel a strong bond growing with each of them.

Shayne and Kerryn continued their visits to Noel. The weeks went by, and the time came for them to review their relationship, as Noel had suggested, three months after Shayne had moved back home. The two walked into the counselling room holding hands, which Noel of course noticed immediately. He commented that this was a good sign.

Both Shayne and Kerryn had the opportunity to share how matters were progressing and both expressed surprise and delight in the way everything was going so well.

'You've both put a lot of work and effort into your marriage,' said Noel. 'It could easily have gone the other way. There are many couples I've seen who are not willing to start afresh as both of you have. Many continue to hold grudges against each other, and they just cannot get past those grudges. Kerryn, you've been willing to forgive a lot. Many wives would have walked out and felt justified in doing so. You have been willing to give Shayne a second chance and it is paying off for you. And you Shayne have been determined to do everything you could to show Kerryn how sorry you are and how you want to be a united family again.'

'I think we've both learned such a lot in these months since we separated,' exclaimed Shayne. 'I've come to understand why I acted as I did, and to forgive my parents too. But I've also learned that I have to be responsible for my own behaviour. I can't blame my parents or anyone else. Ultimately, it's up to me.'

'Not everyone can come to that understanding,' said Noel. 'Some people continue to see themselves as victims.'

'What surprises me,' added Kerryn, 'Is that we can do so many things to help us to bond together. Like our date nights, or the contract for sharing the housework. When Shayne didn't share the tasks equally before, I didn't think there was anything I could do about it. We've learned that we can always talk about anything that worries us. We don't have to bear that burden of resentment.'

'And I'm so pleased with the way that you have listened so well to each other,' said Noel.

Shayne laughed. 'We've had a few times when we stopped listening and hammered the other to try to get them to see our point of view,' he admitted. 'But I think we were both so motivated to get things right, that we usually got back to listening properly again.'

'You've both got tools, now, that you can use to keep yourselves on track,' said Noel. 'You've learned to listen with "I" statements, you've got your contract and meetings and also your date nights. Initially, you were probably following all those things in a legalistic kind of way. But, eventually, you would have started to feel love and trust for each other again.'

'It's extraordinary,' agreed Kerryn. 'I always thought I had to wait until I felt like doing some of those things, like going on a date night. Now I realise that acting in a loving way, even when I don't feel like it, can help to make me feel more loving.'

Shayne agreed with her wholeheartedly. Noel suggested that they see him in another three months or earlier if they thought they needed to. He also suggested that they continue with the practices which they had found so helpful in their marriage, adding that all married couples would benefit from these practices, and it was frustrating to him at times when partners would stubbornly refuse to back down and really work on their marriages.

Shayne and Kerryn walked out hand in hand and decided to celebrate by having coffee and cake at the nearby café.

'I can't say I'm glad it all happened,' commented Kerryn. 'It truly was a very difficult time, and our marriage nearly went under with the strain. But we're so much better off now than we ever were, and I am so glad about that. Maybe we could try sleeping in the same bed tonight,' she added with a smile.

'I'd love that,' said Shayne, reaching out to clasp her hand. 'It would be like the icing on the cake.'

NEIGHBOURS

'Trent,' said Pam. 'The new neighbours have moved in today. It's always a difficult time for people unpacking and getting organised. I'll take a quiche over to them tomorrow and then I'll be able to meet them.'

Pam had grown up in a country town and, whenever a new neighbour moved in, it was the custom to greet them with some home cooking. Although they now lived in the city, Pam had continued with this tradition.

'That's a lovely idea,' said Trent. 'It's Saturday tomorrow, so maybe you could pop in while I'm taking the children to swimming. I'll try to catch up with them in the next few days.' Trent was proud of his wife who was so caring. They were newcomers themselves to the area, having moved in the previous year with their two small children, Sam and Ivy.

The following day, Pam made the quiche and went to see her neighbours whose names were Hilton and Averil. She could see that the couple were exhausted from the move but they greeted her warmly. She sat and chatted to them for just a few minutes and learned that they had moved because of Hilton's job as a manager in the local supermarket.

Trent went to see the couple for a brief visit the following Tuesday evening and also had a quick chat with them, offering to help them in any way they needed it.

Over the weeks, the two couples would exchange friendly greetings when they happened to meet each other and Pam and Averil had morning tea in each other's homes once or twice.

It was nearly Christmas. Pam and Trent always found Christmas a busy time. This year, they had arranged to go to Pam's family for Christmas lunch, and for Trent's family to come to their house for the evening meal. 'It's always such a big day for the children,' said Pam, 'and if they get too tired, one of us can put them into bed.'

'I don't know,' answered Trent. 'I think they might want to stay up, so they don't miss out on anything.'

It was a tiring but happy day for them all. Pam was glad she had prepared as much as possible the day before. Trent's family would bring food, so it was mainly a matter of having the house reasonably tidy and the table set. Soon Trent's family began to arrive. There were 20 people altogether that night and Pam reflected how lovely it was to have everyone together. They lived in a court, and she could see their little court filled with cars.

As usual they all enjoyed the time together and, when everyone had gone, and the children were safely tucked into bed, Trent and Pam had one last cup of tea together while they reflected on their busy but enjoyable day.

The following morning, there was a loud knock at the door. Pam went to answer it and there was their new neighbour, Hilton. He looked angry. Before Pam could say a word, he said, 'Can you tell your visitors not to park in front of our house!'

Pam was stunned at this unexpected rebuke. For a while she could not speak. She could see that Hilton was very angry. After making his point clear again, he went on his way.

Pam talked it over with Trent. 'He can't expect people never to park in front of his house,' said Trent thoughtfully. 'Nevertheless, there were a lot of cars in the court yesterday. That's the problem with living at the end of a court. There is not much parking space. But it sounds as if it was pretty rough for you. I wish I'd answered the door myself.'

'What would you have said to him?' asked Pam. Trent was a very mild and easy-going person. She could never remember him raising his voice to anyone.

'I'd have listened to him and let him have his say,' responded Trent. 'I couldn't promise him that our visitors would never park in front of his place.'

Over the next few weeks, the two couples kept to themselves. Pam felt very anxious about the situation. If they were having visitors, she would ring them to tell them not to park in front of their neighbours' house. When the children were playing in the court with children from another neighbour, she noticed one day how Hilton came roaring into the court in his car and began to fear for the children's safety. When it happened again, they told the children to play elsewhere, either in the back yard or in each other's houses. Then she noticed that rubbish began appearing in their yard, near the fence that divided their properties. There were times when Pam felt sick with worry. She even began to discuss with Trent the possibility of their moving house. She just wanted to get away from the problem.

Pam and Trent were a Christian couple and belonged to a small Bible study group which was held in their home on Wednesday nights. They were studying the book of Numbers. God had promised the people of Israel that He would give them the land of Canaan as their inheritance. The Israelites sent spies into the land who reported that they would never be able to defeat the people of that land. Twelve spies were sent in and only two, Caleb and Joshua, said that, with God's help, they would be able to defeat the enemy. Rather than looking to God to help them, the other spies looked at the circumstances and said that, in comparison with the people from the land, they were like grasshoppers. As a consequence of their attitude, the people had to remain in the wilderness for another 38 years, until that generation had all passed away. Only the faithful Caleb and Joshua were allowed to inherit the land. Trent and Pam's friend Jonathan, who was leading the study, commented that the ten spies saw only two possibilities – to go into the land and be defeated, or to retreat. They failed to see the third possibility – to go into the land and have victory, which would come from trusting in God.

Jonathan went on to say that we can be like those ten spies as we face situations in our daily lives. We can retreat or we can live miserably with the situation, or we can have victory. Suddenly Pam had a flash of insight which she knew came from the Holy Spirit. They could live in misery with the situation with their neighbours; they could sell the house and retreat, or they could live in God's victory. She had not even thought of that possibility in regard to their own situation.

After the others had gone, and they were getting ready for bed, she shared her insight with Trent. He too had not thought of having victory in the situation they were facing. But as they kept discussing it, he was reminded of a couple of Bible verses that explained that God gives victory to those who love Him and are seeking to be obedient to Him. He said, 'I think there's a verse somewhere that says that God always leads us on in triumph. That's victory isn't it? Then there's another verse in Corinthians that says, "Thanks be to God who always gives us the victory through our Lord Jesus Christ." Paul was speaking about victory as we face death, but it would surely apply to other situations as well. Then there's that verse where Jesus was speaking to the disciples at the Last Supper. He said, "In this world you will have trouble, but be of good cheer, I have overcome the world." Surely that means victory too.'

'Somehow, I've never really thought we could have victory in every situation,' commented Pam. 'I've thought we've got to live with some situations and be miserable. But it makes sense. If Jesus, by His death on the cross, has won victory over the enemy, then we need to claim that victory when troubles come.'

'And it doesn't mean that all troubles will go away either,' said Trent thoughtfully. 'But the Scriptures promise that we will not be tempted beyond our strength and, that is victory too, even if the situation is not removed from us. We will be given the strength and wisdom to cope with it.'

By this time, the couple were in bed and Trent suggested that they pray about the problem together before they went to sleep. He prayed for God's victory, strength and wisdom in that situation and that God would give them any insights they needed. He also thanked God that He was working in the situation and now that they had committed it to Him, they did not need to worry about it.

Pam slept better that night than she had for quite a while. When she woke up, she had the thought that it would be helpful to share their problem with their pastor David. Trent agreed and Pam rang and made an appointment for David to come to their home the following Tuesday night.

In the meantime, Pam thought about how terrified she had been of Hilton. Where did that feeling of real terror come from? As she pondered the situation, she thought of her own father. He would go into rages when he was frustrated. As a small child, Pam had found this behaviour truly terrifying. It was as if Hilton's behaviour brought back those same feelings. Her mother had never stood up to her father and this was the behaviour that Pam had learned from her mother, to be passive. As a child, she had felt totally helpless when her father went into his rages. Now she felt the same way with Hilton.

Pam had arranged to go out for coffee with her friend Jeannie, that morning. The children were at the childcare centre and she looked forward to being with her friend and talking the situation over with her.

Jeannie noticed immediately that Pam had something she wanted to share with her. She already knew about the situation with Hilton as Pam had mentioned it the previous week. Pam told Jeannie how they were to see David their pastor and discuss the matter with him. Jeannie thought this was a good idea. She had been concerned about her friend and wanted the situation to be resolved so that Pam and Trent could move on with their lives. Pam also explained to Jeannie about the Bible study with Jonathan. Jeannie was impressed.

'It certainly sounds as if God was speaking to you,' she commented. 'What would victory in that situation mean for you, do you think?'

Pam was thoughtful. 'I think it would mean staying where we are and going on with our normal lives without living in fear,' she said finally.

'That certainly sounds as if you are on the right track,' agreed Jeannie.

Pam then went on to explain the thoughts she was having about her father and his rages and how they would leave her very fearful. Jeannie agreed that it was understandable that she would feel that way when confronted with Hilton.

'I've made the decision to forgive my father,' Pam explained. 'He passed away last year, and I had learned to get on with him as well as possible. We could not be close, but I tried to show love for him by visiting him in hospital when he was ill. He really appreciated that. But even as an adult, I would never have been able to contradict him.'

Jeannie sat pondering what her friend was telling her. It was bringing back some memories of her own. 'It reminds me of when I was bullied at school,' she said. I remember feeling completely helpless when that group of girls attacked me. I was terrified. I also felt so ashamed that I felt I couldn't tell my Mum and Dad. I just tried to keep out of the way of those girls as best I could. Then later on, after I married Sam, I started having nightmares about it. Sam was very concerned and suggested I have some counselling. I think I was a bit like you too, not able to be assertive with anyone who was abusive to me. Well, I did go to counselling, and it was a great help to me. The counsellor explained how we can react in one of three ways when someone is being aggressive with us. We can become aggressive in return. We can simply not react and act in a passive way, allowing them to continue the abuse. The problem with that one though is that we can become resentful. Then we can respond assertively, and maybe ask the person not to speak to us in that way. If Hilton gets into a rage with you again, I wonder how you could respond assertively.'

'I suppose I could just tell him that anyone can park anywhere in the street as long as they are not parking over a driveway,' said Pam.

'Yes. That's right,' said Jeannie, 'And the important thing is to say it calmly and politely. You might be quaking inside, but you can still train yourself to be calm as you speak. And as you become more assertive, it does get easier.'

'I would find it hard,' commented Pam. 'I'm so used to being passive.'

'It takes practice,' said Jeannie. 'I used to practise with Sam. Although it feels particularly difficult at first, you do get used to the idea. I am certainly more assertive than I was. I think I thought I had to please everyone all the time too. I had to tell myself that it wasn't necessary or even possible to do that. Most of our friends will not treat us badly so we don't usually need to be assertive with them. But it's important to be assertive when we really need to be. It's showing self-respect and others will respect us more, too, if we are assertive.

'The other thing I've remembered,' added Jeannie, 'Is to realise that when you were with your father and he got into rages, you were only a child. It's difficult for a child to stand up to an adult. But you're an adult yourself now. You're not that small vulnerable child. My counsellor used to say to me, "That was then, and this is now." You are in a different situation now.'

'That is so true,' agreed Pam. 'You've helped me such a lot today, Jeannie.'

'I hope so,' said Jeannie. 'I don't want you living in fear.'

Pam went home determined that if Hilton or anyone ever spoke to her in an unreasonable way, she would learn to answer them calmly and assertively. Already she was beginning to feel more confident, like a handyman who has to do a job and has the tools which will enable him to do that job properly.

That evening, she shared her conversation with Trent. He too was encouraged. 'I could learn something from that myself,' he commented. 'I'm not always that good at being assertive.'

Pam thought fondly that Trent was usually very calm, kind and stable, but there could be times when he too might need to be assertive.

Tuesday night came around and David their pastor arrived after Trent and Pam had put the children into bed. The couple shared their story with him, and especially how they had been so worried about Hilton's behaviour that they had thought of moving house. They recalled how they had bought their house the previous year. They had been praying about the right house to buy and had actually put a deposit on another house in the area. Then they had realised it would be too small if they would ever want to extend it. After that, they continued their search for a suitable house. At the end of a long afternoon of house hunting, they had found one that they were impressed with, but it was already sold. A real estate agent had told them that a similar house by the same builder was in the next street. They had walked into this second house and immediately felt that it was the right one for them. It had come back on to the market when a couple were not able to make the payments. Trent and Pam believed God had guided them in this process of house-hunting and had loved their home ever since.

David listened patiently as the couple told their story. He said he believed that if God had led them to their house, they should stay there. This was in accord with the insight Pam had received during the Bible study and also with Jeannie's ideas. Pam explained to David the insight she'd had in the Bible study, that they could remain and have victory in the situation. She also explained what Jeannie had shared and how she was learning to be more assertive. David's view that they should remain in the house, because God had led them there, completed the puzzle.

That evening, they prayed with David and affirmed that they believed that they should not retreat in fear but stand their ground. They prayed for strength to handle whatever would happen. David reminded them of a text from Psalm 23, 'I will fear no evil, for You are with me' and explained how the words 'Do not be afraid' were repeated many times in the Bible. He suggested they find some of those verses and write them down. Then they could remind themselves of them whenever they felt fearful.

After David had left, Pam told Trent that she believed they were not to tell their visitors not to park in front of Hilton's place. The following Saturday night, their friends George and Dawn were coming for dinner. 'We'll let them park wherever they want to,' said Pam and Trent agreed with her that that was the right way forward.

Pam could not help feeling apprehensive as Saturday night approached. She had been so shocked by Hilton's attack on her after Christmas. However, she reminded herself that God was with her and would strengthen her. She repeated the 23rd Psalm quietly to herself as she made preparations for the meal.

Sure enough, George and Dawn did park in front of their neighbours' house. Pam was involved with looking after their visitors that night and it was easy not to be fearful when they were all together.

The following afternoon, there was a loud knock at the door. Trent had gone for a walk, so Pam answered it. It was indeed Hilton and he looked very, very angry indeed. Pam felt terror clutch at her heart, but the words of the 23rd Psalm came to her immediately, 'I will fear no evil, for You are with me.' She had a sense of God's presence surrounding and protecting her.

Pam listened politely while Hilton complained loudly about the parking situation. When he had finished, she said calmly, though inwardly anxious, 'Hilton, anyone can park anywhere in the street as long as it's not in front of a driveway. Our visitors were not doing the wrong thing and we are not going to tell them not to park in front of your place.'

Hilton's face was red with anger. 'You'll hear more about this from me,' he raged.

'Goodbye Hilton,' said Pam firmly and shut the door. She had remembered something else that Jeannie had said. She did not need to allow anyone to be abusive to her. She could shut the door and walk away.

When Trent returned from his walk, Pam told him what had happened.

'How do you feel about that now?' he asked.

'Of course, I can't say I wasn't afraid, and I'm still feeling a bit shaky,' admitted Pam. 'But I was able to speak calmly to Hilton, and now I feel really good about it. As if I have worth and value and will not allow anyone to mistreat me. With God's help, I can be assertive.'

'You do have worth and value as one of God's children,' exclaimed Trent. 'And I am so proud of you.'

The weeks passed by slowly. Pam and Trent continued to pray together about the situation and to affirm that God was giving them victory. Pam still felt anxious at the thought of another confrontation with Hilton, but he did not come back to their house, in spite of his threat that she would hear more from him. Pam began to feel a little more relaxed.

Then, one evening the phone rang just as Pam was preparing dinner. It was Carol, the mother of the children in the court that Pam and Trent's children often played with. Carol was still on speaking terms with Hilton's wife Averil. She also knew about Pam and Trent's situation and was very sympathetic towards them. On this occasion, she explained to Pam that Averil had told her that she and Hilton had decided to move house.

'I thought you might like to know,' said Carol. 'Averil told me this morning. I know it's been very difficult for you, and I imagine you would be very pleased to hear the news.'

Pam thanked Carol and agreed that it was indeed good news for them. She also told Carol how she had been learning to be more assertive with Hilton but had not spoken to him for a few weeks. 'I'll be glad when they've gone, but I've learned a lot through having them as neighbours,' she explained.

When Trent heard the news, he said he felt like celebrating. 'I'm taking you out for a special meal on Saturday night,' he said to Pam. 'We'll get a babysitter. What great news!'

Pam thought how very nearly they had put their own house on the market. Now she was glad that they had stood their ground and kept their beautiful house which they were both so fond of.

On Saturday night, they talked over the whole situation and Trent said he could see God's hand in it. 'God promises to care for us as we are obedient to Him,' he commented. 'I know it doesn't always work out as smoothly as this. And we were prepared to stay even if the situation became quite unpleasant.'

'Yes, we were prepared to do that,' agreed Pam. 'And God has brought good out of it as He promises to do in every situation we face. It's been like a course in assertiveness for a start. And I love that verse in the Bible that says we will not be tempted beyond our strength. I am so glad I had that conversation with Jeannie. God really used it to help me to become more assertive in that situation. I feel as if I am a stronger person now. Then the way Jonathan spoke in the Bible study that night! That was God's message for us. And then David confirmed that we were to stay in our house rather than move in fear. I can see that God has been guiding us all the way. I wouldn't want to go through a situation like that again, but it is wonderful to think that God was with us helping us through it in such specific ways.'

'Yes,' agreed Trent. 'It has been wonderful. You know, it wouldn't surprise me if Hilton and Averil have a history of getting into trouble with their neighbours and moving on. We need to pray for them. They cannot be happy people. And I've never seen a visitor at their house ever. That's a clue I believe to their behaviour. They were jealous of us having all our visitors on Christmas Day.'

'I feel so blessed,' said Pam. 'We have our lovely family, then our extended family and lots of friends as well. We have God in our lives and a loving church community. We can afford to be generous and forgiving towards Hilton and Averil.'

With that, the couple ordered another coffee and as they drank it, they shared further on the many blessings God had given them.

HOARDING

Marlene sighed. She was at the home of her mother Helen. Helen had developed a habit of hoarding a few years previously and things had got worse since Marlene had left home to do a course at a university on the other side of the city. Marlene had been away from home for a number of years now, having finished her law degree and then having obtained a good job in a firm of solicitors.

Things had certainly got a lot worse at her mother's. Helen was no longer able to give her daughter lunch. There were so many items in the kitchen that she was not able to use it for cooking anymore. Instead, she tended to buy takeaways. This morning, they had planned to go to a local café for lunch.

Marlene wanted to tackle Helen about the hoarding. She could see that it was simply not healthy for her mother to live like that. Marlene herself dreaded going into the house. On a couple of occasions, she had tripped over articles on the floor, and she dreaded the thought of her mother having a fall when she was on her own and maybe breaking a bone. Then her mother was not able to clean the house in the condition that it was in. Everything looked very dirty, and, to make matters worse, mice had made their home in the house. Marlene did not know how her mother could live in those conditions. She had not always been like that. Marlene could remember times when the house was clean and tidy and would sometimes wonder what had happened in Helen's life for her to change her behaviour so dramatically. Could it possibly be Helen's reaction to the death of her beloved daughter Josie? Josie had been killed in a car crash at the age of 15, a few years ago. Helen had been a single mother with her two daughters. Her husband Paul had left many years before after having an affair. The loss of Josie had been devastating for both Helen and Marlene. Marlene sometimes thought she would never get over the shock of what had happened and could only imagine what it would have been like for her mother. But the hoarding was so extreme. Surely her mother would not have reacted so drastically.

Marlene could see that her mother could not now use her bed for sleeping. There were so many articles on it. Instead, she slept in a recliner chair in the lounge-room. It's a wonder that that's available for her to use, thought Marlene. It can't be as comfortable as her bed would be.

As they sat together in the café, Marlene spoke to Helen about the sadness she felt seeing her mother live in this way. Her mother replied, as she usually did, that she was not hoarding. She was collecting things.

'People who are real hoarders keep things like rubbish,' she said. Helen had read about a man who could never throw anything at all away, even the food wrappings which came with his takeaway food.

'But, Mum, you've got so much stuff that your home isn't functional, and you can never find anything,' responded Marlene. 'I've got an idea. Why don't we go back after we've had lunch and work on the things on your bed? At least if we could clear everything off it, then you would be able to use it to sleep on. It can't be comfortable sleeping night after night in the recliner chair.'

Helen reluctantly agreed that they would work in the bedroom together, but when they got back to her place and began to sort the articles into 'keep', 'throw away' or 'give away' as Marlene had heard was the sensible thing to do, her mother became very resistant. It seemed there was nothing at all she was willing to part with. In the end, the items from the bed were added to a pile of things in the corner and the two women made up the bed. Marlene left thinking they had made very little progress.

A couple of months later, Marlene visited again and was dismayed to see that the bed was once more covered with miscellaneous items and her mother was once more sleeping in the recliner.

Marlene went home heavy-hearted. This was a problem she really did not know how to solve.

One morning, a week or so later, she went to church. The minister was speaking on the Bible verse, 'Casting all your care upon Him for He cares for you.' She explained that there is nothing too big or too little in our lives that God does not care about and wants to help us with. Marlene immediately thought of her mother. She had no idea how God or anyone else could solve the hoarding problem, but at the end of the service, when they were invited, during a time of private prayer, to bring a particular worry to God, she found herself praying about her mother's situation.

The days went by, and Marlene occasionally remembered that she had prayed that prayer. One evening, her friend Coralie rang for a chat. Marlene always enjoyed her chats with Coralie and this time was no exception. During the course of the conversation, Coralie explained how a mutual friend, Rhonda, who was a psychologist, had started a business helping people with hoarding.

'I guess she must have seen a few people with that problem in her practice,' explained Coralie. 'Or maybe the relatives. I know how difficult it has been for you, especially when you cleared the bed and your mother couldn't bear to throw anything out.'

Marlene remembered. 'Yes, it was awful,' she agreed. 'I felt so helpless. I was ready to give up. You can't change someone unless they want to be changed. Maybe I was putting too much pressure on Mum. That's often when people go the other way in reaction. I did pray about the problem though, and I've been trying not to worry about it since. If something's going to happen, I don't think I'm the one who is going to do it.'

'Rhonda works with a team of people,' explained Coralie. 'They help the hoarder to go through all their stuff and to decide what to do with it. Rhonda's trained them to be sympathetic and understanding and to talk things through with the client. And she also has regular sessions with the client as well to help keep them on track.'

'It sounds like a wonderful program,' said Marlene wistfully. 'I would really love Mum to be on it, but frankly, I'm feeling a bit sceptical about whether it would work for her.'

'Why don't you mention it to her and see what she says? Don't put any pressure on her but give her Rhonda's phone number and let the decision be hers,' said her friend.

'I'll certainly do that,' agreed Marlene. 'I'm going to visit next weekend. I'll put it to her when we're having lunch at the café.'

So, the following Saturday, when Marlene was having lunch with her mother, she quietly broached the subject with Helen.

'Oh no! I couldn't possibly do that,' said Helen. 'I want to keep my things. I'm not really a hoarder. I just like having my possessions around me.'

Marlene could see that the conversation was heading to a place where it had often gone before. She would talk about the hoarding; her mother would be in denial and then Marlene would try to convince her that she needed help. This time, however, she remembered those useless conversations and also Coralie's advice about not putting too much pressure on her mother. She bit her tongue while Helen continued to speak and finally said, 'Mum, I'm just giving you Rhonda's details in case you think they might be useful. But the decision is totally yours and I will support you in whatever you decide. I can see that in the past, I've sometimes put too much pressure on you, and I want to apologise. You have to make your own decisions just as I have to make mine. Now, what would you like for dessert today?'

Helen looked at her open mouthed and Marlene could see that she had been expecting an argument. Maybe she even wants an argument, thought Marlene. It's as if she's been convincing herself as well as me that her hoarding habits are all right. She's been so busy defending herself, she hasn't been able to think clearly about what she needs to do.

In fact, Helen brought the subject back again a couple of times as they were eating dessert, but Marlene refused to be drawn into the argument. Each time, she quietly said that it was Helen's decision, and she was not going to interfere. Helen looked a bit crestfallen. Marlene then changed the subject and talked about some of her experiences in the new job she had recently taken on. As she was speaking, she realised how one-sided the conversations with her mother had become since she had left home a few years before. They were always talking about Helen's problems, and it was not a good mother-daughter relationship at all.

When it was time to say goodbye, Marlene kissed her mother lovingly and said she would see her the following month. As she drove home, Marlene felt relaxed. She realised that she had been taking the responsibility for her mother's problem and it felt very good to relinquish that responsibility. Maybe Mum wasn't taking responsibility herself because I was taking it for her, she wondered. Well, whatever Mum decides, it's up to her now. It wasn't working when I took the responsibility, so we'll see what happens now.

The months went by, and Marlene continued to visit Helen and the two had lunch in the café. Whenever Helen mentioned her house, Marlene would be polite but would not put any pressure on her mother to change her ways. She would ask Helen about other things going on in her life and would share what was happening in her own life. She hoped Helen would realise that she needed help, but, even if she never came to that realisation, Marlene knew that she could not go back to that place where she was taking responsibility and arguing uselessly with Helen.

Then one day, she had a call at work. It was from the hospital near Helen's home. Helen had fallen badly at home and had broken her wrist. Marlene left work early and drove across to the hospital. Her mother was still in Emergency and looked very distressed.

'I fell on some of the things in the passageway,' she said dolefully. 'That was yesterday and I was all night on the floor.'

'How did you get help?' asked Marlene feeling shocked.

'At first I thought I could not move at all,' commented her mother. 'And I was in such a state of shock and pain that I could not think clearly. Then I remembered where I'd left the mobile phone. I usually leave it in the kitchen, but this time I remembered it was in the lounge-room, only a couple of metres from where I'd fallen. It was difficult, because I had to get over all the stuff on the floor and try to protect my wrist as well. I moved very, very slowly and it took me a long time, but eventually I got to the phone and was able to call Triple O.

'When the ambulance arrived, they had to break in, and I felt so ashamed at the state of my house. The officers didn't say anything, but I could see they were shocked. It's so long since anyone's been in the house except you. I suddenly saw it more clearly through other people's eyes. Mind you, I felt so terrible after being so long on the floor, that part of me was just relieved to see them. They were so kind and brought me in the ambulance to the hospital. They gave me painkillers on the way and was I glad to have them!'

Marlene sat quietly with her mother holding her other hand. 'I'm so glad they came and found you,' she exclaimed, and that the phone was accessible. What an ordeal you've had. You're safe here now. Just concentrate on getting better.'

Helen's wrist had already been xrayed and it had been confirmed that it was broken. The following day she was scheduled to have surgery to have a plate and screws inserted to strengthen her wrist.

'I don't know how I'll manage when I have to go home in a couple of days,' she confided to Marlene.

'Mum, you can come to my place for a while until you can manage on your own,' said her daughter. 'Meanwhile, I'll go to your house and get a few things for you that you might need.'

Her mother explained where there was a bag and where to look for the needed items.

Following her surgery, Marlene took Helen to her home and looked after her for the next few weeks until her cast was removed, and she was able to function normally. The day before she was due to go home, Helen explained to her daughter that she was dreading going home.

'It's been so lovely here with you,' she explained, 'And you've looked after me so well. I am so grateful.' Tears sprang to her eyes as she continued. 'Your house is so orderly and, well, my house is such a mess. I don't know how I'm going to manage.'

Marlene was tempted to suggest that her mother contact Rhonda and her team, but she restrained herself and simply said, 'I'm glad you could come here and that I could look after you, Mum.'

Helen continued, 'I was thinking about it in bed last night. I was awake for a while thinking about it all, and I've decided to ask your friend Rhonda and her staff to help me. I have enough money in the bank, and I just don't want to go on living like that anymore.'

'That's wonderful Mum,' said Marlene. 'I will support you in any way I can too.'

Helen went home the following day, and she did contact Rhonda who arranged an appointment with her the next week so that they could discuss the situation.

Helen spent the next few days nervously anticipating the meeting. While part of her wanted to be free of her hoarding habit, another part of her dreaded parting with her belongings which somehow represented security to her. But having the broken wrist had shown her that it was not safe living the way she was, and she knew it was not hygienic. She had not enjoyed coming back to the house which was so infested with mice.

Helen met Rhonda on the appointed day and was pleased to see that Rhonda was both professional and caring. She explained that the staff would be free the following week to begin work at Helen's house, that the decisions to be made were Helen's and nobody would force her to do anything she did not want to do.

Rhonda asked Helen if there was any trauma she had gone through as hoarding can sometimes be a reaction to trauma. Feeling that she could trust Rhonda, Helen explained how desolate she had felt when her husband Paul had left her many years previously. She had tended to push her feelings down as she had her two small daughters to raise. But in her heart of hearts, she had blamed herself for her husband's affair. She reproached herself with not being a good enough wife and housekeeper too. Was it her cooking, or maybe she did not give enough attention to her appearance? Should she have noticed the warning signs that he was interested in someone else, and could she have prevented it somehow? Over and over again, she would reproach herself. She rarely spoke about her concerns with anyone, but they would play in her mind unwanted, often when she was in bed at night trying to get to sleep.

Then there had been the sudden death of Josie at just 15. That had been so cruel. It was as if everything she loved and valued had been taken away from her. She knew she would never fully get over the death of Josie and that was when her hoarding began in earnest. It was as if she held on to things as a way of compensating herself for the losses she had experienced – a way of maintaining control over at least one part of her life. Her hoarding had substantially increased again when Marlene had left home, and Helen was left alone.

Rhonda listened to Helen with care in her eyes and, for the first time since her losses, Helen felt able to speak freely about them and how she felt. Even as she shared her story with Rhonda, Helen began to gain more insights. She had never connected the loss of her husband and daughter with the hoarding. Then, when Marlene had left home, it felt like another bereavement as, this time, she was left completely on her own. She could now understand her desire to have at least some sort of control in those situations, even if it meant her life became dysfunctional.

As they continued discussing the issues, Rhonda suggested that Helen may not have allowed herself to grieve fully when she had experienced her losses. 'You had two small children to look after when your husband left. It would have been difficult to find time to grieve when you were so busy. Then, when Josie passed away, maybe you had to be strong for Marlene. Does that sound like a possibility to you?'

'Most probably that was the case,' agreed Helen. 'And in both of those cases, it was very painful to grieve anyway. When the strong feelings came, I would consciously push them down.'

'One of the ways that we get through our grief,' explained Rhonda, 'is to allow ourselves to feel the feelings. I agree that it is very difficult, when we go through such times as the sudden loss of a child. The very suddenness of it means that we are caught unprepared and that can seem worse at the time than the loss of a loved one through a long illness. In that case, we have time to get used to the idea of losing them. That is is very painful too, of course, but not such a great shock.'

Over the next few weeks, Helen continued to meet with Rhonda who helped her to go through the grieving process. Rhonda also talked with Helen about her future. What did she see herself doing? Was there a course of study she would like to do? Or maybe do some paid or voluntary work? Did she want to pursue a new interest or hobby? The hoarding had taken up so much of Helen's life, that she had had little room to do much else, except watch the television.

Rhonda said to her, 'You are still here. Your husband had gone and so has Josie. You can still see Marlene from time to time. I can see that she loves you very much, but she also has her own life to lead. Now is the time for you to carve out a new life for yourself. You will never forget Josie, and you will always have her in your heart. What do you think she would say to you now if she were here?'

Helen thought of her beautiful daughter Josie to whom she had been very close. Josie had had a very caring nature and was particularly concerned for anyone in need. Helen remembered how one of Josie's school friends had been ill, and how Josie would often visit her friend after school just to keep her company. Instantly, she knew that Josie would not be wanting her to live her life as she was now living it. 'She would want me to find something that I enjoyed doing,' she said tearfully. 'In fact, if I do change my life, I'll do it for Josie's sake.'

'And maybe do it for your own sake as well,' added Rhonda.

During those weeks, Rhonda's team had been at Helen's place, going through her belongings with her. Helen was impressed that they respected her feelings and reminded her often that she was in control of the process. They went through one room at a time and encouraged her to either throw things out, to sell or give them away and then to keep the rest. It was a laborious process and at times Helen felt like giving up. Then the team leader she was working with might suggest that she have a short break and come back fresh to the task. With items that were particularly difficult to make a decision about, the team member might enquire about why she was having trouble. She found it difficult for example to get rid of perfectly good items. Then the team member might remind her that she had many other similar items. She had many handbags for example. It was suggested that she choose a small number of her favourite ones.

Clearing out Josie's room was the hardest of all. Her helper suggested that she choose just two or three things which especially reminded her of Josie. She chose a beautiful card that Josie had given her on Mothers' Day not long before her daughter had passed away. The helper suggested that she frame it and put it on the wall. She also decided to keep a few pieces of Josie's school work and some books her daughter had been really fond of.

There were many tears, and the team leader was empathic at all times, listening to Helen's feelings but also reminding her how much more she would enjoy her house when it was put back in order. It was helpful to Helen to have the sessions with Rhonda while they were working on the house. She was able to share many feelings with Rhonda and work through them.

Some items were set aside to be given away, and the helper reminded Helen how others would now be able to enjoy the things she no longer needed. Marlene helped Helen to advertise some items on the Internet and Helen was pleased that she received quite a substantial sum of money with the sales.

It took a few weeks, but eventually the house was cleared, and it was suggested to Helen that she organise to have the house painted and get new curtains and floor coverings. The cost was partly covered by the money she had obtained through the sale of unwanted items.

The day came when the work in the house was completed. Rhonda explained that Helen could keep coming to see her as long as she felt the need and she continued to have the sessions with Rhonda for a few more weeks. Helen had been thinking of Rhonda's idea that she needed to find something else to do with her life and she had decided that she would take up art classes. Then she also had the opportunity to take up part-time work as a carer for elderly people, looking after them in their own homes. Helen also pondered how she would now enjoy having visitors in her home again and giving hospitality. Instead of going to the café with Marlene, she could now prepare a tasty lunch at home for them both to enjoy. She had kept some of her favourite recipe books, although she had disposed of many of them. She could see now that her life would be full and interesting with all the new possibilities in her life.

The time came for Helen's final session with Rhonda. They reviewed the past few months and Rhonda encouraged Helen to see the difference between her present life and the one she had lived when she was hoarding. Helen could see now that she did not need to control her life by keeping things that she did not need. Rhonda also encouraged Helen to book more sessions if she ever felt that she needed more care and support.

Helen left the session filled with hope as she knew she was beginning a new life. She decided she would ring Marlene to see if they could have lunch together the following Saturday to celebrate. As she drove home, she thought of what she might cook for her daughter who she realised had always been there to support her.

ADDICTION

I don't want to keep living like this, said Celina to herself. She was waking up with yet another hangover after a night of drinking. And those nights were becoming more and more frequent. Moreover, Celina had also begun taking drugs. She felt she was living each day in a fog and wondered if things could ever be any different.

She was no longer able to work. In fact, she had been fired from her job after arriving one too many times at work under the influence of alcohol. Nor was she in any state to apply for another job. She got a small amount from the government in unemployment benefits, but that was not enough to sustain her drug and alcohol habits. She had taken to peddling drugs to have more cash in hand, and at times she would steal money in order to satisfy her addictions.

Celina had not grown up in a chaotic family. Her parents, Susan and Roy, had provided a stable and happy home for their family and Celina often thought back to the happy times she had enjoyed with them and her older brothers Ken and Pete when they were all growing up on the farm. Those days now seemed like a beautiful dream, long gone, just as a dream fades with the coming of the morning. Celina's parents were Christian and had taught their children about the faith. They were all in church every week and the family had prayers together each night after the evening meal. Celina had loved life on the farm. She and her brothers had had many adventures. They could roam freely, and they loved the animals. Now as Celina looked back on it, it seemed idyllic.

Celina dragged herself out of bed and tried to have some enthusiasm for the day. She went to the kitchen to get her first alcohol fix for the day. She thought of how she had got started on alcohol. She had been feeling, as a teenager, a bit rebellious about the restrictions her parents imposed on her. They did not want her to go out alone with boys, and, when she went out with a group of friends, they insisted that she get home by 11pm. They also expected her to do jobs on the farm. Looking back now, their expectations were not really unreasonable, but at the time, that's how they seemed to Celina. Then she had been influenced by Max, one of the boys in her class who was a rebel. It was Max who had introduced her to drugs and alcohol. At first, she had experimented just for fun, but it was not long before she was addicted to both drugs and alcohol.

For a while, Celina was able to hide her habits from her parents, but they became more and more suspicious as they noted the changes in her. Her schoolwork suffered and she changed from being a loving teenager, with the occasional times of rebellion, to being morose and angry a lot of the time.

Then, at the age of 16, she had discovered she was pregnant. Her parents had been heart-broken, knowing that she would certainly be incapable of caring for a baby. However, they had encouraged her to have the baby and offered to look after him themselves. Celina had accepted their offer and now, this little boy, whom she had named Jude, was still in the care of her parents. He was now five years old.

Celina had been in an 'on again – off again' relationship with Max. At present, they were together, but, Celina reflected,

Max did not treat her well. Nor did she have the maturity to do her part in maintaining a functional relationship.

There was very little food in the cupboard and Celina knew that she would have to do some shopping. It was not until she'd had another three drinks that she set forth in the battered old car that Max had managed to obtain.

It was on the way to the shop that the accident happened. A small girl had run on to the road and Celina, in an alcohol induced stupor, had seen it all as if it had been in slow motion. Her reflexes were slow, and the small girl had been hit by the car. Celina stopped and got out. The tiny form lay on the road. Celina did not know what to say. She felt horrified. When the police arrived, it was obvious to them that she had been drinking and she was charged with drunk driving. It was fortunate for her that the child turned out to be not badly hurt.

Max and her parents were called, but Max had also been drinking heavily. Celina had been taken to the police station where she had been interviewed. Through floods of tears, she could do nothing but admit that she had been drinking and that her state of intoxication had played a part that could have resulted in the death of the child.

That night, Celina could not get the image of that small figure lying on the road out of her mind. When she tried to sleep, she had nightmares, in spite of dosing herself with drugs and alcohol. She slept fitfully, and, in the morning, she came to a decision. She knew that she could no longer continue as she was. She must get off the drugs and alcohol. She had been to rehab before, and it had worked for a while. But this time, she felt shocked into changing her life in a way that she had not felt before. What if that child had died? She cringed at the very thought and knew her life would have to change. She rang a rehab centre and was booked in for that afternoon. Her parents were delighted with her decision and had paid for her to go to the centre where she could stay for a few weeks and could receive psychiatric help as well as withdrawing from the drugs and alcohol.

It was a difficult time for Celina, as she struggled with withdrawal symptoms. She was grateful for the care of the staff at the centre. As well as the medical help she needed, there was a psychiatrist, Jordan, who talked over her problems with her. He asked her to picture what her life would be like if she were to maintain her sobriety. This was a difficult question for Celina. It was as if her life had been put on hold when, as a young teenager, she had first started on the drugs and alcohol. The psychiatrist explained that any other plans she had for her life would have been let go of at that time. Her sole purpose would have been to secure the drugs and alcohol and to use them to get through the day. Her maturity level would have remained as it was at the time that she had first started taking the drugs and alcohol.

As she thought about Jordan's question, Celina thought that she would like to live a 'normal' life like some of her friends from school were leading. She would like to have a home of her own. She would like to have a husband and children. She would like to train for a job that interested her and where she could be a help to others. She would like to have Jude in her life more. She shared these thoughts with her psychiatrist the next time he saw her, and he asked her what was one small step that she could take on the journey to make her dreams come true.

Celina thought about this question and said she believed the next step was to choose what work she wanted to do and to apply for training in that area. Over the next few days, as she was continuing to go through withdrawal, it was a distraction to her to go through the options. Eventually, she decided that she would like to be a carer for young children in childcare. She looked up places where she could receive training and applied to be accepted in them.

When she next saw Jordan, she told him of her plans and applications and could see that he was pleased with her initiatives. He explained that she was replacing her bad habits with something worthwhile. If she did not find something of value to be involved with instead of those bad habits, she was much more likely to regress, especially when she left the centre and had to manage on her own.

Celina was accepted into a course of training which would begin the week after she would be discharged from the centre. She felt a pleasant feeling of anticipation as she thought of doing the course, a feeling she had not experienced for some time.

Then she thought of her other dreams for the future. She was still living with Max although their relationship had been very dysfunctional. Could it be that Max would also give up his drug and alcohol habits? Then their relationship would have a chance. She remembered too Jordan's warning that it would be more difficult to keep sober if she were living with someone who was not. Jordan had recommended that she find somewhere else to live, maybe with her parents until she could find a place of her own. But as she thought about it, she felt that she could be the one to save Max from himself. If she could turn her life around, why couldn't he do it too, with her help? She decided that she would go back to the house with Max.

Shortly afterwards, Celina left the centre and went back to be with Max. She was to begin her course in child care the following week and she couldn't wait to begin. At times she experienced really strong cravings for the drugs and alcohol. She knew that this would happen, and she also knew that each time she resisted those cravings, it would be a little easier the next time. She had plans of what she could do when she felt these cravings. Jordan had suggested that she take a walk or call someone like her mother, or maybe read a book for a while. He assured her that the cravings would subside, to be patient and to tell herself that things were getting better, and to remind herself that she did not want to lose all that she had gained and go back to her old life.

Celina continued to resist the cravings and was able to begin her course. She loved every aspect of it, especially being with the young children when she had a placement. When the cravings came, she would think back to her dependence on drugs and alcohol and shudder when she remembered what her life had been like. That was enough now to get her back on to the right pathway. It could still be difficult at times, and she knew she would always have to be vigilant, but she definitely thought that she was winning the battle.

Max, however, was another story. He was still holding down his job somehow, but every night he would be at the hotel with his drinking mates. He was still using drugs too. Celina tried her very best to make him see that it was possible to stop. She had stopped and so could he. Apart from her course, she devoted herself to Max. It was her dearest dream that they could have a life together free from drugs and alcohol. She also dreamed of having five-year-old Jude living with them, although, with Max as he was, she knew the time was not yet right. Celina tried to explain to him some of the discussions she had had with Jordan, how he had encouraged her to do the course and made suggestions about what to do when she was bothered by the cravings. But it was all to no avail. If anything, Max became resistant to all her approaches, getting angry with her whenever she tried to help him.

One Saturday, Celina decided to visit her parents. It felt good to see them. She had not visited for a while. She had concentrated so much on her program to reform Max. It felt very good to see Jude too and to note that he was taller than she remembered him. Have I been away such a long time? she asked herself. She wondered if she had been neglecting Jude and her parents by concentrating so much on Max.

As they chatted and were just finishing a leisurely lunch, Celina suddenly felt overwhelmed. It had been difficult for her to become sober, and she was feeling very frustrated that Max could not see her point of view. Then again, there were times when she remembered that still form lying on the road after the car accident and knew that she was responsible for that child's injury. Sometimes, that alone could be overwhelming. She wondered what would happen at the court case which was scheduled for a few month's time.

Celina looked at her father's kind face and suddenly felt the tears rolling down her cheeks. Jude saw Celina's distress and needed to be comforted by his grandmother. As Celina continued to cry, Roy took his grandson out of the room for a walk on the farm, while Celina began to pour out all her frustrations, especially the fact that Max was so resistant to all her attempts to change him.

Susan listened lovingly to her daughter. Finally, Celina came to an end, and they sat for a while in silence with Susan holding her daughter's hand. At last, Susan spoke, acknowledging the trauma that Celina had been through and saying how proud of her she was, that she had become sober and that she was doing so well with her course.

'Thanks Mum,' said Celina tearfully. 'I love the course so much and I definitely do not want to be using again. It's difficult sometimes,' and she explained to her mother the strategies that Jordan had suggested to manage the cravings. 'It's Max I'm worried about,' she continued. 'He just doesn't seem to want to change. He's out drinking with his mates every night. He is still going to work and somehow manages that. I don't know how he does it. But there is no room in his life for anything else. He can be very impatient with me at times, even to the point of being abusive. I thought when he saw how my life has changed that he would want to change too. But it doesn't seem to be happening. My dream is to have Jude to come and live with us. You've been so good having him all this time, but he should be with us. I'd make sure that he spent some time with you and Dad of course,' she added. 'You would miss him if you didn't see him regularly. I know that.'

'We would miss him,' said Susan thoughtfully. 'But it would be good for him to be with his own parents too. We have to think about what's best for Jude in this situation.'

There was silence for a minute or so and then Susan continued, 'I wonder if you're trying too hard to reform Max. You're doing all the work and all the worry too. I read somewhere that when one person over-functions, the other person tends to under-function. You're worrying and trying to change things, so Max lets you be the worrier and doesn't work on the issue himself. He's probably resisting change because he feels the pressure from you. It's understandable that you would try to change him. It would make a big difference in your life, as well as his, if he became sober. It's tantalising for you because you know it's possible. You're achieving it. Your strategies are understandable, but you have to ask yourself the question: are they working?'

'They're not,' said Celina abruptly. 'I can see it so much more clearly now that we've had this conversation. But I don't know what else to do.'

'Give yourself some time to think about it,' said Susan. 'And Dad and I will be praying for you to know what to do.'

'Thanks Mum,' replied Celina gratefully. 'I feel that I've made such a mess of my life, although I've made some good decisions more recently. Do you know,' she exclaimed, 'I think I'd like to go back to church again. Maybe there's a church near me that I could go to. I suppose God is still interested in me,' she commented wistfully.

'Of course He is,' replied her mother. 'God loves each of us with an unfailing love. We can always return to Him at any time, regardless of what we have done and how much we have messed things up. Jesus said that those who have been forgiven a lot love Him more than those that trust in their own goodness and who are critical of others.'

A week or so later, Celina decided to look for a church near her home. She went to different ones and eventually found one where she felt at home. The main thing was that she felt loved for who she was. She began to attend regularly, although Max was critical of her for going to church. One night, she was speaking to the pastor who offered her a tract which explained the way of salvation. Celina took it home and read it carefully and prayed the prayer asking Jesus Christ to come into her heart, to forgive her sins and to fill her with the Holy Spirit. She felt peaceful after praying the prayer and realised there had been anxiety and conflict in her heart which she had come to accept as normal. Now she longed for the peace to continue. She began to read her Bible and looked forward to having fellowship with the people at church each week.

Celina kept thinking about what her mother had said about how she was putting the pressure on Max and it was not working. For the first time, she considered the possibility that, if Max did not change, she would need to leave him at least temporarily, to give him the opportunity to change. One Saturday morning, she talked seriously to him, explaining that she was concerned about his drinking and drug habits and knew that it wasn't doing their relationship any good. She explained further that she had been hoping that Jude could come to live with them, but that she believed it would not be good for him to come with Max the way he was.

Celina could almost see Max's eyes glazing over as she continued speaking. This is how it's been in the past, she thought to herself. He sees it as nagging, and it goes right over his head. Mum was right when she asked me if it was working. It is definitely not working. He'll just go out with his mates again tonight and come home drunk again. He's not going to take any notice of anything I say.

In a flash she knew what she needed to say next. 'Max, I can't keep living with you if you continue to act as you are doing. I am leaving you, at least temporarily. I will give you six months to get sober and change your life, and if nothing has changed by then, I will have to leave you permanently. You have not been treating me respectfully and I can't allow things to go on like this anymore.'

Did she see a spark of concern in those glazed-over eyes? Celina was not sure. Did Max believe that she would carry out her threat? She was not sure about that either. Celina wondered if she had more self-respect now that she was attending church and was more aware of her worth and value in God's sight, and, as a result, less willing to put up with disrespectful behaviour. The love and concern of the church members for her had also been a reminder to her that she had choices in her life. Then there were her parents. Her mother had encouraged her to think of herself and her own needs rather than only being focused on Max and the way he needed to change.

During the day, Celina rang her mother. Her mother had previously offered to have Celina back at the farm if she needed accommodation. Now Susan said her daughter would be most welcome and that she could stay as long as she liked. 'It would be good for Jude to have you here,' she added, 'Good for both of you.'

'Mum, if Max goes to the hotel tonight, I'll take it as a sign that he is not taking me seriously,' she explained. 'And in that case, I'll come to you. I started getting a few things ready this morning, in case I would be leaving. It won't take me long to pack them into a bag. I'll leave the car with Max and get a taxi and should be there about 10.30.'

Susan offered to get her daughter and Celina gratefully accepted when Max went to the hotel as usual. She did not want to be a burden to her mother, but valued Susan's support at this critical time.

It felt strange to Celina to be back with her parents, but she realised that she appreciated them so much more than she had as a teenager. Now she could see their strength of character and their stability, and she valued the way they had looked after Jude. She wanted to get a place of her own if Max continued to go his own way, but, for the moment, it was healing to be with her parents and to develop her relationship with Jude. She had seen very little of him in his five years, and now she found she loved doing activities with him and talking with him. And she could see that he loved being with her too.

Max had called a number of times pleading with her to go back to him, but he would not commit to breaking his drug and alcohol habits. Celina was glad of the support of her parents at these times. They helped her to be strong when her inclination was to rush back to Max's to make sure that he was all right.

'It was my mission to reform Max and part of me still wants to rush back and continue in that role,' she said ruefully one day to Roy and Susan. 'But I can see now that it wouldn't do any good. It might make me feel better at least to begin with, but I don't think it would prompt a change of behaviour in Max.'

Celina was still doing the course on child care that she had enjoyed so much and during the time she spent with her parents, she completed the course and was able to get a job at a local child care centre. She loved looking after the children and it also felt good to be on the road to financial independence.

At the end of six months, she had a meeting with Max. She could see that he was not going to change although he was still trying to persuade her to go back to live with him as before. In fact, she could see that he had been drinking before their meeting. Celina had missed Max. Trying to reform him had taken up a large part of her life. But now she was strong enough to say that she could not come back.

'I'll always remember you Max and have a special place in my heart for you,' she said, 'But I can't come back if you're still going to continue with your drinking and drug habits. I wish you well. I appreciate the good times we have had, but I have to go my own way now.'

As she said these words, Celina pondered that she was a different person from the young woman who had always been at Max's beck and call. Max too looked shocked. He had not expected Celina to be so firm in her decision.

As Celina travelled back to her parents' house, she felt sad that her relationship with Max was finally over, but she also felt proud of herself for being firm with him and for not allowing him to show disrespect towards her anymore.

Celina needed some time to grieve the relationship with Max. She continued to work on her own life. She was able to buy a second-hand car, and this made it much easier to get to work and to church. Then she was able to rent a unit in the small town near her parents' farm. As she was packing to leave, she thought about how she had become so much stronger over the previous year. Then, she could not imagine leaving Max. But now there were so many things in her life for which she was thankful. She had left behind her drug and alcohol habits; she loved her job; she had reconnected with Jude who was going to live with her; she had the church where she felt loved and accepted; and she now appreciated her parents more than ever. Her court case was looming but she felt at peace about it. With God's help and the help of her parents, she resolved she would face the consequences for her actions, whatever they might be.

Susan and Roy had asked if they could look after Jude when Celina was at work, and Celina had gratefully agreed. Jude still needed to spend time with his grandparents and Celina would be able to save the money she would have spent on child care. Eventually, she hoped to put a deposit on a house of her own.

She still prayed that Max would be able to get sober, but if he did not, she knew that his life was now his own responsibility, not hers. Would she accept him back if he became sober? She did not know. Maybe there would be someone else on the horizon. She could dream, couldn't she? In the meantime, she and Jude were a complete little family. With God's help, she could manage on her own. If someone came along, it would be great, but she did not need to be in a relationship to feel complete.

MY SISTER

Athol sat back in his chair and reflected on all the events that had happened in the past few weeks. He thought about the phone call from his sister Merle. Merle was upset.

'Oh Athol. Something terrible has happened. Betty's children have sold her house and put her into care. How dare they do that and just like that. So quickly! Why couldn't they have allowed her some more time? I can't understand it. I always thought they were so caring, but now….' Her voice faded and Athol knew she was close to tears.

'How did they dare to do that to her?' he asked finally. They had both agreed that Betty had been done a terrible injustice.

When he had got off the phone, Athol had thought about Betty and how they had all grown up on the farm together. He had been the oldest in the family and there had been a gap of six years before Merle was born, and two years later, Betty's birth had completed the family.

Athol had loved his two sisters. There were times when he got older that he could find them annoying, especially when they would tease him about a girlfriend, but, in those early years, he loved his two little sisters very dearly. He felt protective towards them, almost like a second father and they in turn adored him. He was the one who would make sure they were safe when playing on the farm and show them interesting things to do, like exploring along the creek and looking for birds' nests. He taught them to look, not to touch the nests, and also to feed the farm animals whom they all loved dearly, especially the three dogs, Rover, Spot and Blackie.

The years had gone by and all three had married and had families. Athol and his wife Amy had three children; Merle had married Eddie and they also were the parents of three children. Betty had married Mike and they had two daughters, Jacqui and Judith.

The families had always enjoyed getting together. Athol had continued to work the family farm. Merle and Eddie were on another farm in the same district and Betty and Mike were not far away in the town. Mike was an electrician and always had plenty of work to do. Betty helped him by doing the books and making phone calls. They had been a good team. Their daughter Jacqui had trained as a nurse in the city but had come back to work at the local hospital. Being a country girl, she couldn't wait to be back in the small town again. Judith had also gone to the city to train as an accountant. After a few years, she had also decided to return to the country town and had been able to get a job in a local firm. Jacqui had married Sam and they'd had three children quite close together, so, what with nursing shifts, it had been a busy time for her, especially when the children were teenagers. Judith had remained single. She had a group of close friends with whom she would go on holidays. She loved her job and had been with the same firm for many years.

And now there was this news of Betty being put into care. Athol felt indignant. He decided to call Betty at the home and see how she was going. She answered her mobile phone immediately. Athol could sense that she was distressed straight away. She quickly explained that she wanted to go home. After speaking to her for a short while, Athol finished the conversation feeling very distressed himself.

Athol knew that Betty was missing her husband Mike who had passed away recently. He had been taken to hospital and, after his symptoms had been assessed, it was confirmed that he was suffering from cancer. Jacqui and Judith, along with their mother had been shocked at this diagnosis and had done all they could to support their beloved father and each other. The sisters had taken turns to take their mother to the hospital and had been with Mike as much as they possibly could in those last few weeks. Mike had died quietly in his sleep early one morning and his wife and daughters had been deeply in grief as they lovingly planned his funeral service. The whole family had been present, and, Athol and his wife Amy, remembering back to that day, just a few months previously, thought how the church had been filled with love and Christian hope.

So, what had been going on since that day? Athol thought he would call Jacqui and find out what had happened. He had hardly spoken to her since the funeral and knew her life was busy, but he needed to talk with her.

A few days later, he managed to catch Jacqui having a quiet evening at home. He hoped he did not sound too accusatory, but he found himself saying that he was very puzzled that Betty had gone into care, and he was finding it difficult to understand why.

'Oh, Uncle Athol, I'm so sorry we haven't contacted you to let you know what was going on,' said Jacqui apologetically. 'We've been so very busy, and things have happened so fast. And we knew you had been very busy harvesting.'

This was true. Harvesting was a very busy time for the farmers. When the grain was ready, they would work very quickly to bring it in before rain could downgrade the crop.

This had happened during harvest the previous year. It had been such a bumper crop too. Some farmers would work all night during harvest to get the crop in as quickly as possible.

'We didn't realise it, but we now know that Mum must have been suffering from dementia for quite a while. When Dad was with her, he must have protected her and done things for her so that it was not obvious. We didn't pick it up, and, as a nurse, I'm surprised I didn't see it.

'It was only when Dad got sick and Mum was on her own, that we began to suspect that something was wrong. Although, even then, we thought she wasn't looking after herself very well because she was so focused on her grief at Dad's passing. She wasn't remembering things so well, but we thought it was the stress she was going through, and that would not have been helpful of course. We were all thinking about Dad of course and somehow, Mum's problems got overlooked.'

'What has happened since your father's death?' asked Athol.

'Well, Mum was at home as usual, and we were contacting her all the time to make sure she was all right. She still seemed to be forgetful but otherwise we did not think anything was too much amiss. She was grieving for Dad, and I thought it was understandable that she was not herself. And then, one day I decided to visit her at home, and everything was chaotic. I had never seen the house like that before and it gave me a shock. When Dad was there, he must have taken over a lot of the housework from her. He must have done the cooking, cleaning and washing. Everything was orderly when we visited, and he was still there. But when Mum was on her own…oh I got such a shock. There were plates of food around the house which she'd neglected to finish eating and then it looked as if she'd forgotten to wash them up. The fridge was in a terrible mess, all sorts of foods that were completely off. I don't know how she got herself anything to eat at all. Then everything was dirty and untidy – clothes everywhere. And the papers and bills were in a complete mess. I had a quick look through them, and I could see that she had not been paying her bills.'

Athol felt shocked as if a bolt of electricity had gone through his body. Could this really have been happening with his beautiful sister? He wondered why he had not visited her. He knew he had been busy on the farm. But then he thought how she had discouraged him from visiting. She always seemed to have a vague excuse for him not to go there. Could it be that she knew she was not managing and felt ashamed for him to see her house in such a mess? As he thought about it further, he remembered Betty saying that she was worried about being forgetful and, also that she was not concentrating on things very well. He recalled her saying that she was glad she did not have to drive very far.

How could I have missed all those signs? he asked himself.

'It must have been a terrible shock to you to find the house in that state,' he commented to Jacqui.

'I knew straightaway that she could not look after herself at home anymore,' continued Jacqui. 'I rang Judith immediately and we agreed that Mum would come and stay at our place for a while, while we worked out the best plan for her future.

'When I had a good look at Mum, I was shocked to see how thin she had become. None of her clothes fitted her. She had lost so much weight. We had to go out and get new ones. Then one day, she got out of bed and just fainted. She had got so weak.' Jacqui's voice shook. 'We could have lost her as well as Dad! We were so sad about losing Dad that we somehow didn't notice that Mum wasn't coping.

'Judith and I consulted about what we should do. We both have busy lives with our work, and we felt that Mum needed care all the time the way she was. We didn't want to leave her alone for long periods of time while we were at work. We applied for government assistance but were told that there was a long waiting list, so we discussed the situation with Mum and decided that we would need to put her into care. Mum was not keen on the idea, but we could see that she was not able to be realistic about what she could manage to do. She thought that she would still be able to manage at her house if she were to go back to it.

'We began to look at the aged care facilities and realised that it was expensive to go into them. Mum would need to pay money regularly based on her income and assets and also a large sum of money as a deposit. Then there would be day to day expenses as well. That was when we knew that we needed to put the house on the market in order to pay for her care. Mum had given us financial power of attorney when she came to stay with me.

'What a lot of work it was to get the house ready to put on the market,' said Jacqui. 'Mum and Dad had been there for so long. I was fortunate to have annual leave, or I don't think we could have managed it. Sam and the children helped when they could and also helped out by taking turns to stay with Mum. They're good kids,' she reflected. 'They're independent of us now, but I'm so glad they've stayed in the area. I was proud of the way we could work together as a family. But all the stuff we had to go through! We had to make quick decisions about it all. I was glad Judith was also able to take some time off work too, otherwise the job would have seemed insurmountable.

Athol could only imagine. He would not exactly have called Betty and Mike hoarders, but they had been in the house for many years, and he knew it would have been a big job sorting everything out.

'What a relief it was when we were finally able to put the house on the market,' continued Jacqui. 'And do you know, it was sold within a week. That must be a record for a country property. Some houses in the town take years to sell as you know. We were certainly hoping that that would not have been the case with Mum and Dad's house.

'In the meantime, we had booked Mum into The Gardens. It seemed like a good place for her. The staff seemed caring and that was the main thing. Also, we liked the layout. We booked her in to have respite for a few weeks so that we could assess after that time whether we should continue.

'The first few days were terrible. Mum didn't want to be there and kept wandering around saying she wanted to go home. We felt terribly guilty, but we did think it was the best thing for her. We thought she should at least stay for the respite time. And then things started to improve. It was like a little miracle. Firstly, she began to go to the activities. Doreen who took the activities made sure that Mum was comfortable and able to take part in them. They did painting one day, and another time, they had a quiz. Doreen said Mum enjoyed the quiz. She's not very good with her short-term memory but Doreen asked questions about what was going on 50 years ago when the residents were all young. Then they have exercises and there's a church service once a month. You know how sociable Mum is. She's really enjoyed being with the other residents. In fact, she's made a friend called Lettie. Lettie has dementia too, but they love having a chat together.'

'That all sounds very good,' commented Athol. 'I didn't know they did all those things for the residents. I know our mother had a horror of going into a home.'

'Maybe that's because the homes weren't so good in those days. There have been a lot of improvements since then.'

'Auntie Merle may have had the same idea,' said Athol. He explained how Merle had rung him and had been shocked by the fact that Betty had been put into the home and the haste of it all.

'I must ring her and explain what's happened,' replied Jacqui. 'I can see now how it must have looked. She would have been shocked – especially if she had such a pessimistic view of nursing homes! In fact, Mum's been doing so well. You remember how I told you that she wasn't eating properly, and she'd lost so much weight? Well, she's really been enjoying the food now and she loves having it cooked for her. They have a good chef at the The Gardens and Mum is looking better than she's been for a long time.

'Of course, nothing's perfect. If we are not happy with anything, we can report it. Mum's not up to doing that now, so we have to have our eyes and ears open to anything that could be improved. Judith and I visit as much as we can, and Sam and the children visit too. Mum's now gone into permanent care after finishing the time in respite.'

'Amy and I will certainly visit as well whenever we can,' said Athol. After a few more minutes chatting, they finished the call. Although Jacqui had said that she would ring Merle, Athol decided that he would contact her as well. He knew she had been worried about their sister.

Merle answered the phone and Athol relayed the conversation he had had with Jacqui. Merle was cautious and still inclined to be critical of the younger generation for their actions. Athol suggested that they visit Betty together the following weekend.

'Amy will probably come too,' he said. 'It will be good for us all to see how Betty's going and I'm sure she would enjoy a visit too. It's a relief for us all to have the harvesting done now and we can think about other things.'

So it was agreed that they would visit Betty the following Sunday afternoon.

Athol and Amy arrived at the home first and were directed to Betty's room. She was so pleased to see them and they could see that she looked well and happy, although her memory was not good and she tended to ask them the same questions over and over. Soon Merle and Eddy arrived and the five of them went down to the little café which was open each afternoon. They had a relaxed and happy visit and were able to meet Betty's new friend Lettie whose son was visiting her.

'We'll have to do this again,' said Merle as they parted. They discussed the idea that if the couples came separately, it would mean that Betty could have more visiting time.

'Why don't we visit all together once a month, say the first Sunday of the month,' suggested Amy. 'And the rest of the time we can visit separately. We thought we might come once a week.' This was agreed on as a good plan.

As Athol and Amy were discussing the situation later that evening, Athol commented to his wife, 'I feel a bit ashamed of myself. I listened to what Merle said about Jacqui and Judith and I think now that I was too quick to judge them. I know they've always been kind to their parents, and they have a lot of common sense too. And that's not surprising as they're the children of Betty and Mike. I should have known they would do the right thing. I can see that Merle was anxious about Betty, and that was understandable. We've all been close as siblings. But I just accepted what she said without question. I can see now how easy it was to jump to conclusions. They've been wonderful daughters, and of course they had to act quickly. It was an emergency situation. They needed to sell the house in order for Betty to go into the home and be properly cared for.'

'You must have had in your mind how your mother did not want to go into care,' commented Amy.

'Yes, and I just accepted that nursing homes were always terrible places to go to because of what Mum said,' responded Athol. 'My mind was closed, and I was prejudiced. Seeing Betty at The Gardens today helped me to see that it is the best place for her. I feel as if I've learned a lesson and I hope it will help me to be less judgmental in future. At least I listened to Jacqui and didn't launch straight into a critical tirade. I'm glad about that at least.

Amy squeezed his hand. 'It's never too late to learn something new,' she exclaimed. 'Now don't be too hard on yourself. What would you like for supper?'

BOUNDARIES

Kim sat in her armchair drinking her coffee and pondered her childhood. Her parents Erica and David had been wonderful Christian people. David had been the minister of a church which cared sincerely for the poor and needy and generally had a strong sense of social justice. Their home was always open, and many took advantage of this situation.

Kim chuckled as she thought about Albie. Albie had been living on the street before her parents took him in to live with them. He was 60 years old and a rough diamond to say the least. He had lived with the family for twenty years before he passed away peacefully at their home following a stroke.

How had her parents managed to do it? They had learned to have firm household rules and that certainly helped. Anyone who got themselves a snack during the day had to tidy up after themselves. And there were rules for doing the jobs around the home. Kim and her brother Brendan always remembered how they had to contribute to the family by doing their jobs, at times reluctantly, but their parents had insisted on it and the result was that, when they left home, they were competent in running their own households. Albie had also been willing to follow these rules. As well, Erica and David had expected him to pay a certain amount of his pension money in return for his board and lodging, and the government subsidised this amount, which was a help to the family.

But then there were all the other people in the home. The family belonged to a church that had taught about caring for others and they had taken this teaching seriously. There was a casserole bank in a freezer at the church so that casseroles could be available for those who were sick or had new babies.

Needy people seemed to know about the church and felt free to call in to the manse at any hour of the day or night, and somehow, Erica and David were always welcoming. At times they gave people the benefit of the doubt. There were sometimes people who would make up a story in order to get money for their drug or alcohol habit. There was the woman who had pretended that she was a single Mum who had a sick child in hospital and four other children to care for. When he found out that her story was not true, David had set up a scheme with the local ministers to help people in need by giving them groceries rather than money. They also decided to communicate with each other in the future as this particular woman had gone round to all the ministers in the area and a number had given her money which she had spent on alcohol.

But it was not just people like this woman who came to the door. Many church members would drop in just for a chat. Others would be going through a hard time, and knew they would be welcomed, and their problem shared with a cup of tea and a sympathetic ear.

It was a real open house, and Kim remembered how, when she had left home to get a teaching job in a country town, her unit had seemed very quiet in comparison. Somehow, she had thought that all households were like her parents' home. In fact, she rather missed the hustle and bustle that she was so used to.

One Saturday morning, the doorbell rang, and Kim went to see who her visitor was. A young lady introduced herself as Meredith. She lived in an adjoining flat to Kim's and said she wanted to meet Kim as they were such near neighbours.

Of course, Kim asked Meredith to come in and got her some morning tea and they settled down to have a chat. Meredith explained that she was rather lonely. She had moved from interstate only a couple of months previously after a break-up with her fiancé. She did not know anyone in the area but had managed to secure a job working in the office of a nearby factory. She was obviously still in grief about the break-up and explained to Kim that she had felt everything was going well, but her fiancé had changed his mind and believed they had become engaged too quickly and that they were not really suited to each other.

'It was such a shock to me,' she explained to Kim. 'I couldn't understand why he made that decision. Later, a mutual friend told me that he had suffered from depression. Maybe that had something to do with it. Oh, I had such hopes and dreams about the wedding and our life together. I don't know that I will ever get over it,' she exclaimed with tears in her eyes.

Of course, Kim tried to comfort her and suggested that she needed to give herself more time. It was only a few weeks since the break-up after all.

'You've been so kind to me,' said Meredith as she rose to leave.

'Feel free to have a chat with me anytime you need to,' responded Kim.

Over the next few weeks, it seemed that Meredith was taking Kim's invitation very literally. She was in Kim's house every day and sometimes more than once. Knowing that her neighbour was going through a difficult time, Kim tried to be understanding. The least you can do, she told herself, is to listen sympathetically while Meredith is struggling so much. She thought of how her parents had always had an open house for those in need and that prompted her to be patient with her visitor.

Meredith did not seem to be getting over the shock she had had when her fiancé broke off the engagement. Then there were other things that were troubling her. She was not getting on very well with one of her workmates and Kim listened to many stories about the disagreements between Meredith and her workmate.

Sometimes, Meredith would even ring Kim quite late at night to discuss something she was unhappy about. Kim would be concerned that she would not get enough sleep and would be too tired to concentrate on her teaching the next day. If Meredith rang or came over earlier in the evening, Kim might be doing some preparation for her class the following day, but Meredith never seemed to be aware of it or to ask if it were convenient for her to visit. And Meredith was never happy. There was always something she wanted to talk about and sometimes go over and over. She talked about herself all the time and never asked Kim how she was going. If Kim occasionally tried to change the subject and talk about what was going on in her life, Meredith would give it scant attention and would always seem to bring the conversation back to herself and her own concerns.

Sometimes, Kim would secretly feel sympathy for Meredith's former fiancé. She could certainly understand that he believed he had made a mistake. Yet she knew Meredith was lonely and reproached herself for not being more patient and unselfish.

One evening, Meredith had been in Kim's unit for more than two hours talking it seemed endlessly about her work situation and the workmate she had trouble getting on with. Kim had been feeling more and more desperate, and, in the end, she felt her patience running out. In anger she accused Meredith of being selfish and always talking about herself. Meredith had been shocked and burst into tears and soon after had gone home.

Kim felt terrible. Why had she acted like that? She judged her behaviour was extremely unchristian. And yet part of her felt relieved. Maybe Meredith would stay away at least for a while. She knew she needed a break.

Over the next day, she knew what she had to do. She needed to talk with her father who she knew would always give her wise counsel. That evening, she rang David and poured out the whole story. 'How could I be so different from you and Mum?' she said at the end. 'You were always welcoming people of all different backgrounds.'

David thought about the situation. It was true that they had been welcoming to many people. 'But you know,' he commented thoughtfully, 'Sometimes I think we could have put firmer boundaries into place. Do you remember Jessie?' he asked.

'How could I forget Jessie?' said Kim. Jessie was an elderly woman who was very lonely and who had practically lived at their home for about 12 months before she had taken ill and had eventually gone to live in a nursing home. 'That must have been difficult for you and Mum at times.'

'It certainly was,' replied David. 'It was when you children were young. I think we thought that we had to be always available to Jessie but now, looking back, I can see that we were not always sensible. Jessie was not really sensitive about all the things we needed to do as a family. For a start, she had never married and had children of her own. And I think she was always thinking about her own needs and problems, so that she didn't seem to think about the needs of others. Your mother would often sit and talk with her over a cup of tea but might have to pay for it later by working into the night to get all the chores done. Eventually, she had to tell Jessie that she couldn't sit and chat for ever and would go on with her work. Jessie would still stay and talk of course, but at least your Mum was getting through the work she needed to do. When she first started doing that, your mother thought she was being a bit rude, but Jessie didn't seem to mind.'

Kim felt she could empathise with her mother in that situation especially as she thought about Meredith who seemed quite similar to Jessie.

'We continued our open house for years,' went on David, 'And I believe that it took a toll on us. Of course, we did a lot of good in that time, but we were looking after others at times to the detriment of our own well-being. We've only recently been able to look at the situation more objectively. We went away for that holiday in August, and both of us felt so relieved to be away – just the two of us. We started sharing how we didn't feel we could face going home again. I was seriously worried about your Mum. She seemed so exhausted. I said to her that maybe the other ministers in the area could have the same problem and I resolved I would talk about it with Tim.' Tim was the local Salvation Army officer.

'When we got back, I met Tim for coffee and told him about our concerns. He said he could definitely identify with what I was describing. Then he had a brainwave. He thought it would be helpful to discuss it at our next Ministers' Association meeting. We meet once a month, as you know, and it has often been helpful to discuss issues like that, which have been concerning us.

'So that's what we did. We had a long talk about it and realised that it was a problem affecting all of us. We shared in confidence all sorts of examples and also our concerns for our spouses and families. Tim had just read a book about setting personal boundaries and he shared quite a lot about that. We realised that, because we are in a caring role, it is difficult to set boundaries. A number of us were not given good examples by our own parents. We discussed how, just as those we minister to are important, so we and our families are important too. Those of us who did not already have a day off decided that we would have one and only a real emergency like a death or serious illness would cause us to break that promise to ourselves. A person like Jessie who just wanted to chat on and on would have to do it another day. And we would also need to say no on any day if it were inconvenient to have that person in our home.'

'I can see that it could be a good idea to set boundaries like that,' commented Kim, as she thought again about Meredith.

'What do you think you could do about Meredith?' asked her father.

'Well, for a start, I see now that I need to say if I am really too busy to have her as a visitor,' said Kim thoughtfully. Like when I am working at night preparing for my classes in the morning. At other times, I could follow Mum's example with Jessie and there might be something I can do while we are talking, like preparing some craft work for the children or cutting up vegetables or doing some sewing. I can see that I might even need to explain to Meredith that the time has come for me to go to bed, and we need to say goodnight.

'I know!' she exclaimed. 'The best thing might be for me to suggest that we meet in a café perhaps once a fortnight. Then I don't need to wait for Meredith to go home. I can just go myself when I am ready.'

'That is a very good idea indeed,' agreed her father. 'One thing that we discussed in the meeting was that we don't need to set boundaries with everyone. Most people will be sensitive towards us and will instinctively know when they need to end a conversation. But some people do not have that sensitivity. They are often needy people and they have not been taught to think about the needs of others, so they tend to think only of themselves. If they do not think of us, we have to be assertive and let our needs be known.'

'How have you put all this into practice in your own lives and ministry?' asked Kim.

'It's certainly been a matter of practice,' explained her father. 'We've been thinking ahead of time what we might say to someone who might be likely to take advantage of us. We even practise role plays in the ministers' meetings. Gradually we have been getting used to being kind and matter of fact, but also assertive about what we can and cannot manage. We try not to be apologetic. And to our surprise, we find that most people don't mind us setting boundaries. We found we needed to support each other, especially when we were just learning to set the boundaries. Even now, we're all aware that we have a lot to learn. Sometimes we go over something where we think we could have done better. We can always learn for next time.

'It's made such a difference to our lives,' he added. 'We feel so much more in control of them. Your mother is certainly looking less stressed and exhausted. You know how she likes to have a nap in the afternoon? Nowadays, if someone comes for a cuppa and chat with her, and I'm here, I explain that she's resting and isn't available just yet. Maybe they could ring and arrange another time.

'You might need some support setting boundaries with Meredith,' he explained. 'We're always here to support you in any way we can.' He laughed. 'Well maybe not on our day off or when Mum's resting!'

Kim laughed too. 'You can't think how much this conversation has meant to me, Dad,' she said. 'I can see it will make such a difference to my life.'

'We should have had this chat years ago,' said her father, 'But better late than never.'

Kim rang off feeling light-hearted. She thought quite a lot about what she might say to Meredith. She decided that first of all, she would apologise for reacting in such an angry way to her neighbour, but also try to explain the need for boundaries. As she thought back to that last conversation she'd had with Meredith, when she had lost her temper, she pondered whether that is a likely scenario when we do not set boundaries with people. We can become more and more frustrated, but bottle up that frustration and anger, not knowing what to do with it. Eventually it is likely to erupt as an angry outburst. It's far better, thought Kim to herself, to be honest and assertive when we first sense the need for boundaries.

The following day, Kim went to Meredith's unit before dinner, feeling rather apprehensive as she rang the doorbell. Meredith answered looking a bit angry and upset, but she asked Kim to come in and got her a cup of coffee.

'I'm so sorry for the way I behaved the other night, Meredith,' said Kim as she took a deep breath and prepared herself to explain to her neighbour the thoughts that she had been practising beforehand. 'There was no excuse for the way I spoke to you. However, I do need to explain something. I am often busy at night preparing for my classes and I just don't always have the time for long conversations. I need the evenings to be free to prepare my lessons and I need to go to bed reasonably early too. Otherwise, I feel tired the next day. Teaching is a job that takes a fair amount of energy! I should have explained this to you before this. You couldn't know without my telling you. I've been thinking about it and wonder if, instead of meeting at my place, we could get together say once a fortnight after work at the café. We could have a chat then and I would be more relaxed.'

Meredith looked as if she did not know how to respond to Kim. She hesitated and finally said, 'I'm sorry. I had no idea I was imposing on you like that. You should have told me earlier. Well, let's try meeting after work as you suggest.'

And so it was arranged. The first time they met, Kim definitely felt more relaxed and found she was able to enjoy the time with Meredith. The best thing was that she felt more in control of the situation. She could be the one to end the conversation by politely saying that she needed to go, rather than having to wait for Meredith to leave her unit as had happened previously. As she thought about Meredith's visits to her unit, she told herself that she could, on any of those occasions, have explained to her neighbour that she had work to do or needed an early night, and resolved that, though it was difficult to be assertive in that way, she would explain what her needs were if a similar situation arose in the future. She reflected that maybe Meredith might ignore her comments and then she would have to repeat them firmly until they were understood. She had discussed this with her father. David had described a situation where a parishioner had ignored their polite comments that they needed her to go because they had planned another activity. At first David and Erica had psyched themselves up to explain the situation to this parishioner and had been dumbfounded to realise that she either had not heard them or her needs were so great, that she was willing to ignore what they said, which, as David said, was disrespectful.

'We had to keep making our point more and more plainly until finally she realised that we meant business,' he had explained to Kim. 'If we were in her situation, we would have understood immediately that we needed to go and might even have felt awkward that we needed a reminder. But then we must remember that we rely on others to let us know their situations. We reminded ourselves that we are not mind-readers.'

As the weeks went by, Kim found that she was not dreading so much the times with Meredith. However, the conversations still tended to be one-sided as Meredith continued to share her hurts and disappointments. Then one evening, Kim plucked up the courage to explain to Meredith that she could see that the conversations were one sided and she would like to share about her life too. This seemed to be a new idea to Meredith. At first, she had looked very offended and Kim had thought to herself that if the relationship were to end, she would have to accept it. It was important to have a more equal friendship.

Although Meredith seemed offended, she did not seem to be changing her ways. She did not seem to be capable of it. She had been so used to having her own problems monopolising the conversation and habits can be difficult to change.

Kim felt the need to have support in this situation, and once again turned to her father for advice and counsel. He asked her to give him time to think about it and decided to bring the situation to the Ministers' Association. After discussing the matter with them, he got back to Kim.

'We had quite a long discussion about the situation,' he commented. 'We had all had similar situations and it felt good to talk about it. In the end we decided that not everyone is going to change, even if we explain the need to them. You must choose whether you are willing to put up with the situation as it is. Maybe decide to give a certain amount of your time to Meredith recognising that she is a needy person. That would mean putting a limit on the time you spend with her. Or you might decide that you are not willing to put up with a one-sided relationship at all. You would need to explain that to Meredith and that could be difficult. But you have already been quite explicit with her and that has taken courage. Remember that we are not aiming for everyone to like us. Sometimes we have to speak the truth in love. Your being truthful could be just what Meredith needs if her relationships are to become more equal and healthy. We all need feedback at times.'

Kim thought and prayed about what she needed to do and eventually decided that she would regard her relationship with Meredith as a ministry rather than an equal friendship. They continued to meet at the café each fortnight. Kim tried to bring her own concerns into the conversation as much as possible to encourage Meredith to listen, but she also recognised that her neighbour was going to major on her own concerns. Kim felt relieved that she could be the one to conclude the discussion.

Visiting her parents one weekend, Kim talked over the situation with them. 'I guess we can't change everyone,' she reflected. 'I feel I have learnt such a lot from this whole situation and I am actually grateful to Meredith because I have had to learn boundaries through the relationship with her. I still don't think I'm perfect at setting boundaries, but I'm learning.'

'It takes practice,' agreed her father. 'We're still learning ourselves of course. We all need to support each other in this area of our lives.'

They all agreed that life had been challenging as they had practised setting boundaries, but there were rewards too as they learned to encourage others to treat them with respect.

IDENTITY

Jennifer looked carefully at her classmate Fiona. Fiona was a quiet girl who seemed to cope reasonably well with her schoolwork. If I could just be like Fiona thought Jennifer, then people might like me.

Then there was Carol. Carol seemed confident and was popular with the boys. What makes them like her? thought Jennifer to herself. If only I could be like Carol. Jennifer spent quite a lot of time thinking about why the boys liked Carol so much, but she could never come up with a satisfactory answer.

Jennifer had not had a happy childhood, and that was an understatement. She had been sexually abused by her stepfather every night for as long as she could remember, and it was still going on. Once, her mother Jean had inadvertently walked into the room and had seen what was happening. Jennifer had hoped against hope that her mother would put a stop to it, but nothing had happened. Maybe she was too afraid of her husband who regularly got drunk and, when under the influence of alcohol would beat her and the children. Sometimes things got so bad, especially on a Saturday night, that they would flee to a sympathetic neighbour who would allow them to stay with her until things settled down.

As far as Jennifer knew, her older brother Ian had not been subjected to sexual abuse, but, like Jennifer and their mother, he had been subjected to violence and ridicule. Ian always looked cowed as if he were trying to be invisible. And that was how Jennifer felt – cowed! She often wished too that she could be invisible.

Neither of the siblings had any self-confidence. They found it very difficult to make friends and their schoolwork had suffered. Things somehow seemed worse when they got into high school and were sometimes subjected to unkind comments from other students. That was when Jennifer had started daydreaming about becoming like one of the girls in her class so that she could be liked and successful. But of course it was impossible to become someone else.

The years went slowly by. Jennifer did not think she had the confidence to get a job, but she had an uncle who worked in a bank and who suggested that Jennifer try for a position there. She always thought that she got the job because of her uncle's influence. She was promised that the bank would train her and resolved to take advantage of this training so that she could do as well as possible. She kept herself to herself and her workmates saw her as a quiet little mouse. Eventually, it was a relief to be able to move out of home and rent a small flat.

Then, one day, one of her workmates, Warwick asked her if she would like to go out the following Saturday night. At first, Jennifer had been inclined to say no. Surely, he could not be interested in her. Maybe he just wanted to torment her. Nevertheless, after a brief hesitation, she accepted, and he arranged to pick her up at her home at seven o'clock on the Saturday evening.

To her surprise, Warwick treated her with respect. They enjoyed the film and had supper together afterwards. Jennifer felt herself begin to relax like a snowy landscape thawing on a sunny day. She decided that they had had a pleasant evening but doubted that Warwick would ask her out again.

So, she was surprised when Warwick approached her at work the following Monday and said how much he had enjoyed the evening with her and would she like to go out with him for dinner the following Saturday night. Jennifer blushed and felt confused but eventually she stammered out that she would be happy to go out with him again.

And then began a time of pleasant evenings together. Jennifer could not believe Warwick would actually be in love with her, but one evening, he explained that he had feelings for her. He did not want to put her under any pressure, but hoped that they would continue going out together.

Jennifer had agreed. She was also beginning to have feelings for Warwick. He was always so calm, respectful and considerate towards her. The whole thing seemed too good to be true. It seemed like a dream that Jennifer would wake up from. But it was true and before long, they declared themselves to be boyfriend and girlfriend.

Jennifer wondered what Warwick saw in her. Her self-esteem was so low. Sometimes she would say to Warwick, 'If you really knew me you would not like me.' But Warwick did seem to like her even though they were getting to know each other more and more each day.

It was not long before they were engaged and then planning the wedding. Jennifer had never been happier, and she noted that Warwick also seemed very, very happy. Their wedding day was special and they settled down to live in a unit that they rented not far from the bank.

They were both very happy and Jennifer loved it that Warwick never seemed to worry about anything. And he was also very thoughtful, thinking of small presents to buy her regularly and always listening carefully when she wanted to explain something to him.

Warwick was a Christian and he explained to Jennifer how God loves each of us and how Jesus died on the cross for our sins. Prior to this time, Jennifer had been unable to believe in God's love, but with Warwick, loving her the way he did, she now believed that she was lovable and was able to accept God's love for her. She also became a Christian and began going to Warwick's church with him and to enjoy the church activities.

But there was still a feeling of emptiness within Jennifer which had come from the terrible abuse she had suffered. She still found herself at times thinking of her identity – who she really was - as she had done when she had tried to 'be' Fiona and Carol when she had been at school. When she had felt safe enough with Warwick, she had explained to him about the abuse she had suffered and he had been truly shocked and sympathetic.

There was a woman in their Bible study called Moira and Jennifer admired her manner and the way she was so relaxed in conversation. Jennifer thought that if she could be like Moira, she would somehow be more acceptable as a person. This was in spite of the fact that Warwick had always insisted that he loved her just as she was and did not want her to change in any way. Then there was Jill their next-door neighbour. Jill was very good at needlework and particularly good at quilting. She had invited Jennifer into her home to see some of the beautiful quilts that she had created. If only she could be like Jill.

Then there was Warwick himself, always so calm. If only she could be like him. Jennifer was constantly thinking that if she could be like someone else, she would be more acceptable to herself and others.

Jennifer enrolled in Jill's quilting class which met each Thursday evening. The members of the group welcomed her enthusiastically and offered to help her in any way they could. But after a few weeks, it became obvious that Jennifer was not suited to quilting. She struggled to get the sewing machine set up correctly. Then she could not seem to sew a straight seam. The other group members were encouraging but Jennifer began to dread going to the class. After a few more weeks, she had to admit to the group that she could see that she was not suited to it and left the class.

On her weekly date with Warwick, Jennifer told him tearfully how discouraged she felt about the quilting class. Warwick listened sympathetically as usual and suggested something different for Jennifer. He had been reading about sexual abuse and learning how greatly it could affect those who suffered from it. He suggested that Jennifer might benefit from counselling. Because she valued Warwick's opinions so much, Jennifer agreed to consider this idea. The following day she rang a Christian counsellors' association and asked to be referred to a counsellor in her area.

The appointment was made for the following week. Jennifer went along in fear and trembling to meet her counsellor, Leanne. Leanne had sounded pleasant and efficient over the phone, but Jennifer feared discussing the subject which she had kept so much to herself over the years.

She soon realised that her fears had been groundless. Leanne was warm and welcoming and assured Jennifer that she need only disclose what she felt comfortable disclosing. She could be in charge of what was discussed. Jennifer began to feel comfortable and to share what her stepfather had done to her for so many years. She cried and her feelings came tumbling out – feelings which had been kept in such tight control over so many years, like a tightly locked box whose contents were kept in strict privacy. Leanne allowed Jennifer to share her feelings for as long as she wanted to and, by her words and manner, showed her care and concern.

After Jennifer had shared her long suppressed feelings, she felt relief and had a sense of hope that she was ready to make a new beginning. Leanne was careful to explain to Jennifer that in no way was she to blame for the abuse. Blame is sometimes put on to the abused person by the abuser, but Jennifer had been a minor and in no way responsible for what had happened.

During one session, Jennifer mentioned her neighbour Jill and how Jennifer had so longed to be like her. Then she thought of Moira in her Bible study who seemed so confident and relaxed in her interactions with the other members of the group and explained to Leanne how much she would like to be like Moira. Then she thought back to how she had admired Fiona and Carol so much that she had tried to 'be' them.

Leanne explained that when we have sexual abuse, our sense of identity is something that is stolen from us. In fact we are given a new identity – that of a sex object that the abuser is free to do what they like with.

'But underneath all that,' she continued, 'is the real you. The "you" that God made and you have your own special identity given by God.' She then went on to ask Jennifer a series of questions. What did Jennifer really like to do? What was she good at? The questions even included such simple things as what was Jennifer's favourite colour, her favourite food? Was she a morning or an evening person? What was her favourite way to relax? Did she enjoy reading? What sort of books did she enjoy? What was her favourite television show, her favourite film? Did she enjoy gardening? The questions went on and on and Jennifer could see that Leanne was trying to find out who the real Jennifer was, not Fiona or Carol, not Jill, Moira or Warwick. Who was she as Jennifer? What gifts and talents had God given her?

As the conversations progressed, Jennifer felt liberated as she realised that she could be herself. She did not need to strive to be someone else. It was all right if she did not enjoy gardening or sewing. She did not have to have a bubbly personality like Moira. She did not even have to have the calm even temperament of Warwick. She did not have to be popular with the opposite sex as she remembered Carol had been or the quiet achiever that Fiona had been. It was enough that she could be herself, enjoying the gifts she had been endowed with, and that she and Warwick had their own unique relationship which she treasured so much.

Jennifer thought hard about what she enjoyed doing and what she was good at. She knew that she was a good listener and genuinely enjoyed hearing people's stories. She had always enjoyed biographies and autobiographies. She also cared for people and loved helping them. Then she was very good at writing and thought that she would like to write a novel one day.

Leanne had encouraged Jennifer to see her gifts as important, gifts that God had given her, talents that she could use in the service of God. When a request was made at the church for volunteers to give pastoral care, Jennifer realised that this was something she would enjoy doing. She joined the pastoral care committee and enjoyed visiting people in need, sometimes too elderly to attend church or maybe having a crisis in their lives and needing extra support.

Jennifer also went to a course for writers, and it was not long before she was planning a novel and writing the first chapter. She would sometimes discuss the plot with Warwick who never failed to encourage her and tell her how proud he was of her. He also encouraged her in the pastoral care work, sometimes visiting parishioners with her.

Jennifer had a deep sense of relief that she could at last be herself. She no longer felt a compulsion to do a particular activity just because others were doing it. Deep inside her, she felt peaceful and calm as she realised that, through the counselling, God was healing her from the abuse she had suffered, and she was developing her God-given gifts. Who knows, she thought, maybe one day I can study to become a counsellor and that would be another way of helping people? The future seemed bright, and she found that she was enjoying life now, rather than enduring it. She knew who she was – Jennifer - and she was feeling more and more comfortable in her own skin.

www.ingramcontent.com/pod-product-compliance
Lightning Source LLC
Chambersburg PA
CBHW051257210726
48287CB00002B/537